WHEN PAUPERS DANCE

The author at age 17, Warsaw, Poland, 1929.

When Paupers Dance

SZLOMA RENGLICH

TRANSLATED FROM THE YIDDISH BY ZIGMUND JAMPEL

Véhicule Press

MONTRÉAL

Acknowledgements

I would like to thank Julian Turkel of Wroclaw, Poland who put me in touch with my translator/editor, Zigmund Jampel; my dear son Henry Renglich who played an important part in accomplishing the translation; Zigmund Jampel, for his inspired translation and editorial assistance; Hannah Fitch and Jim Olwell of the Genesis office on Victoria Avenue in Montreal, who introduced me to my publisher; Louis Dudek, for his encouraging comments; and special appreciation to publisher Simon Dardick for allowing my book to come to life.

Published with the assistance of the Canada Council.
Book designed by Simon Dardick.
Typeset and printed by Les Editions Marquis Ltée.
Cover photograph by Moshe Raviv courtesy of YIVO Institute
for Jewish Research, New York
Back cover photograph of the author by Tom Steiner.

Dépôt légal, Bibliothèque nationale du Québec and the National Library of Canada, 1st trimester, 1988.

Canadian Cataloguing in Publication Data
Renglich, Szloma, 1912-
  When paupers dance

ISBN 0-919890-79-2

  I. Title.

PS8585.E67W44 1987   C839'.093   C88-090007-5
PR9199.3.R46W44 1987

Address all Canadian orders to:
University of Toronto Press
Publications Department
5201 Dufferin Street
Downsview, Ontario M3H 5T8

Address all U.S. orders to:
University of Toronto Press
340 Nagel Drive
Buffalo, New York 14225-4731

Véhicule Press, P.O.B. 125, Place du Parc Station
Montréal, Québec, Canada H2W 2M9

Printed in Canada.

CONTENTS

CHAPTER ONE

The Wheel Turns

DEAR Reader,

This is the story of my life and my plea to all mankind. In telling you how I lived, I hope to tell you more than just my story, for I lived as millions of others did—many had lives as difficult as mine, and many had lives that were far worse. Men, women, and children continue to lead such hard lives today. This is the reason for my call to you, dear Reader. Perhaps all of us together can lessen the need for others to write such life stories.

No doubt you will find in my writing plenty of mistakes, but that can't be helped. I am not a professional writer. I do the best I can and hope that you will do your best to understand me. And so, I begin.

My first name is Schloime. My second name had once been Schmer, but it is now Renglich. Later on I will explain the reason for this change. I was born on September 7th, 1912, in the city of Lublin, which at that time, if I am not mistaken, belonged to the Russians. Today it is a part of Poland. We lived in a small suburb of Lublin called the Volye, but the name of the street I can't remember—if it even had a name. I can only recall that it was a little side street off the main, Kalenovtzisna, and that it led to a mill named Krauzi's Mill after its owner.

Surely, if you are a Lubliner, you'll know exactly where we lived.

Our house was a wooden shack with one small room. It looked as if at any moment it might sink back into the earth. What furniture we had, I only remember vaguely—an old iron bed for my parents, a small wooden crib for me, a table, a few rough chairs, and since we didn't have a sink, a pail of water resting on a low bench. In the midst of this poverty, my father, who was a shoemaker, had his workshop.

Today when I think of our little street, I see at the end of it, as in a dream, a wooden bridge over a long, wide lake. I often went to swim there once I got older. On the other side of the lake stood Mr. Krauzi's Mill, and next to it, painted a shiny white color, stood his three-story mansion. It had large windows with lace curtains and was capped proudly by a waving red and white Polish flag. I never set foot into that place, but I imagined it vividly to be like a king's palace in a fairy tale. Not far from the beautiful house there was a large dovecote, built especially for Mr. Krauzi's pigeons. He had so many that I could never count them all.

My greatest pleasure as a boy was to sit at the edge of the lake dangling my feet in the cool water, watching the pigeons. They would fly higher and higher, glide down, and then suddenly soar up again so high that I became afraid they would fly away and never return. I was unhappy at the thought of a single one of them being lost. I loved to watch how they flew together and I often noticed that if one pigeon tore away from the group, it was immediately surrounded by all the others and led back to sit in their midst in the dovecote. Something about this scene pleased me. I guess that even back then I disliked the thought of being alone.

I would look up at the sky and watch the pigeons for hours. Once while I lay back, lazily cooling my feet in the water, I fell asleep and dreamt that I was flying with the pigeons. I soared so high among them that no one below could see me. When I got tired I flew down onto the roof of our little shack. Suddenly, I became very bitter at the thought that I could have landed on Krauzi's Palace and lived in it like a king. I decided to fly there. But just as I was about to start, rain began to fall, real rain, and woke me up.

How I hated being woken up just then. What bliss it would have been to have sat at the edge of the lake watching the pigeons, to have fallen asleep and dreamt of flying freely among them and then, instead of coming down on the roof of our dilapidated shack, to have flown into Krauzi's Palace, never to leave it again....

Nor can I think of the name Krauzi without seeing before my eyes his huge herd of cows and sheep driven every morning by a herdsman to the pasture to graze. I often tried to count them, as I tried to count the pigeons, without any luck. As soon as they had passed I would ask myself, How did Mr. Krauzi come to deserve such a herd, a mill, a mansion, wagons full of flour, horses to pull these wagons, and so many beautiful pigeons, while we had to live in such poverty? But what the implication of this question was or where I could find the answer I didn't yet know. The only thing I knew for sure was what the rebbi had taught us at *cheder*, You don't bother God with riddles. Back then, I was afraid of God.

Still, whenever I saw Mr. Krauzi with his bloated stomach drive past in his majestic carriage, drawn by four tall horses, his huge dog on a chain sitting at his side, I couldn't help becoming a little resentful of our God. I walked around deeply confused. I thought, If, as everyone says, God cares for us, then why is it that our own Jewish God gives to this German, a Gentile, such wonderful riches, and to all of us, poor Jews of the Volye and Lublin, so little? Where is the justice in this? But I would immediately hear the rebbi's words, become afraid, and stop asking such questions.

No matter. I will never forget nor stop loving that little suburb of Lublin, the Volye. In that small corner of the world are tucked away forever the good and, mostly, the painful memories of my childhood. There, for a little while, I was a child like other children with a father and a mother. We even had a large family of relatives— my father's sister, her husband, and their seven children; my father's brother, his wife, and their four children; my father's stepmother and her unmarried son.... I dream of that place which is surely no longer the same Volye I left behind, and long for the chance to visit it and my memories one last time.

My father's name was Baruch Hillel Renglich. My mother told me that he was such a good shoemaker that when he made a pair of shoes for a customer, my father was never satisfied until he had first weighed each shoe on a scale to make sure that they both had the exact same weight. He even used his tongue to lick the fresh leather of the new soles to prepare them for finishing.

My mother, Roise, was of average height. She had a bright, pretty face, a short delicate nose, vivid green eyes, and a marvelous head of soft, black curls. To me, she was the prettiest woman in the world and I was quite simply in love with her. But she wasn't just beautiful. She was joyful, kind, and ready to help the next person in whatever way she could.

Well, we were certainly not well off because if we had been, would we have lived in such an old shack? But as the saying goes, It would have been a sin to complain. As long as my father pounded away at the leather and sewed with his large curved needle, we always had enough bread on our table. And since time didn't stand still back then either, and my parents weren't always asleep at night, something happened in our little family that often happens to young couples. In 1914, my mother gave birth to a girl. She was named Ruchele. My parents became richer by a daughter, and I, by a little sister.

If life had just continued as it was, everything would have been fine. But things change. The wheel turns. For some it's for the better. For our family, however, life became bitterly hard.

As soon as World War I broke out, my father, along with millions of other fathers, was taken to fight for the Tzar. The effect of this on my mother was devastating. She walked around our one room dazed, knocking into the furniture. She became extremely irritable and suffered severe headaches and stomachaches. From constant anxiety, her hands began to tremble. She couldn't sit in one place for more than a few minutes. When she did calm down, which was rarely, she would sit and talk to herself. When she stopped muttering, she would begin to cry hysterically.

This lasted a few weeks. Eventually she realized that crying and worrying wouldn't fill our empty stomachs. She began to look for a way out of our desperate situation.

After a month, with the help of acquaintances, she found work as a housekeeper for a rich family. The house was large and my mother had to cook, do the laundry, and all the housecleaning.

10

At the same time, she had to care for the family's four children. She would come home late at night exhausted, throw herself down on the bed, and immediately fall asleep.

But wait! I've already forgotten an important detail.

That's what I mean about not being a real writer. I don't think this would happen if I were a real writer. But is it any wonder that I forget details here and there? Perhaps even a professional writer would forget after sixty-two years. But enough of this sidetracking.

Right after my father was taken into the army, our struggling family was enriched by one more member, Babbe Zlate, my mother's mother.

Babbe was then close to seventy years old. She was short, plump, and always had a severe, almost angry, expression on her face— even on the most beautiful summer days. That expression, I was told, my grandmother had inherited from her own father, who was a *Cohen*, a very serious and learned man. But Babbe Zlate, despite her expression, was kind and gentle. She was a widow and had lived by herself as long as she had been healthy. However, a fire which had destroyed her house also severely burned her right arm. Without proper medical care, the burn healed badly, and a patch of skin grew between her forearm and upper-arm. As a result she could hardly move her right arm and usually held it bent against her chest. Crippled, unable to take care of herself, Babbe came to live with us. And so, as if life hadn't been hard enough for the three of us with my father gone, now we had a fourth mouth to share our hunger.

That's the detail I had forgotten.... Some detail.

When I got older, my mother told me that in 1915 the landlord of our old shack decided he wanted it for himself and gave us notice to get out at once. Because of the war a house was almost impossible to find, and rents were going up daily. My mother tried to explain this to our landlord. She pleaded with him to let us stay at least until her husband returned. But the landlord was a brute, a regular dog-killer, and it did her no good. Every evening he would stumble into our house in a drunken rage, screaming as if his teeth were being pulled. A few times he even tried to attack my mother. She would run out of the house and wait on the street until he left. These pleasant evenings made it obvious to us that we had to move.

Miraculously, after exhausting searches in surrounding neighborhoods, my mother found a place she could afford, barely. What she could not afford was the exorbitant security of six months rent which the landlords so patriotically demanded from women such as my mother whose husbands were in the war. But with the drunken dog-killer threatening every night to throw us out into the street, my mother was forced to do whatever she could to get the money. She sold all of my father's clothes, her wedding band, and my grandmother's last piece of jewelry, a pair of gold earrings. The amount my mother received was just enough to pay the security and the first month's rent on a one-room flat. We moved at once.

The Tchurtic, our new neighborhood, was on one of the higher mounts of Lublin. One side of it was taken up by a sprawling fruit garden; the other, by ten little houses. These houses, all alike, made of unpainted redbrick, were carelessly scattered around the Tchurtic without any kind of plan, except for a few that seemed to be standing in a crooked line. One little house stood by the road that led to Lublin, another faced the fruit garden, and one was on such a steep incline that from far away it looked as if it was about to slide off, tumble down the hill, and crash into pieces. It was in one of these little red buildings that we lived.

The house had three floors, each an undivided room. The first floor was actually the cellar. The stairs leading down to it were pitch-dark and treacherous. To go down those stairs without a light was to risk a bad fall and a bloody nose. A good Jewish woman and her three children lived there.

The room on the middle floor was ours. It wasn't large and all we had in it were two small iron beds, one for me and my mother, the other for Ruchele and Babbe, a trunk with all our clothes, a small table, and two chairs. Under the window stood a wooden bench with a bucket for fresh water and a basin for used water. Since we had only two chairs, at mealtimes we pushed the table over to the bed for more seats.

On the upper floor of this house lived a Christian family of seven. The father was a bricklayer, and the mother, a washerwoman. Their four daughters were grown up and well behaved, but their

12

boy was a wild goat with insane notions. As soon as my mother left the house, he would slide down the banister, push at our chained door, and piss in through the crack. That yellow puddle on the wooden floor was no fountain of pleasure to us.

Summer in the Tchurtic, the air was perfumed with the sweet smell of fruits from the garden—apples, pears, plums—and life wasn't at all bad. The adults, of course, complained about the heat and how hard it was to get up and down the mountain. But the children came alive in the summertime. We spent our days sliding down the dusty mountain slope on our behinds, running around, and basking in the hot sun. Whenever 'Crazy' Andreus, the manager of the garden, wasn't watching, we would climb up the wooden fence and shake down whatever fruits we could from the trees. For a few groschen, my mother would buy a bunch of pears at the garden, somewhat spoiled, but all the more delicious for that. And to this day my favorite treat is still a piece of buttered bread and a pear.

In autumn, however, life was far less delightful. As the rains fell, the unpaved road which wound aimlessly around the Tchurtic became muddy, and the limy soil stuck heavily to our shoes. When we came indoors, it was some job to scrape off the chunks of mud. At times it was almost impossible to go out into the street.

In winter, we out-and-out suffered. As soon as it snowed and frost set in, the road iced over and we slipped mercilessly going up and down the Tchurtic. Every winter there were the usual casualties: a broken arm or leg, a few cracked ribs, and nobody escaped without a few bruised bones.

To top it all off, there was no running water on the Tchurtic. In summer, we took a bucket and walked a long way to the next neighborhood to a communal pump. In winter, however, the road was so slippery that it was impossible to make this trip. Water became as precious as gold. Luckily, Lublin had water carriers —men who sold water. Unfortunately, during the freezing weather, these water carriers fleeced us. They charged as much as they could get, but we were stuck. We cursed and we paid.

When our family first moved to the Tchurtic, however, we didn't even think of these problems. We were just glad to have a place to live. And since our house was in Lublin proper, it meant that we had become real Lubliners. The wheel had turned again. This time, for a short while, it turned in our favor.

CHAPTER TWO

"Misery, Where Are You Rushing?"

IN THE YEAR 1915, I was three years old. My little sister, Ruchele, was just one. My mother supported us all as best she could by keeping house for the rich family. Babbe, meanwhile, took care of Ruchele and me so that my mother could work with peace of mind. And my father was somewhere far away, fighting a war.

There is an old Jewish saying, "Misery, where are you rushing?"

"Where else? To the pauper's house!"

What does this have to do with my story? Just listen.

One morning Babbe woke up with a sore throat, a cough, and a warm forehead. My mother thought it was just a cold and would soon pass. She wasn't too concerned. She told me to be a good boy so that Babbe could rest, and she went off to work as usual.

In the next few days, however, Babbe's cough worsened. Her throat became so inflamed that she could hardly eat. The fever, low at first, rose steadily, until one night as we were going to sleep, Babbe began to shiver uncontrollably.

In a panic, my mother pulled me and Ruchele out of bed, hurried downstairs, and asked the friendly woman who lived in the cellar, Frau Liebe, to keep an eye on us. Then she bundled Babbe up and rushed her to the doctor.

Later that night, when my mother returned, she was alone. She took us back upstairs and put us to bed. The rest of the night, my mother spent awake, in torture. After a brief examination the doctor had stated bluntly that Babbe was gravely ill and had to be hospitalized immediately. With a note written by the doctor, my mother had taken her to the hospital. Babbe had been admitted at once. Now my mother's anguish was twofold. Her own mother was near death, and since there was nobody left to take care of me and Ruchele, my mother couldn't go back to work. We would all be starving soon.

After our move to the Tchurtic, my mother and the woman who lived in the cellar became good friends. Frau Liebe was about thirty-five years old, ten years older than my mother, and had three children. She was a religious woman with the heart of an angel, and if her face didn't have an angel's beauty, it certainly had its kindness and warmth. Her head, according to law, was covered by a *sheitel*; and her dark-brown eyes, set in her plain face, looked at the world with deep compassion. Like my mother, she too was without a man, although she had already received the tragic news that her husband had been killed in the trenches that same year, 1915.

Frau Liebe earned her living by baking potato latkes at home and selling them at the Jewish market. Luckily, her three children were old enough to be left home alone. Leibel, a born mischief-maker, was ten. The older girl, Tsutel, another troublemaker, was eight. And the youngest, Elke, a quiet and pretty girl, was six.

As my mother sat worrying that night, it occurred to her that Frau Liebe's children could be the solution to our problem. The next morning she spoke to Frau Liebe and asked if her children could baby-sit for me and my sister, for a payment of course, until Babbe recovered.

Frau Liebe agreed, her children liked the idea, and the deal was closed. As soon as Ruchele and I were dressed, we were brought downstairs. My mother returned to keeping house for the rich family. And Frau Liebe's children went to work on Ruchele and me.

Unfortunately, our baby-sitters were still no more than children themselves, and like all children, they just wanted to play. They

16

soon tired of baby-sitting and discovered that they played best when we slept—and the more we slept, the more time they had to play.

Putting us to sleep, however, was another business. There was a large wooden cradle with peeling green paint in Frau Liebe's cellar apartment. Our babysitters threw me and my sister into the cradle, and they rocked us. As long as it took us to fall asleep, they rocked us.

Ruchele and I weren't too happy to have to sleep so much. We too were only children. We too wanted to play. But what choice did we have? Our babysitters didn't bother to ask us what we wanted to do.

And so it went on for a while. Babbe was still in the hospital. Mother went to work every day for the rich family. Frau Liebe continued to bake her potato latkes at home and to sell them in the market. Our babysitters played. My sister and I slept. And the War didn't even think of ending.

One afternoon, although our baby-sitters rocked and rocked us, I remained as wide awake as the bright day. How much could I sleep! Leibel and his two sisters weren't at all pleased with my stubbornness. They began to rock us harder.

Inside the cradle my sister and I were being jolted from side to side. Ruchele, who had been sleeping like an angel, was startled by the violent motion, woke up, and began to cry. And I, after the brisk shaking, was wider awake than ever.

Tsutel and Elke looked at their brother. What now? they asked.

Let's rock harder, he answered.

With each new swing the cradle jumped a little higher off the ground. Ruchele let out screams as if she were being murdered. I myself was having a great time. I had never had such a wonderful ride before.

Soon the cradle began to jump off its hinges, but still they rocked us harder and faster. It would have been easier to fall asleep on a sinking ship in a hurricane. Suddenly, with a loud crack, the hinges shattered, Ruchele and I were flung out, and the heavy cradle crashed down on top of us.

An uproar rose from the cellar. Terrified by the havoc, our three baby-sitters cowered in a corner and cried. Ruchele lay unconscious on the floor. I, pinned under the cradle, was shrieking from pain. A pool of blood surrounded me.

Alarmed by the noise, neighbors rushed in. At once they pulled us from under the cradle. A man, after a glance at the disaster, ran to get my mother. Ruchele, who was quickly revived, found comfort in a woman's arms and quieted down. I was lifted gently and laid down on a bed. The pain in my legs, however, was so excruciating that I was screaming louder than before.

My mother came in minutes. With the help of two men, who used a blanket as a stretcher, she rushed me to the hospital.

After that, I remember nothing.

To this day I have no memory of having been in the hospital, nor of what happened to me there. I only know that when my mother took me home again, I no longer had two normal legs. My right leg, which had been broken in the fall, was two-and-a-half centimeters shorter than my left.

And that wasn't even the worst of it. After my return home, I stopped walking altogether.

Babbe finally recovered and shortly after I returned, she came home too. When Babbe opened the door to our house and saw me lying on the bed, my leg in a cast from hip to toe, she gasped. She had no idea of what had happened to me. My mother hadn't had the courage to tell her.

Sitting on the bed, Babbe listened to my mother tell the story of how my leg was broken. Babbe cried, pressed me against her frail breast, and blamed herself for all the bad luck; nor could she forgive my mother. If my mother hadn't sent her away to the hospital, she said, none of this would have happened.

That night while I was sleeping, my mother and Babbe had another conversation. It seemed the doctors did not consider the operation on my leg successful. They had told my mother that I would never be able to walk on it again. Their advice was that my right leg be cut off at the thigh and, after it had healed, that I be fitted with a wooden leg. Otherwise, they said, at best, I might learn to hobble on crutches.

My mother couldn't decide what to do.

"Maybe," she said to Babbe, "it would be better to let them operate. With a wooden leg, he could at least learn to walk again."

Babbe's answer to my mother was short and blunt. "If you want to cut a leg, cut your own!" she said. "Don't you dare to let them touch that child! Don't even mention it again. As long as I live, I will take care of him. As long as there is strength in my one good arm, I will carry him."

My mother burst out crying and asked Babbe's forgiveness.

That conversation ended any idea of cutting off my leg.

Babbe had always taken care of me and Ruchele as if we were her own children. Now, she never even let me out of her sight. Every move I made, she was there to see that I didn't hurt myself. I think that she loved me especially because I carried her dead husband's name. She often told me what a good man my grandfather had been and how proud I should feel to be named after him. Ruchele and I were grateful to have our Babbe taking care of us again. We had had enough of our young baby-sitters.

When my leg healed, the cast was taken off. Babbe tried slowly and carefully to help me walk again, but it was useless. Instead of walking, I began to crawl on my behind. As I sat on the floor I would push off with my left leg and pull myself ahead with my hands while my right leg dragged along limply. Babbe and my mother were grief-stricken as they watched me.

Ruchele, however, was already walking and running around. She was one-and-a-half years old then, a beautiful girl with a sweet round face. Like our mother, she had a tiny nose and large eyes as green as the summer grass. Often she would sit herself down on the floor next to me and we would play together. Our toys weren't real toys: a broken pot, a bent spoon, a few blocks of wood. If we didn't make too much of a mess, Babbe would let us have a few drops of water in the pot. Out of rags, my mother had made a doll for Ruchele and a ball for me. Our favorite game was rolling the rag ball on the floor to each other. But every time it rolled away, it was my sister who sprang up on her two little legs and ran to get it. Often, when she brought the ball back to me, she would try to help me stand up. She would struggle awhile, pulling my hands, pushing my shoulders, but soon she would have to give up. I loved her for her kindness. After she sat down again, I would embrace her and kiss her little cheek.

And so time passed. The friendship between my mother and Frau Liebe deepened. They saw each other often, and sometimes when Frau Leibe came up to visit us, she brought along Tsutel or Elke. Ruchele and I, however, stayed away from them.

In the spring of 1916, Frau Liebe married again. The groom was an elderly gentleman named Hertzke Schneidleider. To me, he looked more like a grandfather than a husband. Sadly, right after the wedding, Frau Liebe, her children, and her new husband moved away to Warsaw. My mother felt strongly the loss of her friend.

"Such a good woman that Liebe," she said. "What a pity that she left."

My mother and Frau Liebe corresponded, however, and in their letters they shared whatever few joys they had and a lot of troubles. Frau Liebe expressed so much love for us that when my mother heard the letters read, tears filled her eyes.

The reason my mother heard the letters read to her rather than reading them herself was that, at the time, reading and writing was a privilege of the rich. Among the poor there was only a very small percentage of people that was literate.

One evening, later that same year, 1916, we had an unusual guest. It was my father's sister. She brought a letter that had been sent to us at our old address on the Volye, which the landlord of the old house had given to her. The letter was from my father, the first one that we had received from him in nearly two years. Up until then we had no idea what had happened to him. We knew at once that he had never received any of my mother's letters. He didn't even know that we had moved.

He wrote, "It was impossible for me to write to you sooner because I have never stayed in one place long enough. They have thrown me from one front to the other. Since I left I have been wounded twice. I am now in the city of Irkutsk. My wounds have almost healed. I hope the war will soon be over and we will be together again, happy like before. Please write soon. I kiss you all a thousand times. Baruch."

This one letter brightened our whole house. My mother couldn't stop singing and dancing for joy. She kept on telling us that our father would soon be coming home again and we would be the happiest family in the world. "Soon, soon," she said, "the sun will shine for us again."

It was not until a few months later, at the beginning of 1917, that we had another visit from my father's sister and a second letter. This time my father sent us a photograph of himself with a group of soldiers. In his letter he told us not to worry. He hoped to be released from the military shortly and would soon be home to take care of us.

I was four years old and still crawling along the floor on my behind. I began to ask my mother questions that had no answers and which upset her very much: Why can't I be like the other children? Why doesn't anybody want to play with me? Why do I have to stay home all day, when all the children are outside playing?

Even Ruchele, who had started to make up her own games as she got older, rarely played with me.

One evening, when my mother returned from work, she brought me a gift to cheer me up. It was a clay whistle in the shape of a bird which chirped through a hole in its head when I blew into its tail. It became instantly my favorite toy. I couldn't hear enough of its shrill noise. I made such a racket that evening that my mother finally threatened to take it away from me if I didn't stop. But Ruchele was also fascinated by it.

After dinner, as soon as my mother and Babbe stepped out of the house for a moment, Ruchele grabbed the whistle out of my hands and ran away with it. I chased after her, crawling on the floor, but just as I got close, she ran to another corner of the room. I became furious. While I crawled after her as fast as I could from corner to corner, Ruchele taunted me with the song of my own toy bird. Finally exasperated, I began to scream.

My mother ran back into the house. When she saw what was happening, she picked me up in her arms and covered my tear-drenched face with kisses. Quietly, so Ruchele would not hear, my mother whispered to me, "You'll see, I'm going to break her bones for this."

After a good chiding from Babbe, a somewhat remorseful Ruchele came over to return my toy. I took it, but I was in no mood to play with it anymore. My mother sat me down on her lap, brought out my father's photograph, and we looked at it together.

"Don't worry, Schloimele," she said soothingly, as she wiped away my tears. "Your father will come back soon, he'll take you to the best doctor, and then you'll start to walk again. You'll be able to go out and play with all the other children."

I stopped crying as she spoke, but when I looked up, it was my mother's eyes that were filled with silent tears. After I got off her lap, I crawled over to the low wooden bench that stood under the window. Slowly I climbed up on it and sat myself down between the bucket of fresh water and the basin of used water that were kept there, and I stared out into the street. I kept careful watch over all the men that went by, searching for a tall handsome man with a large upturned moustache, dressed in a military uniform— my father.

I spent long hours at that window, day after day. Many men passed who fit my father's description, but none of them stopped at our house. Still, I held on to my father's photograph, kept watch, and never stopped hoping for that one joyous moment of his return.

It was also at the start of 1917 that my mother befriended Pearl Klapper, known in the neighborhood as Pearl Motorcar. She got that name because instead of walking like a normal human being, she raced. This was probably caused by a nervous condition. She was a wisp of a woman, short and thin, with legs that were no more than two little sticks. She always wore a pair of man's boots that were a size or two larger than her feet. Her complexion was dark; her hair was black, as were her small eyes; her face was pointed; and she looked like a squirrel. Into the bargain, she liked to yell a lot.

Pearl had two children, a boy and a girl. Leibel, who was my own age, four, either took after his father or else had been switched on Pearl as a baby. Leibel was as slow as his mother was quick. He was a hefty boy with a full face, handsome but not too bright, and as nimble as a turtle. Every now and then, Pearl threw a suspicious glance at him as if asking herself, "Where did I get you from?" But Feigele, the daughter, was a miniature Pearl. A sweet two-and-a-half-year old, she was tiny, thin, and as her name suggested, she looked and sounded like a newborn sparrow.

Pearl's husband, like most other husbands, was in the army, which made her the breadwinner of her family. She had no time to waste and had little respect for women who sat around gossiping all day about who-broke-a-leg and whose-daughter-was-doing-what-with-whom. She was especially annoyed at those gossipmongers who talked about her. A malicious rumor had spread that Pearl had saved up a little fortune from her work and that she kept it buried in the floor in the middle of her apartment.

"All those gossiping bastards can kiss my you-know-what!" Pearl would scream whenever she heard about this rumor. Then, she would always add, "If you don't understand—I mean, they can kiss my ass!"

How she could possibly have amassed a little fortune, given the work she did, was inconceivable. Although she liked to think of herself as a businesswoman, Pearl was in fact a peddler of rags. She would race from house to house, screaming. "Old clothes! Old clothes!" All day, she ran up and down stairs, pulling and dragging a large sack on her back, buying whatever secondhand clothes she could get her hands on cheaply. Most often, she did her buying in the rich, gentile section of the city. "What do paupers have to sell," she would say, "but their miseries? And of that I have enough already."

Every so often, Pearl was lucky and ran into a rich housewife who wasn't too sharp. Pearl worked on the woman so fast and made her so dizzy that soon the rich lady had sold her husband's best suit, tie, shoes, and hat for a pittance. On these rare occasions, Pearl had herself a good day. Most of the time, unfortunately, what Pearl had to buy were pants with patches and shiny seats, jackets with rubbed-out elbows, shirts with frayed collars and missing buttons, sweaters with holes, old hats that had lost their shape, and shoes so worn that the leather on the soles were paper-thin.

In the late afternoon, Pearl took her sackful of bargains to a special market of secondhand peddlers in the Jewish section of Lublin. She spread her sack out on the ground, piled her goods on top of it, and began to sell. Her customers were sometimes Gentiles, but mostly they were our own Jewish paupers who couldn't afford much better.

Pearl often worked till late at night to sell enough clothes. But it was by dint of such hard work that she managed to take good care of her family; they had a place to live and food to eat. And this, Pearl said, is what made the gossipers so jealous of her.

My mother and Pearl became such good friends that Pearl invited my mother to be her partner. At the housekeeping work, my mother hadn't even been earning enough to keep us from hunger. She couldn't wait to get rid of that job and jumped at the opportunity for a better livelihood.

"Just you wait and see," my mother said to us happily one evening. "We are going to do much better from now on."

The next day my mother began to peddle with Pearl. And soon our house became happier, brighter, and warmer. Business was good. There seemed to be no end of secondhand clothes to buy and sell. We didn't go hungry anymore. In short, it couldn't have been any better.

Even more blessings did the partnership bestow on us. I had a new friend, Leibel. Ruchele had Feigele. And even Babbe had a new companion. Leibel and Feigele had a Babbe just like ours, Pearl's mother. The two Babbes immediately became friends.

All week long, the new partners were busy buying and selling. Saturdays and Sundays however, became real holidays for us; Saturdays, because our mothers observed the Sabbath, and since most Jews of Lublin kept the Sabbath as well, there was no one to sell the old clothes to. And since Sunday was the Gentiles' day of rest, there were no old clothes to be bought on that day. So the two partners were free the whole weekend. The Family Klapper came over to our house, and every weekend was like one long, happy party for us.

It was too good, of course. When rich men dance, they just get happier. But when paupers dance, watch out for a broken leg.

In February of 1917, wintertime, Pearl's mother became very sick. Pearl was forced to stop working to take care of her and the children. My mother continued the business alone and shared her profits with Pearl.

The old woman suffered for a few weeks, developed heart trouble, and died. Pearl, grief-stricken over the loss of her mother, now also had the problem of how to get back to work with two small children that needed to be taken care of.

My mother asked Pearl to come live with us. She assured her that Babbe would take as good care of Leibel and Feigele as she took of me and Ruchele. But Pearl hesitated. Our apartment was no more than one small room. With her and her children, Pearl said, we would be seven people, and there wouldn't be room to move around in.

Paupers, unfortunately, have as much choice of where to go and what to do in life as cattle in a slaughterhouse. It was soon obvious that my mother's earnings couldn't support both families. Pearl herself realized that she wasn't going to earn a living by sitting at home. She had to act fast.

My mother came up with another plan. She suggested that Pearl and her children move into our house for a while, and with the money my mother and Pearl would save on rent, they could soon look for a larger house. This idea pleased Pearl. In early spring of 1917, Pearl, Leibel, and Feigele moved in with us. They brought with them a bed, a chest of drawers, a big trunk, and the Family Klapper was installed in their new home.

At first it was a bit too crowded and noisy, just as Pearl had predicted, but we quickly got used to it. I had Leibel to play with, Ruchele had Feigele, and the four of us were in heaven. The two partners went back to work in earnest. After a while, we began to feel a little more secure; and soon, we were all thinking again that it couldn't have been any better.

CHAPTER THREE

The Red Passover Eggs

A MONTH FLEW BY. Passover approached. My mother, Babbe, and Pearl began the holiday preparations with a bang. Our lively little home grew even livelier. The house was cleaned from corner to corner. The walls and ceiling were whitewashed. For a few groschen, some of the older boys in the neighborhood who went from house to house took away our *chumets*—the leavened bread—and burned it.

Since we didn't have a set of Passover dishes, the old ones had to be koshered for the holiday. We heated a large stone in the fire of the stove until the stone was glowing-red hot. Next, we put it in a basin with all the tableware. As water was poured over the hot stone, it boiled and everything in the basin was purified and made kosher.

The window was draped with a new curtain. The table was covered with a new tablecloth. The children in our house were dressed up in new clothes. And I was given a new pair of black shoes that reached up to my ankles.

As I watched my mother tie my shoelaces, I asked her, "Why did you buy me a new pair of shoes if I can't even walk?"

Without looking up, she answered, "Don't worry, Schloimele. You are going to walk. Just be patient a little longer."

"Am I going to start walking after Tatte comes back?"

"Yes, my child, as soon as your father comes back."

I could think of nothing else. This was my dearest dream. My father would take me to the doctor, and I would start to walk again. I only had to wait for his return.

After my mother had tied the black leather shoes on my feet, I slid down from the chair to the floor. On my hands and behind, I crawled over to the window. Slowly I pulled myself up on the wooden bench and began again my endless watch for my father.

The preparations for Passover went on for a whole week. Every evening when our mothers returned from work, they brought home a little more of the holiday foods—matzohs, fish, eggs, potatoes, red beets, kosher wine. Finally, one morning, my mother, Babbe, and Pearl began to cook. They worked in the kitchen the whole day until all the delicious Passover dishes were prepared. The smell in the house, sweet and spicy, was like nothing I had ever known before. It was heavenly.

We were only missing our fathers. To make up for it, Pearl had invited her bachelor brother, Schmiel the Shoemaker, to the first *seder*. Schmiel read to us from the Haggadah; Leibel and I repeated the four questions of Passover after him; and we drank the ritual four sips of wine. Later in the evening, a matzoh was hidden, and Ruchele, Feigele, Leibel, and I searched for it. When we found it, each one of us received two groschen.

The following morning, the first day of Passover, I sat at the window as on all other days of the year and kept watch for my father. It was a warm spring morning, perfect weather for playing outdoors. In the empty plot of land beyond the road that passed in front of our house, I saw Leibel and a band of children running, jumping, and chasing each other. Everyone was dressed in new Passover clothes. Even Ruchele and Feigele were out there, on the side, playing together.

I wanted to go out so badly that I had tears in my eyes.

Suddenly a loud, clear voice rang out in my head, "Walk! Don't be afraid. Walk!"

The thought shot through me like an electric shock, and my right leg began to throb painfully.

"Mamme!" I cried out, turning around from the window.

Startled, my mother, Babbe, and Pearl looked at me.

"What's the matter, Schloimele?" my mother asked.

Without a thought to what I was saying, I blurted out, "If you give me two eggs, I'm going to walk again."

In the best of times, I rarely got one egg, two eggs at once was like asking for a roasted duck.

The women were astonished.

My mother gave a nervous laugh. "Are you joking, my child?" she asked.

"Don't you believe me?" I answered, dead-earnest.

She stopped laughing. "Of course I believe you," she said and went at once to the built-in cupboard in the hallway to get the two eggs.

When she brought them to me, I said, "I want them hard-boiled."

My mother pulled a pot from the cupboard. I watched her as she ladled the water from the bucket next to me into the pot with the white eggs.

"And make them red, too," I added.

Pearl stared intently at me with her small black eyes. Babbe's lips began to tremble as she murmured a prayer.

My mother put the eggs on the stove to boil. Then she went back to the cupboard and took out a red onion. She peeled it and threw the red skin into the pot to cook with the eggs.

In the silence that spread through the room, the only two sounds were Babbe's murmured prayer and the burbling of the water as the eggs boiled.

The throbbing in my right leg kept growing. My slightest movement sent waves of painful prickling back and forth from my hip to my toes. Nevertheless, that morning I felt stronger, braver, and more sure of myself than I had ever felt before.

Suddenly Ruchele and Feigele threw open the door and ran in giggling. The atmosphere of the house, however, made them stop. Unsure of what was going on, they sat down next to Pearl on the bed and began to play quietly.

When the eggs were done, my mother placed them in a bowl of fresh water to cool. I was impatient, however, and asked my mother for the eggs right away. She took them out of the bowl, put them on a plate, and brought them to me. I looked down at the two brown-red eggs shining on the white plate. I took one egg and put it in my right pants' pocket. The egg was still very hot. I took the other egg and put it in my left pocket.

No one stirred. Pearl, Feigele, Ruchele, Babbe, and my mother, all looked at me.

"Stand on the other side of the room," I told my mother.

She walked to the door and turned around.

"Here?" she asked.

I nodded.

The two hot eggs in my pockets were like burning spots on my thighs. I moved my left leg and slowly set it down on the floor. I rested and waited for the throbbing in my right leg to stop. Carefully, holding the shiny black shoe in my hands, I set my right foot down. The wave of pain in my leg was so unbearable that I almost fainted. I had to stop until I had caught my breath. I sat awhile staring at my feet on the floor. When I lifted my head and looked at my mother, tears were running down her face.

"Don't cry, Mamme," I said. "I *am* going to walk. I just have to wait for the pain in my leg to stop a little."

Hearing this, my mother clasped her hands together and began to sob violently. "My God!" she cried. "Why do you punish me like this?"

I reached out to comfort her and stood up.

"Don't cry, Mamme, don't cry," I said as I moved to take a step towards her. The bolt of pain that tore through me knocked me off balance, I began to fall, but, at the last moment, I caught the edge of the table.

"Schloimele! My poor child!" my mother sobbed and ran towards me with outstretched arms.

Pearl, however, jumped in her way and held my mother back.

"Leave him alone!" Pearl ordered, as my mother struggled to break away from her. "No one touch him!"

"Don't cry, Mamme!" I shouted. "Don't cry!" And still holding on to the table, I took a step, and then another, and another.

My mother broke free from Pearl, picked me up in her arms, and covered my face with kisses and tears.

The house burst into a joyous din. Babbe thanked the Lord as she wept for joy. Frightened by the commotion, Ruchele and Feigele also began to cry. Pearl embraced Babbe and then kissed the little girls to calm them down.

"Put him down, Roise," Pearl said. "Let him walk!"

Reluctantly my mother set me down on the floor.

I held on to the table and stood still. I had to get used to the pain of just standing on my right leg. Then, very slowly, I took a step. I felt as if long needles were being passed through my leg. In my knee, where I had the sharpest pains, it was as if I were being hit with a hammer. But I didn't allow myself to cry. I took a few more steps and then had to sit down. I sat on a chair; I never again wanted to sit on the floor. After a small rest I stood up. I had forgotten what it felt like to walk, but I soon realized that besides the pain, something else was very wrong. Every time I stepped on my right leg, I sank down sharply. I was limping.

After a few minutes, the pain lessened. I let go of the table and began to walk slowly around the room trying to get used to my limp.

Babbe was afraid that I might still fall and followed me everywhere.

"Rest, Tattele. Don't overstrain yourself," she kept repeating to me. "Enough for one day. Sit down already."

But I was being very careful. The red eggs cooling in my pockets were my treasure and I wasn't going to take any chances of falling and breaking them.

As often as she could, Babbe embraced me and gave praise to God for having answered her prayers. Babbe didn't stop praying that whole day. Ruchele and Feigele, both barely three years old, stared at me with amazement frozen on their faces and followed my every step as if they couldn't believe what they saw. And my mother couldn't even look at me without tears of joy shining in her face.

That day I felt like a king. As I began to walk a little more easily, I took glances out the window at the children playing outdoors.

"Babbe, Mamme, I want to go out and play." I said, unable to hold back anymore.

"Oh my God! Not yet, Schloimele," Babbe exclaimed. "You're still too delicate. They're too rough for you."

I turned to my mother. "Please, Mamme, let me go out," I pleaded.

Laughing between her tears, my mother said, "Go, Schloimele. Go out and play with the children."

Babbe began to protest.

"What're you worried about, Zlate?" Pearl interrupted her. "Let him go out, and thank the Lord he can go."

I looked at the door. Step by step, followed by everyone in the house, I walked up to it and entered the narrow hallway. It was cool and smelled of spring air. The outside door was closed, but I could see sunlight shining through the cracks. I looked back to my mother.

"Go on. Go out, my child," she urged me.

I opened the outside door.

For the first time in four months I stood in the daylight. I felt dizzy. Immense white clouds were floating so low that it seemed they were falling down from the deep, blue sky. The ground was a patchwork of green clumps of grass and light brown soil. The little redbrick houses glowing in the brilliant sunlight appeared to be in flames. The smell of spring, the song of the birds, the warmth of the sun, the whole world before me, made me stop in wonder on the threshold of the door. Suddenly, with the noise of a small herd, the children came running around the corner of the house. Leibel saw me and was paralyzed where he stood. One by one, every other child also stopped. They were amazed to see me standing outside.

"Schloime!" Leibel screamed, breaking the spell. "What are you doing there?" He ran up to me and the others followed him.

I was soon surrounded by all the children from the neighborhood.

"How did you do it?" asked one boy.

"Show us your leg!" said another.

"How does it feel?" asked a third boy.

Walking slowly in their midst, the whole gang moving at my pace, I went back with them to the empty plot of land that was their playground. Leibel took me by the hand and led me to a large stone, the seat of honor. I sat down. When everyone had

31

crowded around me, I put my hand in my pocket and pulled out a red egg. As the boys stared in envy, I reached in my other pocket and pulled out the second egg. The two red eggs were immediately passed around from hand to hand.

When I got them back, I held them before me and said, "I'm going to give everybody a piece of red egg."

Everyone shouted happily and patted my back. One boy ran off to get some matzohs for us to eat with the eggs.

News on the Tchurtic traveled on the breeze and soon everyone who lived there knew about my miraculous cure. As the boy was returning with the matzohs, we suddenly saw Pearl of the Goats, a neighbor who kept three goats in her yard, approaching with a large pot of goat's milk in her hands. And so, with a little piece of red egg on a chip of matzoh and a few sips of goat's milk, we had ourselves a feast, and I became a regular member of the gang.

CHAPTER FOUR

My Flying Father

ONCE I BEGAN TO WALK AGAIN, I left my troubles behind me on
the wooden bench by the window where I used to sit and look out.
And when summer rushed in to the Tchurtic and all the children
rushed outdoors to welcome it, I didn't have to sit at home anymore
merely watching. Every morning, right after breakfast, I ran out
into the street to play, and I didn't return until Babbe had called
me at least three times.

Even though I made new friends, Leibel was still my best friend.
We couldn't have been any closer. Leibel and I even slept together
since our mothers had decided that we were big enough to have
a bed of our own. In the morning, whenever one of us had wetted
the bed in his sleep, we helped each other to hang the sheet out
to dry.

But what brought us even closer was that we shared the same
misery. We were both waiting anxiously for our fathers to return.
My father, at least, had sent us two letters; Leibel's, however,
had gone off and vanished like a stone cast into the ocean.

Unfortunately, after my father's second letter, we also hadn't
received anything else. My mother didn't know what to think. She
wrote to my father often, but we never saw an answer.

The Summer of 1917 flew by like a white dove. Autumn slushed through with muddy boots. And Winter poked an icy, dripping nose through our door.

Our mothers had prepared for the cold by storing up on provisions—potatoes, flour, kasha, and beans. It was cheaper to buy these foods before the winter, and in the freezing weather it was hard enough getting around the Tchurtic without carrying bundles of groceries. Our mothers had also piled up some wood and a little coal to burn in the brick stove on which they cooked and which in winter served to heat the house.

As soon as the cold weather blew in, business slowed down, and during the coldest months our mothers didn't even bother to go out peddling. They had more time to spend with us; they paid more attention to housework; they rested a little; and they began to look around for a larger place to live.

For the long winter evenings, our mothers invited their friends over—other women whose husbands were also lost in the trenches of the war. Over a glass of tea, one at a time, and each in her own way, the young wives poured out their bitter hearts. They spoke of their loneliness, of the cursed war, and of their men, from whom they seldom heard news. From time to time, sobs and sighs broke out softly; then there was silence, as if they had fallen asleep. The silence lasted a while, then slowly the conversation began again.

With the lull of the women's voices, Ruchele, Feigele, and Leibel dozed off. I, however, lay with closed eyes, pretending to sleep, and listened carefully to every word. What I hoped to hear was that the war was over and that our fathers were returning. But the good news never seemed to come. Only after the women had gone home did I finally fall asleep.

One winter night, while listening to the women talk, as my head was swimming with thoughts of my father, I fell asleep and dreamt of him.

Suddenly the door to our house was flung open and a very tall, handsome man with an upturned moustache walked in. Astonished, I stared at him. With growing joy I began to recognize the military uniform, the high, round cap, the sword hanging from his belt, and the long rifle on his right shoulder.

34

I jumped out of bed yelling,"Tatte! Tatte!" and flew into his outstretched arms.

My father caught me and swung me around the room as I clung to his neck. With his free arm, my father clasped my mother and Ruchele to himself and kissed them over and over. We were all laughing and crying for joy.

When he had calmed down a little, my father sat down with Ruchele on his lap.

Suddenly I noticed Leibel sitting on the floor in a corner, his head bent low between his knees. He looked miserable. I went to him, took his hand, and brought him over to my father.

"Tatte," I said, "this is Leibel, my best friend in the whole world. His father is also a soldier. Maybe you know where he is?"

My father looked carefully at Leibel and asked, "Who's your father?"

"Tanchen Klapper," Leibel answered sadly. "He's a tailor."

My father laughed. "Yes! Of course! I know him very well! We were in the same brigade when we went into the army. I don't know exactly where he is now, but I'm sure that he is alive and well."

My father scooped Leibel up onto his lap. "Don't worry, Leibel. The war is over! Your father will soon be home."

Leibel's face brightened with a sweet smile, and I woke up.

When I opened my eyes it was still dark. Everyone, except my mother, was asleep. Lying in her bed, she had been watching me as I was dreaming. I climbed out of bed quietly, not to wake Leibel, went to my mother, and lay down next to her. Under her cover, I felt safe and warm and happy.

"What were you dreaming?" Mamme whispered. "You were tossing so much and making such noises, you frightened me. Did you have a bad dream?"

"No, Mamme," I whispered back, "I dreamed that Tatte came home." And I told her my dream.

When I had finished, my mother hugged me and kissed my head. "What a wonderful omen," she whispered happily. "Do you know what this means, Schloimele? He's coming back. I have a feeling that he'll be back soon."

The room had grown lighter. The others were just beginning to wake up.

I left my mother's warm bed and started to dress. Quickly, I pulled on my cold pants, buttoned up my shirt, and pushed my head and arms through the sweater.

Pearl and my mother said quiet good mornings to each other and began to make the beds.

I couldn't wait to tell Leibel my dream, but he was the only one still asleep. I looked at the window. The last few days had been dark and gray, and the rain had kept me indoors. This morning, however, the yellow square of light on the windowpane was like an invitation from the sun calling me out.

I put on my shoes and quickly tied the laces.

At the bucket, I drew a ladleful of icy fresh water, rinsed my mouth, and spit into the basin for dirty water. To brush my teeth, I used my bare index finger—the only toothbrush I owned till I was twenty-eight. Since water on the Tchurtic was especially expensive during the winter, it had to be used as sparingly and efficiently as possible. To wash up, I filled my cheeks with water and sprayed my hands; the water was warmed up and I could rub my hands properly. To wash my face, I again sprayed a mouthful of water into my cupped hands, which I held close to my face, and rubbed.

Everyone was dressed and the breakfast dishes were already being rattled when Leibel finally stuck his head out from under the cover and opened an eye. But before I could say anything to him, my mother called me into the hallway.

"Schloimele," she whispered, "don't tell Leibel your dream."

"Why not?" I asked, all at once disappointed.

"Because it would hurt his feelings," my mother said.

"Why?" I asked again.

"You're still just a child, Schloimele," she said. "When you grow up you'll understand. Now, promise me that you won't tell him."

I couldn't understand why I had to promise such a thing, but I did.

Leibel at last got out of bed and started to pull on his pants, but I didn't care anymore. I had nothing left to tell him. I ate

36

quickly the piece of thinly buttered rye bread which Babbe had put on a plate for me and drank a glass of weak tea. I was in a hurry to get out.

I had polished off my breakfast before Leibel was even half dressed.

"I'm going out," I called to my mother and Babbe from the door as I pulled on my jacket.

"Hey, wait for me!" Leibel shouted, struggling with his shoe.

But when I yelled back, "I don't have time, Leibel!" I was already out the front door, on my way.

The sun was shining brightly through the cool, windy day— still winter, but Spring already had its foot in the door. The rains that had fallen on the Tchurtic for the past few days had turned it into a slippery mountain of mud, and as much as I was in a hurry I had to walk slowly. Even though the black shoes, my Passover gift, had long ago lost their shine, I still had to be careful not to ruin them any more.

I turned off the main road and crossed a small field to my favorite spot, a large rock at the edge of the mountain. A few days earlier, I had stood there with my mother and she had pointed out to me the Volye and where we had lived when my father was still with us; afterwards, my mother and I had taken a walk and she had shown me our old house.

The sun had dried off the stone. I sat down and felt its coolness through my pants. It was still very early. I was alone. Below me, at the foot of the mountain, ran the cobblestone road to the Volye. On both sides of the road, brown hills spread out in gentle waves. Here and there, a low hill had a small house on top and a long row of steps leading up to it. Further along the road, halfway to the Volye, were the cemeteries: a small Christian cemetery on the left, and a large, well-kept Jewish cemetery, behind tall black iron gates, on the right. Past the cemeteries, the road ran into the Volye, where it became the main street, Kalenovtzisna.

I fastened my eyes on the cobblestone road and began a close watch of the men that passed. I was looking for a tall soldier with a long moustache and a rifle on his shoulder, who was going to the Volye. Since my father didn't know that we had moved, I expected him to go to our old house when he returned.

I saw a few men pass on the road below, but none of them looked like my father. As I kept watch, I wondered why my mother had asked me not to tell Leibel about my dream.

The road became empty except for a rattling wagon driven by an old peasant who was taking crates of live chickens to the market. The wagon was heading away from the Volye, but as I followed it with my eyes, I spotted a small figure, like a toy soldier, in the distance. The dream of my father returned vividly to my mind. Again I saw my father's face and felt his rough kisses on my cheeks and his strong arms as he picked me up.

On the road, the soldier was approaching with quick steps. As he passed below me, I stood up and squinted to see his face. I was disappointed that he didn't have a moustache, but it occurred to me that my father could have shaved it off. Alongside the sack on his back, over his shoulder, the soldier was carrying a long rifle. From where I stood, he looked like my father in the photograph. My dream, I thought, had come true just as my mother had said it would.

Cautiously, I began to climb down the steep slope of the Tchurtic. Because this side of the mountain was almost never used, there wasn't a footpath, only rocks on which I could step for balance. While I picked my way carefully down the muddy mountain, the soldier on the road kept getting further and further ahead of me. I tried to hurry, slipped, and was just able to break the fall with my hands. Luckily only the sleeves of my jacket got dirty.

When I reached the cobblestone road, the heavy layer of mud that stuck to my shoes made it impossible for me to walk. I had to stop at the dug-out gutter that ran beside the road and scrape off the mud against the edge of the stones.

The soldier was already passing the cemeteries when I began to chase after him, but by the time he entered the Volye, I was only a few steps behind. Although I was afraid to speak to him, I decided that if he went to our old house and asked for his children and wife, I would tell him that I was Schloimele, his son, and I would lead him back to our new home on the Tchurtic.

Soon we were only steps away from the street where my family had once lived. When we came to the corner, I was standing next to the soldier. I looked down the block and saw our old house.

But the soldier didn't even notice it. He simply crossed the street and kept on walking.

Maybe after all those years, I thought, my father had forgotten where we had lived. I decided to follow him further. The soldier crossed another street and picked up his pace. To keep up with him, I had to start running. After a few more blocks of aimless wandering, I became afraid of getting lost and stopped. The soldier wasn't my father after all.

I walked back sad and disappointed. Along the way I passed two more men in military uniforms. One was old, the other short, and I could see right away that neither was my father. Some other children would be happy to see them.

When I reached the Tchurtic I was tired, my shorter leg was hurting, but I wasn't ready to go home yet. I crawled back up the mountain. At the top I sat down again on my favorite rock. Although I was sweaty and out of breath, the warmth of the midday sun soothed my exhaustion and I dozed off.

Now and then I would open my eyes, glance at the road below, then fall asleep again. Suddenly, while my eyes were still closed, I heard a faint buzz. It took me a minute to realize that the noise was coming from the sky. I looked up and from the middle of a spanking white cloud I saw a large bird with long, stiff wings fly out. The buzzing became louder, the bird larger, and with growing wonder I realized that it was an airplane. I fixed my eyes on it as the airplane left the clouds, glided over the hills, and came closer and closer to the ground until it disappeared behind a nearby hill. Maybe, I thought excitedly, my father is flying home!

Immediately, I began to run down the Tchurtic again. As I ran, my eyes on the hill where the airplane had landed, I tripped on a stone and started to roll on the slippery earth. I tried to stop myself with my outstretched arms, but it was a small clump of bushes that finally broke my fall. I stood up shakily and saw that my pants and jacket were covered with mud. Miraculously, I wasn't hurt. I continued to climb down more carefully. Near the bottom of the mountain, however, I forgot myself, began to run, and again I slipped. This time, I hit a sharp stone with my left leg. My pants were torn and my knee was scraped. I wiped off the blood with the piece of cloth that I used as a handkerchief. Then I got up and continued to run to greet my flying father.

When I reached the foot of the mountain, I dashed across the road and stopped at the edge of a deserted field. My mother and Babbe had warned me to keep out of it. During the summer, cattle and horses grazed freely on this piece of land. In winter, however, the rain and melting snow turned it into a huge and dangerous quagmire; no person or animal ever crossed it then. Nevertheless, driven by the thought of bringing my father home, I began to run through the field. Almost at once, my legs sank in the cold, brown slush, and my shoes, socks, and the bottom half of my pants got soaked. I was so excited, however, I didn't even think of stopping. I kept my eyes on the hill where the plane had landed and pressed ahead. But no matter how hard I ran, I didn't seem to get very far. Every new step became harder to take than the one before. Soon I couldn't lift my legs at all. As the soft soil gave way under my feet, I began to sink. Now I desperately wanted to turn back but there was nothing under me on which to get a footing. When I tried to push myself out with my hands, they sank too and I almost pitched in with my face. The thick slop of freezing mud began to move quickly up my chest. At the thought that I was about to drown, I was gripped by such terror that I stretched my arms over my head and began to shriek.

"Help! Babbe! Save me!" I screamed. But Babbe was too far up on the Tchurtic to hear me. My throat burned from screeching.

Suddenly, a barked shout broke through my cries. I twisted my head. An old Polish peasant was cautiously leaning forward.

"Help me! Save me!" I begged him as I held out my hand.

He grabbed hold of my wrist with his large, rough fingers and began to pull. With his help I was able to twist around somewhat more and I held out my other hand to him. Pulling on both my arms, the strong peasant dragged me out.

From my chest down, I was covered by icy mud.

The kind old man, dressed like a farmer, led me off the field by the hand. When we reached the road, he said something in Polish which I didn't understand.

I told him that I only spoke Yiddish.

He pointed to the left, then to the right, and by gestures asked me where I lived.

I pointed up to the Tchurtic.

The old man patted me on the back and told me to go home. I gave him a small bow of gratitude. He smiled, nodded, and continued on his way.

I found a few scraps of paper lying in the gutter along the road, and a few pieces of rotted wood, and used them to scrape the mud off my clothes. Then, slowly, I crept back home.

When I entered the house, shivering, Babbe stared at me, her eyes and mouth agape. She didn't yell, but I could see from her face how distressed she was.

"God in Heaven!" she finally exclaimed. "What has happened to you? Look how dirty you are! Where is Leibel?"

"I don't know," I said.

"Heaven protect us! Who knows what's happened to him now? I sent him out hours ago to look for you."

Babbe immediately put a big pot of water on the stove to warm up. She took off my clothes and shoes and threw them to the side. Then she wrapped me up in a blanket and began to rub me with her good hand to stop my shivering.

"What happened to you?" she asked me again. "How did you get into such a mess?"

"I fell into a swamp in the big field."

Babbe gasped. "You could have been killed! God preserve us from such a calamity!"

When the water had warmed up, she poured it into a big basin and told me to get in.

I didn't stop trembling until Babbe was finally washing me.

When I was clean again, she quickly dried me off, dressed me in fresh underwear, and put me to bed.

Suddenly the door flew open.

"I can't find him!" shouted Leibel as he ran into the house followed by Ruchele and Feigele.

"Thank God, you are alive too" said Babbe.

"Here he is! He's in bed!" Leibel shouted again, happy to have found me at last. "Where did you disappear to? We thought you got kidnapped by the gypsies."

"Let him rest," Babbe said as she led Leibel away from me. "He fell into a swamp. It's a miracle that he's still alive."

My eyes closed, and I fell asleep at once.

I woke up when the door opened and my mother and Pearl came in, talking after their day of peddling.

"What are you doing in bed so early?" asked my mother as soon as she saw me.

I quickly closed my eyes and pretended to sleep.

My mother noticed the muddy clothes lying in a heap in the big basin, "Mother, what happened?" she asked Babbe.

"Better just prepare dinner," Babbe answered. "He didn't eat anything all day. I'll tell you about it later."

The women prepared dinner. The table was set and pushed up against the bed.

While we were eating, my mother asked me again what had happened.

Everyone around the table looked at me. I didn't know what to say.

"He's just a poor child," Babbe helped me out. "He was playing in the big field and he fell into a swamp."

"A swamp?" my mother repeated angrily. "Do you have to go crawling in the big field? Don't you have enough places to play around here?"

"I wasn't playing," I said, close to tears.

"Then what were you doing?" she asked me. "Come, Schloimele, I want the truth."

"I was going to bring Tatte home from the airplane," I said.

"An *airplane*?" Leibel almost jumped out of his chair. "Where did you see an airplane?"

Pearl pulled Leibel down by the arm. "Keep quiet and eat your food," she told him.

"What are you talking about, Schloimele?" my mother asked. "What did you do today? Tell me."

I was afraid of being punished for disobeying my mother, but little by little I told her everything.

When I had finished, instead of yelling at me, my mother embraced me. "Poor child," she said. "Don't worry so much. When your father comes home, he'll find us. He'll come back to us on his own."

"But how is he going to know?" I insisted. "He thinks that we still live in the old house."

"The old landlord will tell him, and so will his sister," my mother said. "You must promise one thing, Schloimele. Promise me that you are not going to run after the soldiers anymore."

I promised, reluctantly.

In the following weeks and months, I still kept going back to sit on the big rock at the edge of the mountain. Although I saw many soldiers who looked like my father pass on the cobblestone road on their way to the Volye, I followed them only with my eyes. I spent many days of spring and summer waiting like this. When autumn came, however, it was too rainy and I began to skip days. And in winter it got too cold, and I had to stop altogether.

CHAPTER FIVE

When Paupers Dance

THE WINTER OF 1917-1918 ENDED. Days became warmer, and the air began to smell of spring. Everywhere, trees were spreading out with green finery, each tree giving off its own perfume. On the branches, summer birds appeared as if they had blossomed there like singing fruits. They flew from the trees to the rooftops. They perched on the window sills. When I saw them at our window in the morning, tapping on the glass as if they had come to bring good news, I wished I could understand their chirping language.

That summer again I played as if I were making up for lost time. Often, I would become so engrossed in my games that I forgot everything that had once made me feel miserable.

And one day, in the fall of 1918, people suddenly poured out of their houses, embraced, kissed each other, and danced joyfully in the streets.

"The war is over!" they were all shouting. "The war is over!"

My mother threw her arms around me and Ruchele. She squeezed and kissed us and whirled us around the room. Pearl did the same with Feigele and Leibel. Babbe thanked God with a prayer.

Crowded trains began to bring back thousands and thousands of men in military uniform. They were frightening to look at. Some were without arms; some, without legs; some had lost an eye;

others were altogether blind. A few returned whole. But most of those who had gone to fight were dead and didn't return at all.

Every day the trains brought back more and more soldiers to Lublin. It was as if the streets were filling up with long lost ghosts, and each was slowly searching his way home again.

At our house, a day passed like a year. Our mothers rushed home from work every evening hoping to find their husbands there. But every evening they were disappointed.

Leibel and I became too impatient to wait at home. We went to the railroad station to meet the trains. As the soldiers poured out of the wagons, we asked those who looked like they could be our fathers their names. Some told us. Most, however, after a glance at us, acted deaf. A few asked us whom we were looking for. When we told them our fathers' names, some said that our fathers were on their way and that they would certainly be arriving tomorrow.

Leibel and I would hardly be able to sleep through the night. The next morning we rushed to meet the trains again, but our fathers weren't there, and all of this repeated itself.

We continued to go to the train station for a long time. Then we began to notice that everyday fewer and fewer soldiers were arriving.

One day, near the end of December, Leibel and I gave up. We stopped going altogether.

My dream didn't turn out to be such a wonderful omen after all. The great hope that for a while had been burning so brightly in our house slowly died out, and in our hearts, we were left to stir the cold ashes of a bitter disappointment.

Winter returned. As in past winters, my mother and Pearl stocked up on food and fuel. On Saturday evenings, a few of the young women whose husbands also hadn't returned yet, again visited our house. Now, however, they no longer sat around complaining about their bitter fates. Instead, they brought along two men, musicians, and we spent some very cheerful evenings together.

One of the men, the fiddle player, was blind, and the other, the concertina player, had only one leg, but the two crippled musicians played such lively music that the young women would jump up and dance. And the sight of swaying hips and breasts so excited the one-legged concertina player that he would wink at the women and bellow out a song.

> Lady on high heels
> Decked out like a queen
> Walking down dark streets
> Whom are you afraid to meet?
> Your husband you have long forgotten
> As if the wedding never happened.
> Is it nice?
> Is it right?
> Searching strange men out at night.
> Ladies, you know what I mean!
> Ladies, you know what I mean!

The blind fiddler, who would stamp a beat with his foot as his bow flew over the strings, heard the excitement in his friend's voice, felt the room shake, and squinted his empty eye sockets, trying to catch a glimpse of what went on.

Ruchele, Feigele, Leibel, and I, following the example of our mothers and their friends, would also grab hold of each others' hands and jump around. Although, at first, I had trouble dancing because of my shorter leg, after a few minutes, I forgot my limp and everything else that had bothered me. It was the same with our mothers and their friends: the moment they began to dance, their faces beamed with joy as they forgot all their troubles. Even Babbe, although she disapproved of the songs, would smile now and then. And in this merry way, hardly able to wait from one Saturday to the next, we approached the end of winter, 1919.

On a Saturday night, as the musicians were playing with zest, we, the children, became too rowdy. Leibel, who had been capering about like a wild goat, slipped. Everyone treated his fall as a joke. But when Leibel wasn't able to get off the floor and began to howl in pain, the music suddenly stopped, and a doctor was called in. After the doctor's examination, Leibel was immediately taken away. He had broken a leg.

While Leibel was laid up in the hospital, I went to visit him. Unfortunately, visits by children were not allowed, and so I had

46

to see Leibel from outside, through a window which was above my eye level. I stood on the tip of my toes and stretched my neck for a glimpse of my best friend. All I could see, however, was half of his broken leg in a white cast. And the only reason I could even see that much of him was because his leg was tied to a plank of wood and kept high in the air by a rope. I assumed the doctors had tied him up to keep him from escaping.

When Leibel came home, he had to use crutches until his leg healed. Leibel wasn't selfish, and his friends, who were all curious to see what it was like to walk with crutches, used them as well. Since I was Leibel's best friend, I was allowed to use the crutches most often. And I enjoyed them. I felt that I walked better when I used a crutch on the right side, where my leg was shorter. I told this to my mother and asked her to buy me just one crutch.

"Sure," she said. "I'll buy it for you right away."

After a month, I gave up waiting for it.

Eventually the cast was taken off Leibel's leg, the crutches were returned to the hospital, and Leibel was himself again. We went back to playing our old games, although Leibel refused to dance.

But the year 1919 held much deeper grief for Pearl. In the summer, Feigele, who was five years old then, became very ill. The doctor came almost every day to examine her and write out prescriptions. Pearl rubbed ointments on her daughter's little body, made her gargle, and tied wet towels to her feverish head. From time to time, an old woman came in to apply cupping glasses to Feigele's back, chest, and sides to draw up blood to fight the disease. The little girl's treatment went on for a long time, perhaps half a year or more, because when Feigele died it was already cold, and the snow had begun to fall.

After Feigele's death, a silent saddness spread through our home. While our mothers and Babbe were in mourning, Leibel, Ruchele and I kept out of their way. But my sister was the one who was affected the worst. Ruchele had stayed at Feigele's bedside until the very end, and after her best friend's death, my little sister walked around as if she were dragging something dead inside herself.

Another winter, 1920, came, and as in previous winters, the two partners had more time to spend at home. They cleaned, cooked, sewed new clothes for us, but they gave up looking for a larger house.

The young women who used to visit us on winter evenings stopped coming. Many of their husbands had returned and they had forgotten about us. On rare occasions when one of them did drop by, it was only for a short visit.

Although we continued to wait for our fathers to return, we were far less impatient. I would often hear my mother say, "Who knows what's happened to him? So many men have come back already. Who knows?..."

Pearl hadn't heard even once from her husband since he had gone off to war. She gave him up for dead and began to mourn him along with her daughter. My mother tried to comfort and encourage Pearl with a hope for their husbands' return which my mother herself no longer felt.

Every evening after they had put us to bed, our mothers sat up until late at night trying to figure out what they should do next. I would lie awake and listen to their conversations. I heard how jealous they were of those women whose husbands had returned, and how they lamented the fate of those women who knew that their husbands had died in the trenches and would never come home. And I heard how they cursed to hell those who were responsible for the war. They sat and talked softly for hours until they finally tired themselves out. Sometimes, they fell asleep sitting in their chairs.

And this was how we spent the winter of 1920: without music, without singing, and without dancing.

CHAPTER SIX

The Rebbi with Itchy Legs

THE SPRING OF 1920 was full of surprises for Leibel and me.

On a perfect morning in early May, our mothers shook us out
of bed and told us to get ready. The water for tea was already
boiling. Babbe was busy cutting the bread and buttering it for
breakfast. Ruchele, awakened by the commotion, sat up in her
bed and stared with sleepy eyes. Leibel and I wondered what was
going on as we quickly washed and dressed.

After breakfast our mothers rolled up their peddling sacks, put
them under their arms, and stopped to inspect us. From the look
on their faces it was obvious that they weren't all that pleased with
our appearance—a patch on my pants, a hole in Leibel's sweater—
but it had to do. They told us to come along.

Outside the air was cool and lightly perfumed with the smells
of blossoming trees. We followed our mothers, running a little to
keep up with their fast pace as they led us into the poorer section
of Lublin, not far from where we lived, to a white, two-story
building with sky-blue window frames. A large garden, enclosed
by a wooden fence, surrounded the beautiful building. My mother
took my hand, Pearl took Leibel's, and we walked in through the
tall front doors. Inside it was very clean and quiet. As our mothers
led us down the long hall, Leibel and I exchanged a knowing
look: we were in a school.

We stopped at the open door of the principal's office. Pearl knocked to attract his attention. The principal looked up from the book he had been reading and asked us to come in. Moishele Mishgiach, a man in his late fifties, was youthful in appearance, with a healthy pink complexion, and a white beard. The clothes he wore, a dark-gray suit, a glistening white shirt, looked as new as if he had just bought them that same morning. His office was full of books, and all the furniture, made of dark-brown wood, was highly polished. He looked at us carefully through the gold-rimmed spectacles that hung from his vest pocket on a long golden chain and asked how he could help us.

Our mothers explained that they wanted us to learn Torah and Jewish history, however, because our fathers hadn't returned from the war, and our mothers had to struggle just to keep a roof over our heads, they couldn't afford to pay.

The principal, himself a philanthropist, told our mothers not to worry about the cost. The school, he said, was supported by concerned Jewish men of means, mostly from America, who wanted every Jewish boy, rich or poor, to have a good *cheder* education. The Talmud Torah, the principal said, had many boys whose fathers hadn't returned from the war and whose mothers couldn't afford to pay. He assured our mothers that not only would our schooling be free, but we would be well looked after. Next to his office, he said, there was an infirmary to treat any medical emergency; at the end of the hall there was a lunchroom where the students ate breakfast and lunch everyday; and behind the lunchroom there was a kitchen, run by women who volunteered to cook and serve the food to the boys. And best of all, he said, there was a big yard where the students played.

Leibel and I liked what we heard. And our mothers asked if we could start school at once.

The principal opened a large ledger with a brown cover, picked up a pen, and said that as soon as he took down some information, Leibel and I would be officially enrolled in the Talmud Torah.

As our mothers answered the principal's questions, he wrote everything into the school records in a beautiful handwriting. When he was done, he reached across his desk, shook my hand and

50

Leibel's, wished us both "Mazel Tov" and "a successful scholarly career," and we became students.

Our mothers told us to behave, to go straight home after school, then they kissed us and went to work.

"Come with me, boys," said the principal. He took us by our hands and we walked up the stairway next to his office.

On the second floor, we passed large, bright classrooms with tall windows. There were about twenty-five students in a room.

The first-grade classroom, into which Leibel and I were led by the principal, was a cheerful room with white walls. In the middle of it there was a table with a bench on each side on which the students sat. The rebbi sat on a chair at the head of the table.

When we entered the room, everyone, including the rebbi, stood up.

"Good morning, Reb Schmiel," said the principal. "And good morning, little children."

The boys, who were between five and eight years old, shouted together, "Good morning, Mr. Principal!"

Leibel and I were impressed by this greeting. Our principal was obviously an important and highly respected man. The rebbi who stood before us, on the other hand, was far less impressive. He was a small, skinny man, dressed in a worn-out, black gabardine suit. Everything he wore was creased. Only his face was more creased than his clothes, even though he was just middle-aged. He was so short that his gray beard covered half his body. The older boys in the school had nicknamed him Schmiel *Krutsik*— Schmiel Dwarf. To the first-graders, however, he seemed quite normal, he was just their size.

"Reb Schmiel, I brought you two new scholars," the principal said, handing us over to the rebbi. "This one is Schloimele Schmer, and this one is Leibel Klapper. Teach them well and make sure that at least one of them becomes the Chief Rabbi of Lublin."

With these words ringing over our heads, the principal left.

"Why only of Lublin?" muttered the rebbi as he led us to a bench.

The boys in the class followed us with their eyes, and made me self-conscious of my limp.

"Sit down here, Schmer," said the rebbi. "And you Klapper, next to him." He picked up two large cards from a pile lying in the middle of the table and gave one to each of us.

"This card has the *Aleph-beis* written on it." said the rebbi, pointing to the dots, dashes, little circles, and boxes. "Look at it carefully and listen while the other boys study with me. When it's your turn, I'll teach it to you too. Any questions?"

Leibel and I shook our heads no.

"Good," said the rebbi as he shuffled back to his chair at the head of the table. A thin, pale boy with a worried face sat next to the rebbi's chair, awaiting his lesson.

"So, Hershele, my Talmudic genius," said the rebbi to the boy, "how are you going to mangle the poor *Aleph-beis* this time?"

The other boys in the class laughed.

Hershele began nervously to recite the letters to which the rebbi pointed with his bony finger. "*Aleph...*" he said in a faint voice, "*Beis...Dalled...*"

I heard a swishing noise and saw Hershele wince in pain as he rubbed his arm.

"*Dalled?*" asked the rebbi, suddenly waving a little whip with thin leather straps. "Aren't you rushing the *Aleph-beis* a little?"

"*Vuv?...*" Hershele tried timidly, afraid to say anything, but even more afraid to say nothing.

The rebbi picked up the little whip menacingly.

Leibel looked at me with bulging eyes.

"No! *Tuv!*" the boy quickly corrected himself.

"Wrong," said the rebbi and again hit him on the arm with the little whip.

"*Gimmel!* It's a *Gimmel!*" Hershele cried out.

"Are you sure this time?" asked the rebbi.

Hershele looked carefully at the little whip, which was now resting on the table, and nodded.

"If you're so sure of yourself, why didn't you give me the right answer in the first place? Did you want to keep *Gimmel* a secret from your teacher?"

"No, rebbi," said Hershele, holding his sore arm, "I forgot."

"Then maybe next time you will try harder not to forget so I won't have to remind you. All right, enough. You can go," the rebbi said.

At once Hershele jumped up and ran out of the room.

All of this seemed very strange to me. Leibel, I could see, was especially afraid of the little whip. But the next boy who studied with the rebbi knew his answers better and wasn't hit at all. When he was finished, the rebbi said, "Enough," and this boy also ran out of the room. Then the next boy moved closer to the rebbi, and everyone else on the bench moved up a seat. Everytime we moved, I noticed that the little rebbi was looking intently at me and Leibel. I imagined he was trying to decide which one of us should become the Chief Rabbi of Lublin.

The lesson continued like this until Leibel and I were the only ones left in the room. The rebbi told us to sit one on each side of him. He pointed to the letters on the card and told us what each one meant. Finally, he pointed to a letter and asked what it was.

Leibel sat frozen and stared at the card. I, however, remembered how every boy had begun his lesson by saying "*Aleph,*" and said the same thing.

"Very good, Professor Schmer," the pleased rebbi said with a tug at my ear. "You're a smart boy."

Gathering up my courage, I told him what I had been thinking throughout the lesson. "I want to become the Chief Rabbi of Lublin."

"Don't worry," he said. "I can tell that you're going to be as great a scholar as your father."

"But my father wasn't a scholar," I said.

"Is that so?" asked the rebbi, raising his eyebrows. "So, what did become of your father? A doctor, at least?"

"No, a shoemaker," I said proudly.

"Well, I'm not surprised. He always had the brains of a shoemaker."

I wanted to ask the rebbi how he knew so much about my father, but I felt shy.

"You can both go home now," the rebbi said at last. "But make sure that you're back here tomorrow morning at eight o'clock, no later."

On our way home, Leibel said that he was finished with school. I, however, feeling suddenly grown-up, wanted to learn to read and write. I told Leibel that I wanted to become the Chief Rabbi of Lublin. Leibel said that he didn't care what he became, as long as his mother didn't send him back to the Talmud Torah.

Later that evening, as we ate supper, my mother asked me how I had liked my first day of school. I told her that I wished that she had sent me sooner.

"And you, Leibel," Pearl asked, "how do you like it?"

"I hate it," said Leibel. "I don't want to go anymore."

"You will go," Pearl said sharply. "Are you so smart all of a sudden? Do you want to be stupid all your life?"

Ruchele said that she didn't want to go to *cheder*, either. She was happy to stay at home and have Babbe to herself all day.

"Mamme, how does the rebbi know Tatte?" I asked.

"Who says that he does?"

"He told me so. The rebbi said that I was going to become a scholar just like Tatte."

"Your father, a scholar?" my mother laughed. "I suppose your father must have studied with the same rebbi."

"But why did he say that I was going to become a *great* scholar like Tatte? You told me that Tatte was a shoemaker."

My mother looked around the table at Babbe and Pearl.

"By that," Babbe said, "he meant that you're going to be a good student, just like your Tatte was when he was a *cheder*-boy like you."

My mother and Pearl couldn't help laughing. But I was proud to be a student of the same rebbi who had taught my father. To me, this was an important link to my father.

That night I thought more of school than I slept. The moment I saw daylight through the window, I jumped out of bed and began to get ready. Leibel, however, just wanted to be left alone. He pulled the cover over his head and went back to sleep.

After washing up, I found a rag, dampened half of it, and cleaned the dust from my shoes. With the dry part of the rag, I wiped some thick black soot from the bottom of an old pot standing on the stove. I spat on the soot to make it stick, and smeared it on my shoes until they were black again. Then with a clean rag, I polished so hard that the shoes started to shine like new. Next I began to brush my clothes.

Babbe, seeing me work so hard, asked, "Schloimele, are you getting ready to go to a wedding?"

I told her my plans to become the Chief Rabbi of Lublin, and to do that, I said, I had to be as well dressed as our principal, Moishele Mishgiach.

When Pearl saw that Leibel was still asleep, she pulled off his blanket and slapped his behind. Forced out of bed, unhappy, Leibel began to dress slowly.

After breakfast, when we were ready to go, Babbe gave us each a sandwich to take along.

This time, Leibel and I went to school alone. It was a quick walk and we got there early. In the hallway we met our principal. He was wearing a new suit of clothes. Amazingly, like his suit the day before, it looked as new as if he had just bought it. He greeted us and told us to go up to our classroom.

Many boys were already in the bright room, sitting and waiting. As the rest came in, they raced to get the closest empty seat to the rebbi's. At eight o'clock, the rebbi himself walked in.

On his way to his chair, the hunched-over little rebbi began to murmur *Hamotsi Lechem*—the blessing of bread before eating it. I assumed that he was about to have a snack. But when he reached into his coat pockets for a piece of bread, he didn't even find a crumb. Having said the blessing, according to Jewish law, it would have been a sin for the rebbi to utter a word before he had eaten some bread. He began to search frantically from pocket to pocket but came up empty handed every time. Finally, he turned to the class, pointed to his mouth, and using gestures he begged for help out of the trap in which he had caught himself. The boys, who seemed to be already trained in this little game, raced each other to give the rebbi a piece of the bread which they had brought from home. The rebbi devoured the bread on the spot. Feeling better for having eaten, the rebbi thanked the boy who had saved him from committing a sin and sat down at last to start the lesson.

As the day before, the rebbi studied with one boy at a time and then allowed the boy to run out. Leibel and I couldn't wait to find out where the boys went. Before my turn came up, however, I noticed again how every so often the rebbi would twist an earlock while he stared at me and Leibel.

My turn finally came. I paid attention to the rebbi as he told me the names of the letters, and I was able to repeat many when he questioned me.

"If you want," the rebbi said when I was done, "you can go out to the yard. But don't get it into your head to run home like your father used to do."

I ran out of the room and down the stairs to the first floor. When I came out into the yard, I knew at once why every boy wanted to be the first to finish studying. All the children in the yard were playing. The rougher boys were running around, fighting, and rolling over each other in the dust. The quieter ones were sitting to the side, playing jacks with pebbles.

I edged over to the quieter group. After watching awhile, I was invited to play with them. Soon, Leibel came out and also joined us. When we became tired of playing jacks, we began to tell each other stories. On my turn, I told some of the stories which I had overhead the young wives tell during their long winter evening visits to our house. These stories made me very popular with the boys. I became especially friendly with an older boy, Lazerel, who was in the second grade and already smoked cigarettes.

I could not have been any happier with my life as a student. Not only was I on the way to becoming the Chief Rabbi of Lublin, I was enjoying myself at it. Even Leibel began to like going to school.

The next morning, Leibel and I both jumped out of bed early and rushed out of the house. When we ran into our classroom, there were only three boys ahead of us. We took our seats, picked up the cards with the *Aleph-beis*, and waited.

As soon as the rebbi came in, he began the lesson. After the first boy was done, all the boys quickly moved up a seat. This time, whenever I looked up, I noticed that the rebbi was no longer eyeing Leibel; now, he was staring only at me.

The second boy finished studying, and again we moved up a seat. There was only one student in front of me. I couldn't wait to be done so I could run out to play. Suddenly, I saw the rebbi calling me with a crook of his finger.

I stood up and went to where the rebbi sat.

He took my hand, leaned close to me, and said, "If you'll be a good boy and do as I tell you, I'll make sure that you and nobody else becomes the Chief Rabbi of Lublin."

I nodded eagerly.

"Then get under the table," he said.

I heard some boys snicker, but most became stone-silent.

At first I didn't understand him and stood confused.

"Do as I tell you, get under the table," the rebbi repeated and pointed to the floor.

I thought that maybe he had lost something and wanted me to find it for him. Without knowing what I was looking for, I bent down to search around the benches.

"Under! Get under the table," the rebbi urged me.

I crawled under the table, among everyone's feet.

As I sat there, stunned, the rebbi reached down and carefully rolled up one of his pants' legs, then the other. Suddenly, he stuck his head down, pointed to his naked shin, and said, "Give me a little scratch, there."

The smell from his feet was so foul that I felt like throwing up.

"Give me a *scratch*," he said again.

I didn't know what to do, but since I made no motion to scratch him, he took my hand, put it on his shin, and showed me how to do it.

I didn't want to touch his leg at all, but how could I say no to the rebbi? I started to scratch. Immediately one of my fingernails caught on something hard. The rebbi screamed and jumped in his seat. His head suddenly appeared under the table. "Be careful!" he said.

I felt something moist on my fingers. Blood. A trickle of blood ran down the rebbi's shin. Inexperienced as I was at leg scratching, I had ripped off a scab. I stopped scratching.

"Did you fall asleep?" I heard his voice above. "Wake up," he said as he poked me with his foot.

I started to scratch again, very gently this time to avoid breaking any more of the scabs that covered his scrawny legs.

"Can't you scratch a little harder?" came the immediate direction from the annoyed rebbi.

I gave a harder scratch, and he jumped again and almost fell off his chair.

"Not so hard!" he yelled.

The boys in the class roared with laughter.

"Softer!" "Harder!" "Slower!" "Faster!" the rebbi kept on giving me directions.

I kept scratching and when I finally scratched him the way he liked it, the contented little rebbi sighed and murmured quietly, "Ah... Ah... Ah..."

He sounded as if he were simply in heaven.

I wished that he would go to hell. And if this was the training to become the Chief Rabbi of Lublin, I thought, I would rather be a shoemaker like my father. But I didn't know what to do. I was even afraid of the rebbi's little whip. I decided that the next day I would come to school as early as possible. That way I would be the first to study and leave the room, and he wouldn't be able to put me under the table again.

The next day, however, when the rebbi came in and saw me and Leibel at the head of the bench, he told me to move my seat to the end.

Hurt and humiliated, I moved. Soon, he called me again with his finger and pointed under the table. I became extremely resentful that I was forced to sit among the boys' feet, scratching the rebbi's itchy legs. I began to think that I would rather stop studying altogether.

That day on our way home, I told Leibel and Lazerel that I was not going back to school anymore.

"Are you crazy?" Leibel said. "Your mother'll kill you."

Lazerel asked me why I wanted to quit school.

I told him what was happening to me in class.

"I know how you can get away from that stinking rebbi," said Lazerel. "You don't have to tell your mother anything. Just meet me here tomorrow morning before school."

The next morning, a warm spring day, Leibel and I met Lazerel on the way to school.

"You go on, Leibel," Lazerel said. "But first swear on your life that you're not going to tell anything."

"What should I not tell?" Leibel wanted to know.

"Never mind what," said Lazerel.

"If you want to be my friend, Leibel, just swear," I told him.

"All right," said Leibel, "I don't even know what I'm swearing to, but I swear."

"After school, wait for us on this spot," Lazerel said to Leibel. "Don't go home without Schloime."

"Aren't you two coming to school?" asked Leibel, amazed as if the sun had started to shine in the middle of the night.

"Not today," Lazerel said with a smile towards me.

"What do I tell the rebbi when he asks where you are, Schloime?" Leibel asked.

"Tell him that Schloime is sick," Lazerel answered for me.

"I don't like this," Leibel said.

After Leibel left, Lazerel told me that all I had to do was tell the rebbi the next day that I had been sick. My mother would never know, he said, because we would go somewhere far away to spend the day where no one would recognize us.

Lazerel knew his way around the city. We walked far into the richer streets of Lublin. As we strolled along we told each other stories and looked for cigarette butts. Lazerel showed me how to smoke and we spent that whole day smoking, coughing, and spitting. When it was almost time for school to be over, we headed home.

As soon as Leibel saw me, he exploded with questions. "Where were you all day? What happened to you? Why didn't you come to school?"

"If you had to sit under the table a whole day," I said, "scratching the rebbi's stinking legs, you wouldn't want to go back to school, either."

"That's not true," said Leibel. "I had to scratch his legs today, and I'm going back to school tomorrow."

"You know, Leibel," I said, disgusted, "you're not very smart."

Leibel looked angry and hurt. I felt bad for what I had said, but that put an end to his questions.

At home, we let Babbe know that we were back from school.

Leibel was still angry and didn't want to go out and play with me. I went out alone and stayed out until it got dark and I heard my mother calling me to supper.

As soon as I walked into the house, I saw that something was bothering my mother. I decided it was best to act as if nothing had happened.

We sat down at the table.

"Where were you today?" my mother asked.

I shot Leibel an accusing glance. I felt betrayed and doomed.

"Don't look at me, Schloime," said Leibel in self-defense. "I swore that I wouldn't tell and I didn't say anything."

"What were you doing in the city today?" my mother asked, getting angrier. "Answer me! Why didn't you go to school?"

I tried to think of something quickly.

"I wasn't in school," I said, "because the rebbi's son died."

My mother stared at me with a look of astonishment. She almost started to laugh, but then she grabbed a big, wooden cooking spoon that was lying on the table, pulled me over her lap, and began to beat my behind savagely.

"Roise, you'll kill him!" screamed Pearl.

"Let him go, Roise! Let him go!" Babbe pleaded.

"I'd rather kill him than have a liar for a son!" my mother shouted back.

She was furious and the spoon burned into my skin, but I felt too guilty to cry. Babbe and Pearl couldn't stop her. When my mother let me go finally, I crawled away into a corner with my swollen behind, cried myself out, and fell asleep.

The following morning, after breakfast, my mother asked me, "What excuse did you prepare for the rebbi?"

"I don't want to go back to study with this rebbi," I said. "Send me to another one."

"What's wrong with your rebbi?" she wanted to know.

"He tells me to go under the table and scratch his stinking legs."

My mother looked at me with disbelief. "What's happened to you? How did you become such a liar?"

I didn't answer. I was afraid of getting another beating.

"He's not lying," Leibel suddenly said." I had to scratch yesterday because Schloime wasn't there."

"What are you saying?" Pearl asked Leibel.

"The rebbi has itchy legs and he makes us scratch him under the table," Leibel said.

My mother was aghast. "You little fool!" she said to me. "Why didn't you tell me this sooner?"

"Idiot!" Pearl screamed at Leibel. "Why did you let him talk you into it!"

My mother and Pearl were livid. They grabbed our hands and ran off with us to school. Halfway there they stopped and asked us again if we weren't lying. Leibel and I swore that we were telling the truth.

At the school, Pearl called the principal out of his office and without stopping, our mothers, followed by the bewildered Moishele Mishgiach, went right up to our classroom. When the little rebbi, who had just started the lesson, saw our mothers advancing on him, he almost slid off his chair.

Pearl grabbed the rebbi by his thin arm, and as if he were a child, she pulled him out into the hall. Our mothers spoke in low, but angry voices.

Although Leibel and I couldn't hear what they said, we saw the little rebbi, his face twisted by fear, cowering between the principal and our mothers. Every now and then the rebbi tried to murmur a word in his own defense, but whatever he had to say made Pearl so angry, that he quickly shut up, afraid she would hit him. The conversation was finished in the principal's office. And when the rebbi came back to class, he seemed to have shrunk to half of his already small size.

After my mother and Pearl had the talk with the rebbi, I never had to scratch his legs again, nor did Leibel. In fact, nobody had to scratch. I could see that the rebbi was a little angry with me and Leibel, but I didn't care; I was happy to spend my days above the table rather than under it.

Following this strange beginning, my first year of school continued quietly. By the end of the year, I had learned to read and write. Leibel, hadn't learned much of anything. He was, actually, one of the worst students in the class. Still, we were both passed on to the second grade, and we were both glad to get away forever from the little rebbi with the itchy legs.

CHAPTER SEVEN

With the Buttered Side Down

THE FIRST THING LEIBEL and I noticed when we entered the second grade was that our new teacher, Moishe Yusifover, wore high boots which reached up to his knees. We took that as a good sign that nobody would have to scratch his legs.

More things were different in the second grade. There were only fifteen students in the class. We sat at school desks which were joined in pairs. And all of us studied together. Everybody started and finished the lesson at the same time.

In appearance, our new rebbi was the exact opposite of Schmiel Dwarf. Moishe Yusifover was not tall, but he was broad-boned and fleshy, which made him look large. He had a rosy complexion. When he smiled, his round cheeks glowed like two small red apples. He had a habit of running a little white comb through his short, blond beard as he was teaching. He was always well dressed, and the brown leather of his high boots shone like 'balls on a tomcat.' Best of all, our new rebbi never became angry; he did everything with a wink and a smile.

Despite these differences, however, one unfortunate fact remained the same. We soon learned that like Schmiel Dwarf, our new rebbi had his own insane ideas of how we should be educated.

One morning, at the beginning of the school year, Moishe Yusifover suddenly stopped the lesson. In the back of the room, a distracted boy had been rolling a ball of paper on his desk.

"Are you having a good time, Mottele?" asked the rebbi with a smile.

The boy immediately tried to hide the ball in his pocket.

"Come up front, my shining example of scholarship," the rebbi said.

Mottele, who knew that he wasn't a shining example of scholarship, only went up because he had no choice.

"For being such a good student," said the rebbi as he took hold of the boy's wrist, "I have to give you a candy." The rebbi then dug his thumb and middle fingernails sharply into the boy's skin and began to pinch without pity.

"Well?" asked the rebbi cheerfully, "what do you say to this candy? Don't you like it? Don't be shy, tell everyone how good it is."

The 'candy' pleased the boy so much that tears filled his eyes. "I like it! It's *good!* It's *very good, Rebbi!*" screamed the boy, twisting and turning like a top.

"I'm glad you enjoyed it so much," said the rebbi, finally letting go of the lucky boy's wrist. "If you keep on being such a good student, you will get many more candies. Is that clear?"

One taste of this 'candy,' however, was enough to last a boy a long time. And the rest of us, seeing how delicious the rebbi's 'candies' were, did our best not to earn any. Sooner or later, however, most boys slipped, and the rebbi never spared them. Because I was short, I sat right in front of the room, and I had to be good. I was one of the few lucky boys who never got a 'candy.'

But as lucky as I was in school, at home our luck took a strange turn.

On a quiet winter evening in 1921, as my mother, Babbe, and Pearl were chatting and sewing up holes in our clothes, and Ruchele was playing with her rag doll, and Leibel and I were discussing our new rebbi, there was a sudden loud knock on our door. We were all startled. But before any one of us could get up, the door was opened from the outside and a man stepped in.

He was tall, heavyset, with a brutish face. Although he was elegantly dressed, we recognized him immediately as one of the criminals from the neighborhood—a thief, at the very least.

"I want to speak to Roise Schmer," he said in a hoarse voice that sent shivers through us.

We looked at each other fearfully. What business could he possibly have with my mother? I wondered.

"Yes, I'm Roise Schmer," my mother said defiantly. "What do you want?"

"I want you to move out!" he said. "Right now! I bought this house and I need it."

We were stunned.

"But it's the middle of the winter," said my mother. "It's impossible to find another house. Don't you see we have children and an elderly woman? How could we start moving now? Give us at least until the spring."

"I'll give you one day," the well-dressed gentleman said. "And if you are not out by tomorrow, I'll throw you out."

"Oh, my God! What has Avraimele done to us?" my mother cried out. She turned to Pearl. "Go and get Avraimele right away."

Pearl jumped up, grabbed a coat, and was out the door before the new landlord could stop her.

"It won't do you any good!" he shouted after Pearl. Turning angrily to us, he said, "Avraimele sold this house to me. I can do what I want with it."

"Why don't you sit down and have some tea?" said my mother as she put the kettle on the stove.

"Take my advice and start packing right now," he said gruffly.

Our old landlord, Avraimele *Samdtreiger*, lived close to the Tchurtic. He was called *Samdtreiger*, Sand-Carrier, because he earned his living selling sacks of sand. His customers were mostly the poorer people of the area who used the sand in their homes to cover the floors which would otherwise have been the bare earth.

In less than ten minutes, Pearl returned, dragging old Avraimele behind her. The bewildered little man was out of breath and drenched in sweat from scurrying up the Tchurtic at Pearl's pace.

The moment Avraimele set foot in our house, my mother turned angrily on him. "What have you done to us! Without a word, you sell the house and throw us out? What are we to do now in the middle of winter? You want us to live in the street with our children?"

Avraimele, whose shoulders were stooped from a lifetime of carrying heavy sacks of sand, was so frightened by my mother's shouting that he could hardly stand up.

"Stop yelling, *please*," he whined. "Better let an innocent Jew have a chair. My legs are buckling under."

My mother took him by the arm and sat him down on a chair next to the thief.

"Is this the way an innocent Jew acts?" Pearl now turned on him. She pointed a finger in his face. "Have you got stones in your heart? Where's your fear of God? A plague will consume you for this."

Avraimele realized that he wouldn't get away from our mothers without doing something. He got up and pulled the thief over to the other side of the room for a private talk. The new landlord, who was much taller than the old one, bent down, while Avraimele stood on the tips of his toes to whisper into the thief's ear. For a few minutes, they murmured back and forth. Suddenly, the new landlord turned to us and said, "I give you two weeks to get out of here. After that I'm throwing you out on top of your junk." Then he stormed out, banging the door behind him.

There was nothing to do but move as quickly as possible. Pearl soon found a place for herself and Leibel. It was just a small room, however—too small for us to move in with them. And a few days later my mother found a place for us, a flat to share with a Jewish family. Since our new apartment was even more crowded than Pearl's, it put an end to our hopes of living together no matter how much it hurt us to separate.

Our new home had a small kitchen and one large room. For one family it wouldn't have been bad, but we were sharing it with five other people, and that made nine of us altogether living there. The space that our family occupied could only fit one bed, a trunk, and a small iron stove. All four of us, Babbe, my mother, Ruchele, and I, slept in that one bed. Not only was our space small, but since the house had been built under a mountain, the little window in our corner was constantly dark. And we still had to hang a piece of cloth as a divider, which made the room even smaller and darker. Because we didn't have electricity, a naphtha lamp had to be kept burning all day. In addition to these fine features, the walls were constantly damp; a cold sweat seemed to pour from them. And that's how we had to live: in the dark, cramped, damp, and cold.

Schmiel Mottel, the head of the family from whom we had rented that corner, was a tanner. He was a short man with a long goatee, a shiny bald head, and a wife, Zissel, who was twice his height. Notwithstanding heights, they had three children. The oldest, a girl of thirteen, was sickly and quiet. The youngest, a girl of seven, was so healthy and overactive, she made enough noise for herself and her sister. And the middle one, a boy my age, for reasons which I never understood, always wanted to fight me. He took after his mother, was quite tall and strong, and any time he caught me, I got thrown all over the house. He was also thick-headed, because no matter how hard I tried, I couldn't make him understand that I had no interest in fighting and just wanted to be left in peace.

After our move from the Tchurtic and forced separation from Pearl, our life began to change drastically. It was as if the little piece of bread which we had been eating up until then had suddenly fallen out of our hands, with the buttered side down. How else does a piece of bread fall from a pauper's hands?

Pearl had a sister whose husband became so sick he couldn't work, and she was forced to take her sister on as a partner. Since there wasn't enough business for three, Pearl had to break off her partnership with my mother. Pearl felt badly about it. Every time we visited her, she apologized to us.

My mother continued to peddle on her own. She worked harder than ever, but business simply grew worse and worse.

Leibel and I still saw each other in school. We were ten years old then, not more than children, but our hardships were quickly robbing us of our childhood. We saw how our mothers struggled for survival, and we understood how desperately they needed their missing husbands. Out of class, Leibel and I spoke constantly about our fathers. We made a pact that as soon as we were old enough to travel on our own, we would search the whole world until we found them.

66

My mother was young and pretty, and while she was waiting for my father to return, she had a few proposals of marriage. One was from an American Jew, an elegant gentleman who traded in currency. On his visits to Poland, he brought money to Lubliners sent to them by their relatives in America. He was set to move our whole family to America if only my mother would marry him.

I was beginning to suspect that it was useless to wait for my father. I urged my mother to accept the American's offer. But she wouldn't even hear of it. She was still married, she said, and until she knew for certain what had happened to my father, she wouldn't remarry. Although she put a quick stop to my attempts to talk her into marriage, she decided to make every effort to find her husband. At the time, the Council of Jewish Congregations was involved in finding Jewish men who had been lost in the war. My mother applied to our congregation for help. She gave them the addresses of the two letters which we had received from my father during the war. If her husband was found, my mother said, she wanted to know whether he intended to come back to her; if he did not, she asked that he be told to send her a divorce.

A few months later, in the summer of 1922, a young Hassidic man came to our house looking for my mother. Babbe told him that she was working.

"I have been sent by the Jewish Congregation," he said, "to tell her that she has an appointment there tomorrow at one o'clock in the afternoon. Tell her to go straight to the Rabbinate."

The young man's brief message, which Ruchele and I also heard, upset Babbe greatly. Her eyes started to blink as she tried to hold back tears. When I asked her what was wrong, Babbe said, "Heaven protect us. That call for your mother to go to the Rabbinate is a very bad sign. I just hope that I'm wrong in what I think it means."

Ruchele and I were frightened by Babbe's answer.

That evening, my mother knew that something was wrong the moment she entered the house and saw us.

"Why are you all sitting around with such faces?" she asked.

Babbe looked at her sadly and said, "They're calling you to the Rabbinate."

"What's that about the Rabbinate?" my mother flared up angrily.

Babbe's answer was a resigned silence.

The next day, when I returned from school, I found my mother at home. She was distraught and tearful. Babbe and Ruchele had also been crying.

"Your father has left us," my mother said quietly. "He has divorced me." And she began to cry again.

Although I was expecting to hear bad news, when my mother said those words I became wild. I ran to the trunk, threw it open, and quickly pulled out my father's photograph. With a kitchen knife, in quick slashes, I cut out his face, tore it up, and threw the pieces to burn in the flames of the black iron stove.

My mother and Babbe ran to me. When I had calmed down somewhat, I began to feel remorse for what I had done. But only for a moment, because as soon as I remembered how easily my father had thrown me, Ruchele, and my mother away, I felt that he wasn't worth much more than that.

It was then that my name, which had been Renglich, changed legally to Schmer, my mother's maiden name. Not until many years later did my name change back to Renglich again.

So ended our eight years of waiting and hoping for that joyous moment of my father's return and those better times that we had always looked forward to. The divorce seemed to destroy all the hopeful prospects of our life. My mother lost the will to live. Her eyes were always red and swollen from crying. She felt bitterly ashamed to have been deserted with two small children by her husband. Her pitiful appearance tore at me, but I didn't know how to help her. As much as I wanted to speak to her about what had happened, I was afraid to reawaken her misery, and so I held myself back from saying anything. I wanted her to forget my father as soon as possible.

I, however, like my mother, also couldn't make peace with our woeful fate. After my parents' divorce, I began to feel nervous and angry. I constantly asked myself what I had done to deserve such pain. Up until then, I had believed that bad things happened to people as a punishment for sins they had committed. But how had *I* sinned? It seemed to me that I kept the commandments better than many of the adults around me. Then why did such awful things happen to me? And if it wasn't my fault, whose fault was it? I brooded about these questions, but the only conclusion I came to was that if there hadn't been a war, we wouldn't have been sentenced to so much suffering.

I decided, as soon as I could, to learn a trade. I wanted to earn money to help my mother. As for my father, I decided that if I ever found him, I would settle accounts with him for all the pain he had caused us.

CHAPTER EIGHT

The American Delegation

DESPITE MY ANGUISH AT HOME, I continued to do well at the Talmud
Torah, and except for one incident, I enjoyed Moishe Yusifover's
class. Although I had only stayed out of school once, in the first
grade to avoid scratching Rebbi Schmiel Dwarf's legs, I suffered
for it in the second grade.

It was a neighbor, I had found out, who had reported me to my
mother after he had seen me and Lazerel strolling through Lublin,
smoking cigarettes. Leibel had not betrayed me, after all. But I
was convinced that it must have been Leibel who told the story to
the boys in school. How else could they have known that I had
told my mother that I didn't have school that day because the
rebbi's son had died?

The story spread through the school like the plague. The boys
began to taunt me that I had wished the rebbi's son dead. Their
pestering became so aggravating that every time someone started
it, I had to run away. Idiots! I thought to myself when I was alone.

When I told my mother and Babbe what was happening in
school, they sympathized; but when they began to reminisce about
the incident, they started to laugh. It kept them in stitches for
some time, and Babbe seemed to enjoy it the most. Soon, even I
began to laugh.

When the story reached Moishe Yusifover, he also chuckled. One day, during class, he turned to me with a wink of his eyes and said, "Schloimele, if you're planning to skip my class someday, remember, I don't have sons, only daughters." The whole class broke up laughing. After that comment from the rebbi, the boys stopped taunting me. For a few days, I even became some sort of a hero.

The school year continued quietly. When it ended, I was passed from the second to the third grade. Leibel, unfortunately, wasn't passed. He had barely gone from the first to the second grade, and there he got stuck. Leibel was a little ashamed about being left behind, but not too disappointed. He figured that since he had already gone through the second grade once, the second time would be easier, and he wouldn't even have to study much. Studying was the only thing Leibel didn't like about school.

My third grade teacher, Reb Heniach *Gaver*, or Heniach Drooler, was a man in his seventies. He was a bit absent-minded and sometimes a thin trickle of drool ran from the side of his mouth. Above his white beard and sunken cheeks, he had sad, watery brown eyes, like those of a dreamer, always slightly upturned as if at any moment he expected a message from Heaven.

On the first day of school the rebbi handed us each a book of *Chumish*, the Pentateuch, with commentaries by Rashi. The new rebbi's method of teaching was to have the class read a line of *Chumish* aloud. The rebbi would then translate the Hebrew into Yiddish, and the class in unison would repeat the Yiddish translation.

I was a good reader and did well with the *Chumish*, which was printed in large letters at the top of each page. When we started to study Rashi, however, I was suddenly lost. The letters in which the commentaries were printed were so small that all I saw was a blur. I didn't know what to do. I was ashamed to tell the rebbi that I couldn't see, nor did I want to be teased by the boys in the class for my poor eyesight. I decided that as long as no one asked me whether I could see the small print, I would say nothing. I pretended to read the Rashi along with the class. After a week of repeating the same passages, I realized that if I listened carefully to the lessons, I could memorize what I couldn't see to read. I was so good at memorizing that not only did no one suspect that

I couldn't see a word of Rashi in the book, I actually became one of the best students in the class.

Reb Heniach Drooler turned out to be a gentle and quiet man. In his class, it was soon obvious, the students could do as they pleased. Of course, some boys took advantage of the situation. The classroom often became so unruly that it was pure hell. Balls of paper, pencils, and even books would suddenly fly through the room like birds in summer. The moment a boy started to pay attention to the rebbi's lesson, he got hit on the head with something. Fights broke out. Every now and then, one of the hooligans in the class would jump up from his seat, leap over a few desks like a wild goat, land on top of a cohort, and the two of them would go rolling around the room, murdering each other. Although it was impossible to hear the old rebbi over the noise, he continued the lesson calmly as if nothing at all were happening. Perhaps the rebbi really was so deaf and blind that he didn't notice these incidents. Or maybe he simply knew that he couldn't stop them anyway, so he sat back, glad that he himself wasn't attacked. He was probably just waiting each day for the hours to pass, hoping to go home in one piece.

Occasionally, as the rebbi sat at his table teaching, his eyes would slowly close and he would doze a little. No one would wake him, nor did the bedlam which broke loose seem to disturb his nap. But he never snoozed for more than a few minutes at a time, and when he woke up, he simply continued the lesson from where he had left off. One day as the rebbi had just dozed off, one of the hoodlums who sat in the back of the room crept under the rebbi's table and tied the rebbi's shoelaces to the legs of his chair. Still not satisfied with this mischief, the boy crumpled a piece of paper, put it on the table next to the snoring rebbi's face, and as we all watched in horror, set fire to the paper. The heat startled the rebbi awake, and the rebbi, seeing a fire burning under his nose, naturally assumed that the whole building was in flames.

"Fire!" the rebbi jumped up, screaming. "Save yourselves! Run for your lives, boys!" He took one step and crashed to the floor, the chair on top of him.

The idiots in the back of the room laughed like a pack of hyenas, while we, the good boys, full of pity for the poor rebbi, covered our mouths with our hands to hide our laughter.

The rebbi slowly untied himself from the chair and, by God's miracle, stood up without any broken bones. He walked up to us, the good ones, and asked who had played this prank on him. We were afraid, however, to say anything. Any boy who dared mention a name would have had his head broken, nothing less. We looked down at our desks, ashamed of our cowardice, but what could we do?...

One day, halfway into my third year at the Talmud Torah, painters appeared at the school and started to paint it inside and out. Cleaning women came to wash the floors, windows, doors, even the desks and seats. In the hallways and classrooms, every small lamp bulb was taken out and large ones, as bright as the sun, were screwed in. It became an absolute pleasure to walk into the *cheder*.

Those of us who weren't the best dressed—to put it bluntly, whose clothes were torn—were given new outfits. I received a new *chalate* (a light coat), new shoes, a cap, and a new *leibtzudekel*, the ritual, fringed, body covering. Much attention was paid to the *leibtzudekel*, and our teachers began to check us every day to make sure that we were wearing it.

The Talmud Torah, we were soon told, was preparing to receive distinguished visitors. A delegation of American philanthropists was on its way from America to see how the *cheder* was being run.

Finally, one morning instead of our usual school breakfast of a piece of plain bread and a cup of weak tea, we were served milk and a roll smeared not just with butter, but with a delicious marmalade as well. And for lunch, instead of the usual corn meal soup, which tasted bitter and nobody liked, we were given real soup cooked with meat. The Americans had arrived! Even the teachers were decked out like Yentel-for-her-divorce. I thought to myself that if the Americans were to live with us all year round, life would simply be heavenly.

And the following morning, soon after breakfast, the American philanthropists began their tour of the school. They went from room to room and listened to the students, judging their progress.

It was not until after lunch that the Americans came to visit Reb Heniach's third grade. Their appearance surprised me greatly. They didn't look at all the way I had expected Americans to look.

In my imagination, Americans wore tuxedos, high top hats, and black patent leather shoes with white spats. The men who came into our room, however, were so ridiculously dressed, they almost made me laugh. They wore pants with little colored boxes, shirts with all sorts of flowery designs, and on their shirt collars they had pinned something that resembled a dead, black butterfly. To me, they looked more like the circus performers who put on shows in our courtyards than Americans.

The philanthropists greeted our rebbi in Yiddish, exchanged a few friendly words with him, and then they asked to hear a student read. The rebbi brought them over to me and said that I was one of the best readers in the class.

First they asked me to read some *Chumish*, which I did very well.

"Not bad," said one of the Americans. The others nodded their heads in approval.

Next, they wanted to hear some Rashi commentaries.

I recited for them what we had been studying that week.

They liked that too. But suddenly one of the Americans picked up my book, turned a handful of pages, and asked me to read some Rashi that we had not studied yet in class.

I was dumfounded. I sat, dead-still, staring at the open book like a rooster staring at a chopping block. The smiling Americans waited for me to start. The rebbi sensed that something was wrong and said, "Why don't you speak up?... Read... Did you lose your tongue?"

I didn't know what to do.

"Read like they tell you!" the rebbi said, trying to give an order which came out sounding more like a pitiful plea.

One of the Americans bent down and said gently, "Read, little boy, don't be afraid. You recited the *Chumish* so well, why don't you try the Rashi?"

I caught a glance of the rebbi. His eyes looked about ready to well up with tears. I felt badly for us both—pity for him, and fear of the outcome for me.

Another American bent down and asked me, "Are you sick? Don't be ashamed to tell us."

I couldn't keep silent anymore and I said, "How am I supposed to read the Rashi if I can't even see the letters?"

The boys in the class burst out laughing.

The American straightened up, turned to the rebbi, and said indignantly, "I don't understand this. How could you have been teaching him all this time without realizing that he can't see?"

The rebbi stood in a daze.

"Take this boy to the infirmary to have his eyes examined right away," the American said to the dumbstruck rebbi. "And later on, we would still like to speak to you about this, Reb Heniach."

The American delegation trooped out of our class. The minute they were gone, the rebbi came back to life. "How have you been reading Rashi all this time if you can't see? Why didn't you tell me?"

I felt that at least I owed our poor rebbi an explanation. When I had finished telling him everything, the rebbi shook his head in amazement. "You smart aleck, you!" he said. "Do you realize what you've done to me? You shamed me before the Americans."

I tried to apologize, but before I had said two words, the rebbi gave me a slap on the back and started to laugh. And he laughed until tears rolled from his eyes and the whole class was laughing with him.

Later that same day, the rebbi took me down to the infirmary and told the school doctor that the Americans had ordered an examination of my eyes.

The doctor, a plump, elfish man with a ruddy face, asked me to sit at one end of the room. On the wall, at the other end, a signboard had been hung which had ten lines of numbers in different print sizes. The doctor pointed to the numbers with a stick and asked me to read them. The first line was large and easy to see, but just a few lines down the numbers were so small that I had to guess at them. Next, the doctor looked into my eyes, shining light into them from a small round mirror strapped around his head. Then he began to try out different lenses over my eyes. As he changed the glasses, he kept asking me how I saw through them. When the examination was done, he sat down at his desk, wrote out a prescription, and handed me a folded piece of paper.

"Give this note to your father," he said, "and tell him that you have to wear eyeglasses."

If the doctor had had any idea of where my father was, I thought, I was sure he wouldn't have told me to take the note to him. I decided to give it to my mother instead.

When she came home from work, I told my mother what had happened to me that day in school and handed her the note. She eyed me suspiciously, as if she didn't believed me. She opened the doctor's scribbled prescription and looked at it carefully. I was glad to have that paper as proof of what I was saying.

A sad, weary look clouded my mother's face.

"Why didn't you tell me that you were having trouble seeing?" she asked.

"I am not having trouble seeing!" I said. "It's only the Rashi that I can't see because the writing is so tiny."

I knew that my mother couldn't afford to buy eyeglasses for me, and I didn't want them anyway. The bitter truth was that ever since my mother had stopped peddling with Pearl, we had little to live on. How could she buy me eyeglasses when she could barely afford to buy food?

"I can see very well," I assured her. "I don't need glasses."

In school, I began to feel miserable. The boys started to tease me again, now, for having made a fool of the rebbi in front of the Americans. Instead of giving me credit for memorizing all the Rashi which most of them barely managed to read, those fools laughed at me. And not a day passed that those same ruffians didn't play some horrible trick on the old rebbi. It made me sad and angry the way Reb Heniach Drooler allowed himself to be led around by the nose by a bunch of no-goods. I would have liked to have seen them try their tricks on my second grade rebbi, Moishe Yusifover. He would have given them what they deserved—'candies' until their eyes popped out.

Our poverty became so serious, and I grew so disgusted with school that I decided to quit the *cheder* altogether.

After supper, one evening, I told my mother that I would rather learn a trade than go to school.

"But you're still so young," she said. "I don't want you to start working yet."

"The sooner I start to work, the sooner I'll be able to help you out," I told her. "I know that you need help."

My mother looked at me sadly, her face drawn and tired from worry and hard work, and suddenly she embraced me.

"Not yet, Schloimele," she said as she hugged me tightly. "Not yet."

But I was determined. Night after night I spoke to her about it until, eventually, she realized how serious I was.

"Let's wait a little longer, to the end of the school year," my mother said one evening. "Then we'll see what to do."

I was glad to have this promise.

Although my mother and Babbe kept on trying to persuade me to stay at the Talmud Torah, I held firmly to my resolution and waited impatiently for school to end. The rebbi, who hadn't forgotten that I couldn't see the Rashi, asked me every day when I would finally get my eyeglasses. I stopped making up excuses and told him that my mother and I had decided not to get the eyeglasses because I would soon be leaving the *cheder* anyway to learn a trade.

"I am sorry to hear that you will have to stop," he said. "But if that's the case, you can read just the Chumish. And as far as the Rashi goes, continue to learn it by heart. That is the best way to learn it anyway, in your heart."

I took his advice and continued to memorize the Rashi. I realized that despite the way he was treated, the old rebbi was a kind, learned man, and I grew to like him very much. When the school year ended, I was sad to leave him.

Leibel, once again, did not pass the second grade. But he didn't mind; he already felt quite comfortable there. In fact, Leibel liked the second grade so much that he never left it. After repeating it for a few more years, he was graduated from the Talmud Torah without having to go through any other grade.

As for me, when my mother realized that I could not be talked into going back to school, she looked around and found me an apprenticeship as a shoemaker.

Just a few blocks from where we lived, there was a shoemaker's shop that was run by four brothers. My mother had come to an agreement with them: in return for being taught the craft, I would work in the shop without pay. On the first day of my apprenticeship, my mother and I left the house together early in the morning. We walked quickly since she also had to go to work. When we came to the workshop there was such loud hammering going on that at first no one noticed us standing at the door.

The four brothers worked at home, where they lived with their widowed mother and teen-aged sister. My mother told me that their father had been killed in a train disaster. Their whole house consisted of just one large, poorly furnished room. It had a kitchen cabinet, a few chairs, a trunk, a small table leaning against a wall, and two beds which somehow accommodated the mother, daughter, and four sons. The workshop was in the middle of this room.

For a few minutes my mother and I and watched with amazement as the shoemakers worked with quick and precise motions. Each brother stood at one corner of a high workbench. A metal pipe stuck up from each corner. They slipped a shoe-mold on the pipe. To the bottom of the mold, they fastened a heavy piece of cardboard which became the inner sole. Over the top of the mold, they fitted a piece of leather for the upper part of the shoe. They joined the leather and cardboard with little metal nails and glue. Then they nailed on the outer sole. And a shoe was finished. This was a factory, and the brothers produced about forty pairs of cheap shoes a day.

When one of them finally saw us at the door, he motioned to the others and all four stopped working.

My mother introduced me to my new bosses and left at once.

As soon as she was gone, one of the brothers handed me an iron shoe-mold, gave me the address of another shoemaker in the neighborhood, and told me to deliver it there. The mold was heavy and I wasn't sure where I was supposed to go. On the street, I asked passers-by for directions and found my way.

The moment I returned, before I could even rest, I was given another shoemaker's address and was sent out again, this time, to borrow a shoe-mold which the four brothers needed.

The molds were expensive, and since no one shoemaker could afford to own all the different sizes, the shoemakers in an area borrowed from each other.

This was my main job with the four brothers. Every day, at least four or five times a day, I was sent back and forth to borrow and return the heavy iron molds. My hands became sore and my arms ached.

If the parents of a child paid for his apprenticeship, a contract was drawn up specifying the time in which the child would be taught the trade. But since we couldn't afford to pay, how much I was taught was left up to my bosses. After a few weeks, I realized that they had no intention of teaching me a thing. They just used me in whatever way I came in handy. And because I was short, I couldn't even see what they did at the high workbench. That's how I became a shoemaker at age eleven. Like someone might say that he works at the opera. "At the opera? What do you do there?" "I sweep the floors and take out the garbage." That's the kind of shoemaker I became.

At home, when my mother asked me how work was going and how I liked shoemaking, I told her that I would rather have been a tailor's apprentice.

"But what about your eyesight?" said my mother. "How would you be able to thread a needle or make a fine stitch?"

I thought for a moment of asking for a pair of eyeglasses, but I knew that we couldn't afford it. No matter how aggravated I felt by our poverty and helplessness, I said nothing to my mother. I reminded myself that I had asked to be sent to work and now I had to make the best of it.

At the shoemakers' shop I spent a lot of time trying to figure out some way of learning the trade. In the end, I simply took a chair, pushed it to the high workbench, and stood up on it. At last I was among the shoemakers.

"Look how much he's grown since we took him on," said one of the brothers. They all laughed and without wasting time to teach me even the simplest task, they continued working.

I picked up a hammer, found myself a piece of leather, and tried to imitate what the shoemakers were doing. As I was hammering, however, my chair started to wobble, I lost my balance, fell.

The shoemakers, who hadn't stopped work for a second, looked at me over their shoulders and laughed as I lay on the floor.

I got up, pushed the chair back against the table, and stood up on it once more. Angry tears welled up in my eyes as I picked up the hammer and started to pound the leather. But the wobbling chair almost slipped away from under my feet again. At the last moment I caught the edge of the workbench.

This was so hilarious to the four brothers, they finally couldn't go on working because they were laughing so hard.

I threw down the hammer, stepped down from the chair, and ran out crying.

Outside, I calmed down and decided to go home. I realized that all I would get from dragging around the heavy molds would be a broken back.

When my mother came home that night, I told her the truth about my apprenticeship. She listened, shook her head sadly, and agreed that I should quit the four brothers. "Just continue to work there a little longer," she said, "until I can find you some other place."

I began to feel sorry that I had left the *cheder*. I missed the old rebbi, the *Chumish* and Rashi, and my school friends. But I couldn't stand watching my mother struggling alone to take care of us all. I felt that I had no choice. Somehow, I had to help her.

CHAPTER NINE

My Father's Good Friend

WITHIN A FEW WEEKS, my mother found work for me with another shoemaker, and I was happy to be rid of the four brothers. I had learned everything I could about dragging heavy molds around. My new boss was a good craftsman who only made shoes to order. I was relieved to see that the molds he used were wooden, not metal, and that he sat while he worked; I would at least be able to watch him as he made shoes and maybe learn something.

His workshop was in his home, and his home was the corner of a large, dark cellar which he and his family shared with three other families. My boss had a wife and three young children, and the other families weren't any smaller, so there was quite a small crowd living down there. The floor in that cellar was the dug-out earth itself. It was bumpy, and the little children were constantly tripping and scraping themselves. For privacy, each family had covered its corner with a curtain, but since there were no windows, large naphtha lamps had to be kept burning night and day. These lamps fouled up the air and left a layer of soot over everything and everyone.

I liked my new boss from the moment I met him. He was tall, thin, had a long face blackened from his work, and a full, rich voice. His large hands were dark from shoe polish and as tough as the leather they handled. During the week, my boss, who was nicknamed Sruel Grime, never washed. Only for the Sabbath did he take a bath, because that was the day he went to the theater. His wife, who loved him deeply, said it was a blessing that Lublin had a theater or her husband would never have bathed. But above all, my new boss was a friendly and cheerful man. While we worked, he would often sing songs and tell jokes he had heard in the theater. I was delighted to be working for him.

Sruel Grime even began to teach me the shoemaker's craft. First I learned to make cobbler's thread. I would twine a few strands of thread into one, then smear it with tar. When it dried, this thread was used to sew the inner sole to the upper part of the shoe. I also learned how to hammer in a sole; tiny, wooden pegs with sharp points were used, instead of nails. The sole had to be perforated along the edge with small holes, and then the pegs were fitted in and hammered into place.

For these lessons, I did whatever Sruel asked me to do in the workshop and sometimes helped his wife with housework. When she had to run out for a while, I even looked after their children. Although there were still times when I had to carry shoe-molds to and from our shop, now I did it gladly. I was finally becoming a real shoemaker.

And my new boss liked me very much too. One Friday afternoon, only a few weeks after I had started working for him, Sruel asked me, "How would you like to go to the theater with me?"

I couldn't believe my luck. "Yes," I said quickly.

"Good," he said. "Be here tomorrow at two o'clock, and I'll take you along. You're not so big. I can probably get you in for a half ticket."

Although I had heard much about the wonders of the theater, I had never been to one. My mother had told me that before the war, my father used to take her almost every week. After he left us, of course, we could never afford it. I could hardly wait for the next day. I worked as fast as I could, to show Sruel my gratitude and make the time go by as quickly as possible.

At the end of the day, as I was leaving, my boss said to me, "Don't forget, Schloimele, tomorrow at two o'clock. Sharp!"

"I won't forget," I assured him.

I ran home to tell my mother the good news.

I walked into our house cautiously, on the watch for Moishe, the landlord's son, who thought it was a good joke to jump on me from out of nowhere and send me rolling across the floor. Thankfully, only his mother and sickly older sister were at home. I wished them a Good Sabbath and went through the curtain to our part of the house.

My mother, Babbe, and Ruchele were already setting the table for the Sabbath-eve meal.

I told my mother what a wonderful man my new boss was.

"Why is he so wonderful?" she asked.

"Because tomorrow afternoon Sruel is taking me to the theater," I said, glad to get out this piece of good news.

My mother laughed. "So that's it," she said, obviously happy for me.

Babbe, however, wasn't at all pleased. "Are you letting him go into that *church*?" she asked my mother sharply. "Is that a decent place for a Jewish child?"

To Babbe the theater and the church were one and the same place, and as often as she went to church, that's how often she went to the theater. Never.

My happiness began to evaporate quickly. Until that moment it hadn't even occurred to me that my mother could forbid me to go.

Ruchele, who had been listening to every word, became jealous. "I want to go to the theater too," she began to cry. "Take me with you, Schloime."

But I wasn't sure anymore that even I was going.

"Please let me go, Mamme," I began to plead with her; it was useless to try and change Babbe's mind. "I've never been to the theater, and I want to see it so badly. You told me that you used to go with Tatte."

"What harm will it do him?" my mother asked Babbe. "Let him have some fun. He works so hard."

Babbe said something about my mother buying me a cross next, asked the Lord to forgive her for those words, but she let it go at that.

"You can go, Schloimele," my mother said.

My happiness returned doubled.

"Mamme, I want to go too!" Ruchele cried.

"You know that we can't afford it," my mother said. "Your brother is going only because his boss is taking him."

"How much does it cost?" Ruchele asked.

"Twenty-five groschen," said my mother.

"So much?" Ruchele said sadly. Even as young as she was, Ruchele seemed to understand that those few groschen were a fortune to us.

"I'll take you someday, Ruchele," I said. "As soon as I start to earn money. And you, too, Mamme. You'll see. I'm going to be a good shoemaker soon and we won't have to be poor anymore."

"I'll *never* go to the theater," said Ruchele. "You're not going to make any money and you're never going to take me."

"Do any of you still remember that it's almost the Sabbath?" said Babbe.

Quickly, before the Sabbath started, I asked my mother to help me prepare my clothes for the next day. While she took a brush to my pants and jacket, and ironed a white shirt for me, I found some rags and polished my shoes to a shine befitting a shoemaker's apprentice.

I was so excited that night that I couldn't sleep. I lay awake in the dark, trying to imagine what the theater would be like.

In the morning, I dressed up in my clean clothes, and right after breakfast, I left the house. Luckily, I managed again to avoid the landlord's son, who would have liked nothing better than to have wiped the floor with me in my good clothes.

Since it was still too early to go to my boss's house, I went to the city for a walk. But when I got there, I spent most of the time waiting around Lublin's city clock, watching the hours and minutes pass. The city clock was big and had a balcony surrounding it. At exactly twelve o'clock, I saw a man with a trumpet who came out on the balcony to announce the hours, play a little march four times, once in each of the four directions.

Although I was still two hours early, I couldn't wait anymore. I figured that the walk to my boss's house would take another half hour, and I decided that it was better to be a little early than late.

When I walked into the cellar and saw my boss, I almost didn't recognize him. I couldn't believe that the clean, shaven man, dressed in a suit and tie, was the same Sruel Grime who was so dirty all week. He even smelled good from the shaving lotion the barber had sprinkled on him.

He took a glance at me and nodded approvingly. "Very good," he said. "For the theater, you should always wear your best. And I'm glad that you came early because the sooner we get there, the better seats we'll find." He said goodbye to his wife and children, and we left.

The theater was on one of the shabbier streets of Lublin. It was a gray corner building with two big brown doors in front and a smaller side door. Although the theater was still closed, a large crowd was already gathered around it. I followed Sruel to the side entrance, and we mixed in with the people. As we waited, we kept trying to get closer to the door. When it finally opened there was such a wild rush that I was knocked off my feet. I was about to be trampled when my boss quickly reached down, scooped me up, and sat me on his shoulders. On my own, I never would have made it into the theater or up the stairs.

As soon as we got to the balcony, my boss grabbed two good seats for us. It was like an insane asylum up there. People ran and pushed and shoved each other, and even after every seat was taken, more people still kept piling in. Those who could, sat on the stairs; and those who couldn't, stood.

Finally, when the house was fully packed, the lights slowly began to dim. As the theater darkened, it became quieter, and when the lights were completely out, there was a moment of eerie silence in the audience. In that instant the curtain rose; the stage lit up like a summer day; and the band began to play such bouncy music that it made us dance in our seats. What I saw and heard then was unlike anything I had ever known before.

A man and a woman with faces painted like circus clowns danced out on stage wearing costumes that looked like huge, blown-up balloons. Only their heads and feet stuck out. The striped material of the costumes was so colorful that it seemed to have colors that I had never seen before. As they swayed from side to side, they sang:

Listen to me Motke

Here is what I say,
Get a fresh new broom and
Sweeping up is play.

There's a fad going 'round
Everyone can see,
Husbands and their wives
Divorcing—one, two, three!

Listen to me Motke,
Isn't it a shame?
Father, Mother dark as coal,
Children—Red as flame!

Up there in the balcony,
They really have no class;
There's a fine young lad
Fooling with a lass.

What he's doing with her
Isn't so discreet;
He just had the dumplings,
Now he wants the meat!

When they had finished, I applauded with all my strength. The theater not only lived up to my imagination, it went far beyond. More dancers, musicians, and comics followed. Before I knew where the time had flown, the same couple who had started the show came out again and sang:

Now that we have sung for you
And made your hearts so light,
You may want us to continue
Singing through the night.

We know a lot of verses
And the night is very long,
But you can keep applauding,
This is still our last song!

Because from all your clapping,
Whistling, shouting, Bravo! More!
We'll be traveling to America
By foot and get there sore!

When the show ended, I was so drunk with music and laughter that I floated home as light as a balloon myself.

Outside our house, Ruchele, who had her own friends and usually wanted nothing to do with me, was waiting for my return. Before I had even walked through the door, she started to ask me questions. I waited until we were inside and then I told her and my mother everything. I couldn't wait to start earning money, I said, so that I could take them to the theater too.

When I went back to work the next day, Sunday, I heard all the songs from the show again, this time, sung by my boss. He had such a mellow voice and sang with so much feeling that it was a pleasure to listen to him. After a song which I especially liked, I paid him a compliment.

"Sruel," I said, "you sing as well as the artists in the theater themselves." I knew the compliment had pleased him because he smiled as he kept on working. "If I could sing like you," I continued, "I would rather have become an artist than a shoemaker."

"What's the big deal with being an artist?" my boss said. "You envy their lives, I see. I don't. They have to drag themselves from city to city like gypsies. Only a few, the very best, manage to earn a living. The rest are even bigger paupers than us shoemakers."

"I only envy how they can make people happy," I said. "In the theater you forget all your troubles."

"That is true," said my boss, nodding his head. "That is very true."

A few weeks later, on a Friday afternoon, as we were working— I, preparing cobbler's thread, and my boss, finishing a boot—he looked at me and said, "Schloimele, did you know that your father was a good friend of mine?"

I was startled. I had had no idea of it until that moment. My heart began to pound with a strange mixture of emotions—anger, curiosity, shame.

"Yes, I knew him very well," said Sruel as he continued to work. "He was a good man. He also loved to go to the theater. I used to meet him and your mother there every week. Why he disappeared after the war, I just can't understand... Something strange must have happened to him...."

"I even remember when your father fell in love with your mother. She was a very pretty girl, one of the prettiest. And your father was very handsome—tall, strong, always dressed up like a gentleman. But your mother's father, Reb Schloime, after whom you are named, was a very religious man, and he wanted nothing less than a Hassid for his daughter. Your father was a good Jew, but a Hassid he wasn't. Well, your father and your mother loved each other very much, but her father wouldn't allow them to get married. Do you know what your father did then?"

"No," I said without looking up from my work, although I could no longer concentrate on what I was doing.

"I wonder if I should tell you this," my boss asked himself. "Well, you're soon going to be Bar Mitzvahed, right? You're old enough to know. One day, your father ran off with your mother to another town, and there, quietly, he married her. When your grandfather found out about it, he got very angry. He worked himself up to such a rage that he had a heart attack. He was in bed, sick for a couple of weeks, and then he died."

With a few blows of the hammer, my boss nailed the sole of the boot on which he had been working. He set the boot down and put his hand on my head.

"That wasn't your father's fault. Can you understand, Schloimele? If they had already gotten married, your grandfather should have just blessed them and welcomed them back. After all, your father was a fine man, a good Jew, and a top-notch shoemaker. What more can you want from a man?"

I sat with my head bowed down, silent, waiting for my boss to finish telling me about his good friend. All I could think was that if my father had been such a fine person, then how could he have abandoned us? That wasn't the way a fine person acted. And if he was such a great shoemaker, what good did it do us now? It made me so angry to think about my father that I didn't want to hear another word about him.

"I know that you must miss him very much," said my boss, misunderstanding my silence.

At the end of the day, as I was about to leave, my boss called me over to his workbench. He took my hand and put a two-zloty bill on my palm. "From now on," he said, "every Friday evening, I will pay you two zlotys for your work."

I was so surprised that for a while I just stared at the bill, hardly believing that it was real.

"Be careful with the money. Don't spend it," my boss advised me. "You should give it to your mother. I'm sure that she needs it."

"Thank you very much, Sruel," I finally stammered.

The instant I came out of the cellar, I remembered my promise to my mother and Ruchele. Despite my boss's warning and my fear of spending the money without my mother's permission, I headed straight for the theater. On the way, I still had one last problem to resolve, whether to buy three or four tickets. Babbe, after all, was also one of us. I decided, however, that from the way she spoke, I would probably insult Babbe more if I bought her a ticket than if I didn't.

At the theater, I walked through the front doors into the lobby and went straight to the ticket window. Reaching up to the high window with my outstretched arm, I laid the two zlotys down and asked for two half-tickets and one adult.

A man's head peered out from the little window to see to whom the money and the hand belonged. When he saw me, he put the two zlotys back in my hand. "Sorry," he said. "I can't sell tickets to children. Did someone send you?"

I realized that if I told him the tickets were for myself, he wouldn't sell them to me. "My mother sent me," I said.

"You're going to the theater with your mother?" he asked. "Why not with your father?"

I became angry. What business was it of his? "My father," I said, "still hasn't returned from the war."

"Sorry to hear that," said the ticket seller, but he took my money, gave me the three tickets, and a zloty change.

I left the theater carrying such treasures with me, I didn't dare put them into my pocket. Holding the tickets and money tightly in my fist, I ran all the way home.

When I walked into the house, the tanner's family was already sitting at the table eating. I wished them all a Good Sabbath and passed through the curtain to our part of the room. The Sabbath candles were already lit. Babbe, my mother, and Ruchele were waiting for me to start the meal.

"What happened to you?" asked my mother. "It's the Sabbath already."

Inside of me, my heart began to dance. "Mamme," I said, "do you remember my promise to you and Ruchele a few weeks ago?"

"What are you talking about, Schloimele?" my mother asked.

"Sruel paid me two zlotys today for my work and I want to keep my promise." I showed her the three tickets. "I'm taking you and Ruchele to the theater."

My mother's face suddenly sparkled with amazement and delight when I handed her the tickets. It had been a long time since I had seen her look so happy. And Ruchele, when she realized that what I had said was true, simply began to skip for joy.

"When are we going to the theater?" asked Ruchele.

"Tomorrow afternoon," I said.

"Weren't you afraid that I might be angry at you for spending so much money?" my mother asked.

"Yes, Mamme, I was," I told her. "But I made a promise to you and Ruchele, and I had to keep it, right? I still have a zloty left over." I gave my mother the money. "From now on, I'll be getting paid two zlotys every Friday."

"You are becoming a man," my mother said, embracing me. "A provider. And I'm proud of you for keeping your word."

Babbe, however, became very upset. She stood up and walked away from the table. As if lost, she took a few steps around the room and finally sat down on the bed.

"Mamme, are you all right?" asked my mother.

"How can I be all right," Babbe answered angrily, "if he's so young and already he's buying tickets to that sinful place. And you encourage him to do it. What will happen when he gets older? He will convert, Heaven forbid. May it fall on the head of our enemies. I was sure that he would take after his grandfather, may his soul rest in peace, but I see that he's beginning to follow in his father's footsteps."

"Mamme, please don't talk like that," my mother said. "You see what a good child he is. He works so hard the whole week, what's wrong with a little enjoyment?"

"You are no better than him," Babbe said, still angry. "Do all of you have to go on the Sabbath?"

My mother, Ruchele, and I looked at each other guiltily.

"You're right, Mamme. I'm sorry," my mother apologized to Babbe. "But since he already bought the tickets, we'll make this the first and last time that we go on the Sabbath."

Although Babbe called us pagans, she was somewhat appeased. And we, the three pagans, smiled at each other, anticipating the pleasures that awaited us the next day at the theater. I felt very proud of myself for being able to provide my mother and Ruchele a little pleasure. I hoped that I would soon become a real shoemaker and be able to help my mother out as I had planned.

But just as soon as things got a little better, just as quickly they fell apart. Less than a month after I had begun to get paid, Sruel Grime started to have less and less orders for shoes. Soon we were no longer working a full week. And before long, whole weeks passed without any work at all. My own boss went to work for another shoemaker, a friend of his, and I was left with nothing to do. For a few days, I still kept going to my boss's house, hoping that business would pick up, but it didn't. One day his wife told me that I should stop coming there because her husband had given up his shop altogether.

I decided not to wait for my mother to find me another job, and I began to look for work myself. I spent whole days going from one shoemaker to another. Often when I walked into a shop and asked for work, the shoemakers laughed at me. "Look at this worker," they would say. "How old are you anyway?" When I told them that I was twelve, they didn't want to believe me. I was so short that I didn't look older than eight or nine. The few shoemakers who didn't laugh at me told me to come back in a year or two.

Weeks passed. I couldn't find work. My mother, who was also looking for me, couldn't find anything either. Every evening when she came home from her peddling and heard that I still had nothing to do, she would ask me, "What's going to become of you?"

I didn't know what to answer her.

CHAPTER TEN

Cockeyed Yankel

ONE EVENING, to my surprise, my mother asked me if I would like to be apprenticed to a tailor.

"I think Moishe Nutte needs someone to help out," she said. "I could speak to him. Maybe he'll take you on."

"How can I become a tailor's apprentice if I have trouble seeing small things?"

"I know, Schloimele, but maybe you should at least try it. What have you got to lose? Tailoring isn't as small as Rashi, and if you really won't be able to see, I'll get you eyeglasses. Let's just hope that Moishe Nutte takes you on."

In all honesty, I had begun to enjoy not working at all. I wasn't fully twelve years old yet, and I still felt like playing with my friends in the street. If not for our poverty and my mother's lonely struggle for our survival, I wouldn't have wanted to become a shoemaker or a tailor.

A few days after our conversation, my mother told me that she had spoken to Moishe Nutte, who had accepted me as an apprentice. In the spring of 1924 my career as a shoemaker ended, and I began my career as a tailor.

Moishe Nutte was an unusual tailor. He was a specialist, a pants-maker, and he worked for other tailors who made uniforms for high-ranking officers of the army. He had the reputation of being the best pants-maker in Lublin. When I told my friends for whom I was working, they didn't want to believe me. They were jealous. Unfortunately, as I found out soon enough, my new boss was also unusual in ways that had nothing to do with tailoring. At first, however, I was very happy with my new job. Although I didn't have a salary anymore, my new work was cleaner than shoemaking. I no longer had tar-smeared hands at the end of each day; nor did I have to help the boss's wife with housework or the children. Now I was truly an apprentice.

Moishe Nutte, my new boss, was a handsome burly man, about thirty-five years old. He had dark, curly hair, and eyes so black they seemed wild. He was always elegantly dressed, even at work. To me, he looked more like a famous actor than a pants-maker.

He had his shop in his home, which was a very large, bright room with many windows. He lived there with his wife, who was a small, pretty woman, their two children, well-behaved boys of four and six, his wife's mother and sister, and his own brother. My boss had so much work that all the adults in the family worked for him.

Gedalie, the boss's brother, a handsome bachelor with a playful character, was a well known womanizer; while Leah, the boss's sister-in-law, was a pretty, temperamental girl of eighteen, with long, blonde braids. A few times as we were working late and the women were already asleep, Gedalie tiptoed over to Leah's bed and gently lifted the cover off the pretty girl. "Come here, Schloimele, and take a peek," he would whisper to me. "A little beauty, no?" When he felt especially playful, Gedalie lifted her nightgown too.

I knew that if she had woken up and caught us looking at her, Leah would have poked our eyes out; but I was so curious, I couldn't resist. As I gazed upon her, my heart racing with fear and wonder, I had to agree, she really was a beauty.

The first thing I learned from Moishe Nutte was to sew a border of wide stitches around the cut cloth to prevent it from fraying at the edges. I found it hard at first to keep the needle from slipping off the open thimble and pricking my finger. But with a little practice, I overcame this problem. No amount of practice, however, could help me with the difficulty I had threading a needle. At home, I talked about it with my mother. She promised to buy me eyeglasses as soon as we could afford them. Unfortunately we could never afford them, and all I got was the promise.

My boss soon noticed that I spent a good part of each day aiming the thread at the needle. I was afraid that he would send me home on the spot. Instead, he found me a needle with a bigger eye, which helped somewhat, and I was able to get by.

I was learning quickly and it even seemed that my eyesight might have been good enough for me to become a tailor, or at least a pants-maker. I felt grateful to my mother for having found me this job. As I worked, I began to dream again of earning money and becoming the breadwinner for our family.

But when summer came, strange things began to happen in the tailor shop. There were times, I noticed, when my boss would stop working, lay his hands down limply on his lap, and sit staring at the wall with a glazed expression. He could remain frozen like this for as long as half an hour. I assumed the pants-maker was a deep thinker. Who knew what important matters were occupying his mind?

On a hot day in July, as we were working and sweating, I saw my boss in one of these trances. This time, however, his eyes were wilder than usual and rolling around in their sockets in an odd way. I wondered what could be affecting him so strongly. All at once, he jumped up from his chair and began to pace furiously back and forth across the room shouting curses and gesturing wildly as if he were arguing with someone. Everybody stopped working and looked at him. Soon the pants-maker began to throw things: spools of thread, dishes, pots, chairs, anything he could get his hands on.

I was terrified by now. Something had obviously angered him. But what? I hoped his wife or brother would speak to him and somehow stop him, but they only kept watching. Then, to my total horror, I saw the pants-maker grab a large pair of shears. I was sure he was going to kill one of us. But still no one stirred, and I sat frozen too.

Waving the shears over his head, Moishe Nutte ran up to a window and smashed it. Then he turned around wildly, found another window and lunged again. Only now did the members of his family jump to their feet. His wife grabbed the two little boys by their hands, and as we scrambled into the street, the mad pants-maker turned on us. At the last moment, when we were all out, Gedalie slammed the door shut on his crazy brother and held it closed with all his strength.

While we stood there trembling, we heard inhuman screams and sounds of furniture bouncing off the walls coming from inside. The noise lasted about ten minutes, and then there was silence.

Cautiously, Gedalie opened the door, looked in, and crept into the house. We waited to see if he would come running out. When he didn't, the boss's wife went in, and the rest of us, the mother, sister, the two boys, and I, followed after her. Inside, Moishe Nutte was sprawled out on the bed, asleep. The women went quickly and quietly around the room and straightened it out. Soon we were back in our seats, working silently not to disturb the boss's sleep.

An hour later Moishe Nutte began to stir. I was terrified. I expected the pants-maker to go berserk again. But he simply went back to his sewing machine and continued to work as if nothing had happened. He didn't even seem to notice the pleasant breeze that blew in from all the broken windows.

Whenever we had a week of very hot weather the pants-maker had one or two of these attacks. His family, however, was used to them, and most attacks weren't as bad as the first one I had witnessed. I began to get used to them too.

On a hot day towards the end of July, Moishe Nutte dropped his work and went to the clothes closet. We sensed that something was up. But all he did was put on his best suit, hat, and gloves as if he were going to a ball. It was a little strange, but compared to his other attacks, this one seemed the mildest. We hoped he would soon go back to his sewing machine. Instead, he called his two boys to himself and started to dress them up too. The children submitted like little lambs. When he was done, the pants-maker took their hands and went out for a walk.

His wife asked me to come with her, and we began to follow her husband and children.

It was a sweltering day. The two little boys were inhumanly overdressed. The tailor led them down a few dusty streets, across a field, and approached a deep lake. We thought that now he would surely turn back. But the insane Moishe Nutte simply kept walking, and dragging a child on each side, he strolled right into the water. The children began to cry and struggle desperately to free themselves from his grip. It was useless, however; their father held on tightly to their little hands and pulled them further into the lake. As the water crept up the children's necks, the pants-maker's wife began to scream for help. A crowd gathered and suddenly two policemen appeared. They ran straight into the water, fought Moishe Nutte down, and barely managed to pull him and the children out alive.

I was very shaken by this incident. If his wife and I hadn't followed him, the pants-maker would certainly have drowned himself and his two small boys.

That summer I had also begun to go to the Volye on my days off to swim in the lake next to Krauzi's Mill. On a warm Saturday afternoon, on my way there, I came upon Moishe Nutte in the middle of a green pasture, head to head with a brown bull, in a butting match. He and the animal were mooing and bellowing at each other. At any moment, my boss was going to be trampled and gored to death. I looked for help, but since there was no one around I carefully began to approach the two contestants, hoping that I would be able to talk the pants-maker into leaving before he was killed. The instant he saw me, however, Moishe Nutte let go of the bull and, with a savage scream, took off after me. I started to run as fast as I could, but with my limp, I couldn't outrun him for long and he was soon close on my back. As I felt his hand upon me, I suddenly ran into a group of men. I imagine that the men, seeing a lunatic chasing a limping boy, must have blocked his way. I don't know because I didn't look back or stop running until I was home.

What happened to the deranged pants-maker after that incident, I have no idea. When I caught my breath and calmed down a little, I told my mother about my narrow escape. "Mamme, I'm afraid to go back to work for him," I said.

"I wouldn't let you go back even if you wanted to," my mother said. "I never realized how crazy he was. He could have killed you."

96

"What is wrong with Moishe Nutte?" I asked.

"Before the war," she said, "he was as normal as everybody else, but he was wounded in the head while fighting on the front, and from then on, he began to have these attacks."

"If it weren't for the war," I said, "Moishe Nutte wouldn't have gone crazy and I could have become the best pants-maker in Lublin."

I thought about that for some time. The same war which had taken my father from us had also destroyed Moishe Nutte's mind, and seemed to have caused all our suffering. As young as I was then, I already began to curse the mere idea of war and all those great leaders of the world who caused it.

But right after I quit my apprenticeship with Moishe Nutte, a new problem arose. We had to move again. The tanner Schmiel Mottel, whose one-room house we had been sharing, lost his job and was being forced to leave Lublin.

We started to look for a new apartment. But before we had a chance to find anything, Mottel sold the house, loaded up his belongings on a wagon, and took off with his family to Warsaw. The house was bought by a Gentile and it became impossible for us to continue living there.

I asked my mother if perhaps the new landlord would let us stay on for a few days until we had found another place.

My mother was astonished at my suggestion.

"Have you lost your mind?" she asked. "How could we spend even one day under the same roof when we have to keep a kosher house and he doesn't? At any minute he'll take the *mezuzah* down from the door. How will you say your prayers with a *cross* hanging on the wall? And what will the neighbors say? They will stone us. Don't you dare to repeat your idea to Babbe, do you hear?"

I couldn't help wondering why if there was just one God, he hadn't made everyone of the same religion. Then maybe people could have lived in peace with each other.

On the same day that Mottel left, the Gentile landlord began to move his belongings into the house. We had to get out fast. Since we couldn't live on the street, we took the only way open to us. On 6 Tchwarteck Street, in the poorer Jewish section of Lublin, close to the Tchurtic, lived my mother's older sister, Simke. She was Babbe's oldest daughter. My mother asked her sister to put us up until we found ourselves another flat. Simke couldn't refuse her own flesh and blood, even if her husband wasn't happy with the idea, although he also felt that it would be unseemly to turn us away. For our part, we insisted on paying rent.

We moved in with Uncle Yankel and Aunt Simke and their six children. They lived on the fifth floor of a big, old building, in an apartment made up of a large room with cracked walls, and a small kitchen. It was into the kitchen that Uncle Yankel helped us move our belongings. We barely squeezed our iron bed and trunk in there.

"If only these brick walls would stretch," said Uncle Yankel with a sad smile, seeing how cramped we were.

Babbe, Ruchele, my mother, and I slept in that one bed. We had learned to fit ourselves into it so that there was plenty of room for everyone. That first night at Uncle Yankel's, however, we slept very little. As soon as we had laid down and closed the light, bedbugs began to crawl on us. They bit us so viciously that we couldn't lay still. We spent the whole night hunting and squashing them in our bed and on the wall next to the bed until our hands stank from the dead bugs. But no matter how many we killed, there were always more. Like armies, they marched out from the cracks in the wall. Finally, a little light from the sun accomplished what our massacre couldn't; at dawn, the bedbugs scurried off and let us get some sleep.

When we complained to Uncle Yankel, he laughed. "What's the problem?" he said. "You're only paying rent for the kitchen. I'm not charging you an extra groschen for the bedbugs. You think that they're biting only you? They're not ashamed of me either. But why do you come to me? Did I make the bedbugs? If it was up to me, the world would get along without them. If you have any complaints, why don't you take it up with their Creator?"

But none of us bothered to take it up with the Creator. We were glad just to have a roof over our heads.

I wouldn't have believed that Aunt Simke and my mother were sisters if I hadn't heard Babbe address them both as daughter. Simke didn't seem as bright or capable as my mother, nor as pretty. If Simke had any beauty, it was well hidden by her harassed and bedraggled appearance; taking care of her six children was a lot of work. She had five boys and one girl, ranging in age from two to fourteen, and none of the children went to school, although the oldest two boys were apprenticed to shoemakers.

But Aunt Simke fit Uncle Yankel perfectly. He was a simple man, in his middle thirties, who earned his living as a porter— a human beast of burden. He did that work not because he was especially suited for it, but simply because he had never learned anything else. Although he was stocky, Uncle Yankel was of average height and somewhat bowlegged. His nose was bulbous; his black beard grew unevenly and sparsely; and on his head, there wasn't a shadow of a hair left. His eyes, which were as blue as the sky, were crossed; their beautiful color only called more attention to their defect. He looked as if he were amazed by his own bulb of a nose and couldn't take one of his eyes off it.

My uncle's parents had died while he was still a child, and he was brought up by strangers. His foster parents had been butchers. They didn't send him to school, nor did they teach him a trade. When he was old enough, they put him to work in the butcher shop. His job was to lead the cattle to the slaughter. This was the easy part of his work: the animals could still walk. The hard part was when he had to drag the carcasses back. That was how Uncle Yankel had lived, worked, and grown up—like a wild shrub in the forest.

I suspected that he couldn't read and had never even learned the prayers. Every Friday, before our Sabbath-eve meal, Uncle Yankel and I read from our prayer books. I noticed, however, that after my uncle had almost shouted the first few words, he buried his nose in the book and mumbled the rest. I was afraid that it was like me and the Rashi. The first few words my uncle had probably picked up in the synagogue, to which he went often, and as for the rest, he pretended to be praying silently. I thought to myself that God couldn't possibly punish Uncle Yankel for this falsehood. My uncle wanted to be a good Jew; he prayed as well as he could. It wasn't his fault that no one had taught him how.

My mother told me that when Uncle Yankel married Aunt Simke, he had received as dowry a horse and wagon with which he was to keep himself and his wife from starving. The very first time that

Uncle Yankel rode off on his wagon to the city to earn some money, Aunt Simke noticed that he didn't keep to the middle of the road. He drove awhile on the left side, awhile on the right, and sometimes off the road completely. Outside of the city there wasn't much harm in it. People just watched and laughed. But the moment Uncle Yankel entered the crowded city, he drove the horse and wagon straight into the big display window of a clothing store. The horse was badly wounded by the broken glass, and my uncle himself barely escaped alive.

Had the store belonged to reasonable people, something might have been worked out. But they were heartless. It didn't help to plead with them. They prosecuted Uncle Yankel and he was sentenced to pay for all the damage. Since he had no money, he was forced to sell the horse and wagon. His days as a wagon driver were over before they had even started. This was how he had earned himself the nickname Cockeyed Yankel.

When my mother told me this story, I asked her, "Why did they buy him a horse and wagon? Couldn't they see that there was something wrong with his eyes?"

My mother laughed. "Who knew? Do you think that if your grandfather had known that Yankel was half blind, he would have bought him a wagon?"

The story filled me with pity for my uncle.

Since he no longer had a horse, Uncle Yankel harnessed himself up and became his own horse. He wound a big rope around his stomach, hung around the commercial streets, and waited for businessmen to hire him to pick up or deliver loads of merchandise. From his meager earnings he had to support a wife and children. Porters never became millionaires. When Uncle Yankel came home after a good day at work and he had some money, life wasn't so bad. On evenings when he returned with empty pockets, however, it was impossible to stay in the same house with him. He could pick arguments with the bare walls. Whenever I saw him in such a mood, I would leave and not return until late, after he was asleep.

At first I was angry with my uncle for these outbursts, but I soon realized that it wasn't sheer pleasure that was driving him into fits of rage. And I began to feel sorry for him instead. My mother and Babbe were also deeply disturbed by my poor uncle's carryings-on, but how could they help him? They were in desperate need of help themselves.

Occasionally, however, when Uncle Yankel was in a good mood, he would tell us all the story of how he had driven the horse and wagon into the display window. His children rolled on the floor with laughter, tears streaming from their eyes. And for a change, Uncle Yankel laughed too.

One evening, after he had told the story and the laughter had died down, my uncle suddenly became very serious. After a short, thoughtful silence, he said, "The Devil knows why life is like that. May the Almighty forgive my words, but why does He give so much wealth to some, and such poverty and misery to others?"

This was a question which my uncle taught me to ask. The answer he didn't know, and I soon realized that neither did anyone else.

CHAPTER ELEVEN

A Whisper Like a Bolt of Lightning

TOWARDS THE END OF 1924, Uncle Yankel found work for me with another tailor. Chaim Zecherman, my new boss, a man in his mid-seventies, was a very kind and pious Jew. He had a small shop in back of which he lived with his wife. My boss handled only the measuring, cutting, and fitting of the suits. He employed two assistants to do the sewing.

My job was to stoke the press irons with coals, run errands, and, at the end of the day, sweep out the shop. Chaim Zecherman and his wife knew that I didn't have a father and treated me well. Between chores, everyone in the shop made sure that I learned tailoring. I even began to earn money again. Every week my boss paid me two zlotys. From my errands, which were mostly to buy supplies and deliver finished suits to customers, I made about a zloty a week in tips. And the two workers in the shop always gave me a few groschen whenever I went out for them. Each Friday I brought home three or four zlotys to my mother, a good salary for me. With four zlotys I could feed myself for a week.

Ruchele, already ten years old, started to work for a dressmaker, a neighbor who lived on the first floor of our building. My sister helped the dressmaker with the housekeeping, and in return was taught to sew. The dressmaker even gave Ruchele fifty groschen a week for her work.

But as much as we wanted to move out of that cramped kitchen, we never seemed to have enough money for the rent security. One evening, when I saw my mother becoming discouraged, I tried to reassure her.

"Don't worry, Mamme," I told her. "As soon as Ruchele and I learn our trades, we'll help you out. We won't let you work so hard."

"I know what good children I have," my mother said. "But when will we ever be able to move out of here? When will that blessed day come already?" Then, half smiling, she added, "May your father starve until then."

"Amen," I said, and we laughed bitterly, both of us sad and angry at the thought of him.

All in all, however, we couldn't complain. My mother continued peddling. Babbe helped with the housework. Ruchele and I contributed our salaries. We were eating; we had a roof over our heads; and we got through the winter of 1924-1925.

At the beginning of spring, as Passover approached, my boss, out of sheer kindness, sent me to a children's tailor and had a suit made for me for the holiday. The assistant tailors gave me a new pair of shoes as a gift. My mother bought me a shirt and hat. And on Passover, when I went to the synagogue with Uncle Yankel, I was dressed up like a rich man's son.

I began to dream of my coming Bar Mitzvah. I was finally becoming a man. I had no doubt that Chaim Zecherman would help me to become a tailor. I made plans for the future. In just a few years, I thought, I could be earning enough money to support all four of us by myself.

One evening in the summer of 1925, when I came home from work, I saw Babbe sitting in the kitchen, crying. Tears ran down the deep wrinkles of her face like little rivers. Ruchele lay on the bed, her head buried under a pillow, sobbing hysterically. Aunt Simke and her children stood at the entrance to the kitchen and looked at us with gloomy faces. The scene plunged at my eyes like the blade of a knife. One thought suddenly struck me, *Where was my mother?*

"What's the matter, Babbe?" I asked. "Why are you crying?"

Her mouth twisted in agony, but she couldn't form any words. She covered her face with her hand and gave out a cry of pain.

Ruchele was sobbing so much, I couldn't say a word to her.

I turned to my aunt. "What's going on? Why are they crying?"

Aunt Simke reached out her arms and embraced me. As she held me to her breast, she whispered into my ear, "Your mother went away."

My aunt's whisper ripped through me like a bolt of lightning. I tore myself out of her hands and began to shout, *"What do you mean, went away? Where did she go? Tell me! Where is she?!"*

"Don't scream. Calm down," said my overwrought aunt, on the verge of tears herself. "I would tell you where she went if I knew. When she left, all she said to me was goodbye, nothing else. Yankel knows everything. He'll be back soon. He just went to take your mother to the train station."

I threw myself against the door and flew down the stairs. The train station was far from where we lived, but I ran most of the way. When I got there, I began to search every corner. I asked the people behind the ticket windows, the porters, the policeman. No one had seen my mother or my uncle. I wanted to go out to the platform to look for them on the trains, but the ticket collector at the gate wouldn't let me through. I tried explaining to him, I begged him, nothing helped. I began to cling to the hope that they still might not have reached the station. I decided to wait.

After an hour, I realized that what I was doing was useless. I went home. On my way, I kept looking around me, hoping to catch a glimpse of my mother and Uncle Yankel.

When I returned to the apartment, Uncle Yankel was already in bed. Everybody else, except Ruchele, was sleeping. My sister, lying next to Babbe, was still sobbing quietly.

With a muffled cry I fell on my knees by my uncle's bed. "Where is she?" I begged him to tell me. "What happened to her? Why didn't she tell me anything?"

"Stop crying," my uncle said in a whisper and pulled me off my knees. "Sit down on the bed, and I'll explain everything." Uncle Yankel fixed the covers around him and slowly began saying, "Your mother has gone to Warsaw—"

"Why did she go to Warsaw?" I cut him off.

Uncle Yankel became angry. "If you want to know, shut up and don't interrupt me, alright?"

I nodded silently.

"Your mother has a cousin in Warsaw. A rich man. He owns a dry goods store. He and your mother wrote a few letters to each other. Last week she had a letter from him saying that if she wanted, she could work for him in his store." My uncle looked at me and smiled. "Well? Now do you see why she went to Warsaw? Don't say anything yet, listen. You have nothing to worry about. Your mother told me to tell you that the minute she's all set up, she'll send for you, for all of you. What could be better? Warsaw is a big, beautiful city. You want to live in that stinking kitchen forever?"

I waited until I was sure he had finished, and I asked, "Why didn't she tell me this herself? She never had any secrets from me. Something's wrong, Uncle! Tell me the truth. What really happened?"

As well as he could, my uncle pointed his crossed blue eyes at me and laughed quietly. "Listen, you little fool, do you want to know why she didn't tell you anything? Because your mother knew that you wouldn't let her go. Just look at the way you're acting now. That's why."

I spent that first night without mother, lying in bed next to Babbe and Ruchele, crying softly to myself. One desperate thought kept going through my head, to catch a train to Warsaw. All that stopped me from stealing out of the house in the middle of the night was that I didn't have the money for a train ticket, and I didn't know where my mother was, if she was in Warsaw at all.

The next morning at work, my boss noticed at once that there was something wrong with me. He took me to the back of the shop and looked at me closely.

"Schloime, you don't seem well this morning," he said in a low voice. "Are you sick?"

"No, Reb Chaim, I'm not sick. I feel fine. Really." I smiled to reassure him. I was afraid that if he knew the truth, he wouldn't want me as an apprentice. What would he think of me, a boy abandoned by his father and his mother?

"Are you sure, Schloime? You needn't be afraid to tell me," he said. "If you are sick, you can go home and take care of yourself. You will only make yourself sicker by working."

"I'm feeling *very* good, Reb Chaim," I said, continuing to smile and even attempting a little laugh.

My boss let me go back to work, but from the way he kept watching me, I didn't think he believed me.

"What's the matter with you, Schloime?" one of the two assistant tailors asked.

"You look terrible," said the other.

"Nothing is the matter."

"What do you mean nothing? Are we blind?"

I had to tell them something, so I said, "I don't know, I just didn't sleep very well last night."

But as soon as the boss's wife came in, I knew that I was in trouble.

"My God in Heaven, look at that child," she said, "as white as a sheet! What's the matter with you men? How can you let a poor child work in that condition?"

"I asked him if something was wrong," her husband defended himself. "He tells me he's fine. They asked him. He tells them he didn't sleep well last night. I can't get an honest word out of him this morning. He looks like a ghost, but he won't stop grinning."

"Come to me, you poor child," she said. "Let me feel your forehead."

I couldn't escape her. She placed her palm against my forehead, against my cheeks.

"Dear Lord! Cold as a piece of ice!" she exclaimed and started to drag me out of the shop. "Come with me, I'm taking you right to the doctor."

I couldn't go on lying any longer. To go to the doctor, to bring on that unnecessary expense to my good boss, would have been to carry the whole thing too far.

"I'm sorry, Reb Chaim, for not telling you the truth right away," I said. "Last night my mother...my mother..." But I couldn't finish. Each word stuck in my throat like a stone. I broke down and began to cry.

My boss's wife put her arms around me. One of the tailors got me a chair. My boss ran into the kitchen and brought me a glass of water. I couldn't stop crying for a long time. When I was able to speak again, I told them what had happened the night before.

"Poor, innocent child," said the boss's wife. "Don't take it so to heart. The Almighty will watch over your mother. Soon you will be with her again."

My boss placed his hand on my shoulder. "Your worrying, Schloime, won't help the situation any," he said. "It will only make you sick. From what you've told us, I think that everything is going to turn out all right. This was a good opportunity for your mother and she had to take it. Trust in Providence."

The two tailors were of the same opinion as my boss.

Everyone seemed to be convinced that it was all for the best, except for me.

When I came home from work that evening, Babbe and Ruchele had red eyes and swollen noses from crying. I tried to comfort Ruchele. I told her what Uncle Yankel had told me, that our mother was preparing to move us to Warsaw, that we would have our own apartment there, that with our mother's new job she would earn enough money to end our poverty. The only effect my words had on my sister was to make her start crying again. She threw herself on the bed and shook with sobs. How could I convince her of what I myself didn't believe? I asked Babbe, who had been sitting on the bed, watching us quietly, if our mother hadn't told her anything.

Babbe shook her head sadly, her eyes brimming with tears. "I told you, Schloimele, not a word. She packed up her bag and ran like a thief. May I better be struck dumb than say anything bad."

"Why did she leave without us?" I asked.

"Who knows? If I could have stopped her, do you think I would have let her travel alone? I only pray that the Lord may have brought her safely to Warsaw, and that He keeps watch over her there."

Uncle Yankel, who was returning from work, opened the door and saw us in the kitchen in tears. "Fools!" he yelled and started to laugh. "What's wrong with all of you? What did she dump on me, a bunch of professional criers? Didn't I tell you everything already? What more do you want? We'll have a flood from all your tears and drown. Enough! I can't wait for her to take you off my hands!"

But Babbe, Ruchele, and I couldn't believe that Uncle Yankel was telling us the whole truth. What we found hardest to understand was why my mother had left without an explanation, without even saying goodbye.

I began to have trouble sleeping. The moment I dozed off I would dream that I was searching for my mother. I felt lost as I ran looking for her through strange, deserted cities. There seemed to be no one left in the world. Sometimes, in these dreams, I would see my mother on a street corner or at the window of a house. She would smile and call to me, and I would at once chase after her. I ran up endless flights of stairs; I dashed from room to room; but I never found her. Sometimes, unexpectedly, I caught her, and then I clung to her desperately. If I managed to wake up with this feeling I was lucky. Most often, as I held her, she vanished from my arms. This left me with such a suffocating feeling of grief and terror that I had to struggle to tear myself out of my sleep. My thrashing would always wake up Babbe. After I woke up from such a nightmare, I would be afraid to close my eyes again.

At work and at home everyone tried to cheer me up and give me hope. But as the weeks passed without even a word from my mother, the situation seemed worse and worse. Babbe, Ruchele, and I spoke very little to each other. Every time I tried to comfort my sister, she would cry. Not to disturb her any more, I began to leave her alone. To Babbe, I didn't know what to say. Sometimes when Babbe and I did talk, we saw such horrible suspicions about my mother in each other's eyes that we avoided looking at one another. We didn't dare to mention our painful thoughts. And yet, strange as it was, when the situation seemed completely hopeless, I began to hope again.

A month passed. One evening, as I approached our building on my way home from work, Ruchele came running up to me. "Come, Schloime! Fast!" she screamed and started to pull me by the hand.

"What's the matter?" I asked as we ran up the stairs.

"You'll see! Come on," she said out of breath.

Ruchele banged open the door to the apartment. "He's here!" she screamed and dragged me into the living room where Uncle Yankel, Simke, and Babbe were seated waiting for me.

At once my uncle handed me a letter.

I took it. The address was written in Polish, which I couldn't read.

"Open it up," Uncle Yankel said. "We want you to read it to us aloud. I can't make out the handwriting."

I quickly pulled out a thin piece of paper from the envelope and unfolded it. As soon as I saw the first few words, my hands began to tremble.

"Well? Let's hear it already!" Uncle Yankel snapped at me.

I looked at Babbe and Ruchele and told them that it was from Mamme. Then I started to read aloud: "Dearest Mother and Children, I am in Warsaw, working in Cousin Yakob's store. I am feeling well. It was a difficult decision for me to make, but a good one, to come work here. I am finally earning a decent salary, enough for our needs. Very soon, my dearest Mother and Children, I will be able to rent an apartment, and I will send for you. We will be much happier here. We just have to be patient a little longer. Warsaw is a very large and beautiful city. Schloimele, don't give up your work. Keep on learning to become a tailor. Tailors make a very good living here. And take care of your sister. Ruchele, be a good girl and help your Babbe. Dear Mother, please don't be angry with me. You see that I had to do this. We can't ask Simke to keep us forever. How are Yankel and Simke and the children? Read this letter to them and let them know how much their help means to me. I hope you are all well and healthy. I hug and kiss you with all my heart. Roise."

Uncle Yankel jumped up and started to tickle me. "Well? What do you say now, smart aleck?" he said as he suddenly lifted me up in the air.

"Put me down, Uncle! Please!" I screamed, struggling and laughing.

"You didn't want to believe me, did you?" he said, setting me free. He turned to Ruchele, caught her in his arms, and tossed her up in the air. "And you, you big girl? Do you promise to stop crying now?"

Squealing with laughter, Ruchele promised, and she was set free.

"Tell me, big genius," Uncle Yankel asked me, "when you move to Warsaw will you at least write a few words to your Aunt and Uncle?"

"I'll write you a long letter, Uncle Yankel, and tell you everything about Warsaw," I assured him.

"Praised be the Lord," said Babbe. "Maybe the time has finally come to get rid of those bedbugs."

We were overjoyed. For Babbe, Ruchele, and me, receiving that letter was like waking up from a nightmare. Our darkest fears and suspicions were immediately turned into a bright, fresh feeling of hope.

One evening a few weeks later, when I came home from work, I found everybody assembled in the living room again, waiting for me with a second letter. I opened it at once and read: "Dearest Mother and Children, I am working hard to have you with me as soon as possible. You must be patient a little. Meanwhile I am sending you 20 zlotys by the Savings Bank of Poland. Don't worry, everything is fine and we will soon be together. Give my love to Simke and Yankel and the children. I have met Frau Liebe here, and I visit her often. She says that she can't wait to see you all again. Schloimele and Ruchele, be good children and listen to your Babbe. I hug you and kiss you with all my heart. Roise."

"It's not going to take much longer now," said Uncle Yankel when I had finished reading. "You can start packing up."

The next day I told my boss, his wife, and the two tailors that we had received a second letter and that I would soon be moving to Warsaw. Everyone was very happy for me.

"You see," my boss said, "you worried unnecessarily."

At home we had not only stopped worrying, we were singing for joy.

In a few days a card came from the bank. Uncle Yankel took me with him and we picked up the twenty zlotys.

After the second letter, however, a few weeks passed without word from my mother. At first we thought that she was preparing our new apartment and was too busy to write. Then we became afraid that she might be sick. We began to worry again and decided to write a letter to Cousin Yakob asking him for news.

No answer came back. We didn't know what to think. I wrote another letter to our cousin. Three more weeks passed, and then one evening, when I came home, I found a third letter from Warsaw waiting to be read aloud. It was from Cousin Yakob and it said: "Dear Aunt Zlate and Children, I'm sorry for having let all this time pass without answering your letters, but I didn't know what to write to you. I still don't know what to tell you. It's been over a month that Roise stopped working for me, and I haven't seen her since. I don't even know where she is. She moved out of her room and didn't leave a trace. I am continuing to look for her. You can be certain that as soon as I find her, I will let you know. Yakob.'

CHAPTER TWELVE

Some Sort of Scoundrel

IN HER SECOND LETTER, my mother had mentioned that she often visited her old friend Frau Liebe in Warsaw. I rummaged through our trunk and on the bottom, among our clothing, I found the letters Liebe had sent us after her move from the Tchurtic eight years earlier. I wasn't sure whether her address in Warsaw was still the same, but I wrote anyway, asking about my mother. The answer, which came quickly, was the same as Cousin Yakob's: Roise had suddenly stopped visiting over a month ago and hadn't been heard from since. That final letter drained us of our last drop of hope. Not even Uncle Yankel had any more explanations to offer.

Under these circumstances the day of my Bar Mitzvah arrived. Without my father's or mother's presence, I took on the responsibilities of an adult through the ritual in the synagogue. In reality, however, it was the bitter struggle for survival that forced me to become a man at thirteen. Ruchele was still a child and Babbe was almost eighty years old; I was now the head of our little family of three.

My uncle let us live in the kitchen and helped us as much as he could, but instead of seven people, he now had ten to feed. During the worst days of winter, Uncle Yankel was forced to stay home from work, and since he had no savings to fall back on, there was little for any of us to eat.

On a cutting cold day, he took me aside and said. "Schloime, don't be angry with me for asking, but what are we going to do? Let's forget about the rent, but I still have to feed all of you too. Where am I supposed to get it from? If only I had.... But you can see for yourself. I don't have to tell you. If I don't work a day, we're starving. What are we going to do about this?... We have to find a way out...."

I was speechless as I listened. What could I possibly answer him? He was absolutely right. The few zlotys I earned each week at the tailor shop were not enough to take care of Babbe and Ruchele. And I was still far from being even an assistant tailor. My only consolation was knowing that there were grown men, much older than I, who also did not earn enough to feed their families.

To me, Uncle Yankel had spoken softly so that others in the house would not overhear him, but he was far less sparing of his own wife. Whenever he got angry at his bleak fate, he let out his rage on her. "I should have broken both my legs before I stood under the canopy with you! You're burying me alive, you and that family of yours!" Then, with a hiss that we heard in the kitchen, he said to her, "If you don't chase them out, I'll break your jaw!"

Poor Aunt Simke. She would wail, beat her breast with her fists, and curse herself twice as hard as her husband did.

Sometimes, however, after a good day at work, Uncle Yankel would have a few drinks on the street and come home happily drunk. When he was in this state, he caught Aunt Simke in his arms, kissed her, and apologized. "Forgive me, Simkele," he pleaded. "You know it's my miseries that yell at you, not me."

"I know, I know," said Aunt Simke, kissing him back. "Go to sleep already."

As the winter grew worse, so did our life, and Uncle Yankel called me aside for more *talks*. How was he supposed to provide for us all? he would ask me. How much longer would we have to depend on him? How would it all end?

These questions threw me into despair. More seriously than ever, I began to look for ways to take Babbe, Ruchele, and myself off my uncle's hands. I decided to try to get help from my father's family.

On a Saturday afternoon, I went to the Volye to visit my father's sister. When she opened the door, her face blanched. She wasn't at all pleased to see me and only begrudgingly did she allow me into her home. As I told her our problems, her look of disgust made it obvious how ashamed she was of us and our poverty. When I had finished, rather than offering help, she offered criticisms.

"It's your own mother's fault," she said, her tight lips trembling angrily. "If she hadn't been so hot to divorce my brother, you and that little sister of yours would still have a father. He would have come back in time. It doesn't surprise me in the least that now she has dumped all of you too. What do you want *me* to do about it? What kind of a mother and wife does what she did? I'll tell you what kind...."

Her vicious words angered me so that I ran out of her house, slammed the door, and left her talking to herself. As I walked away from the Volye, I knew that Babbe, Ruchele, and I would get no more help than we were already getting. Somehow I had to start earning more money than I was making at the tailor shop. I had a few street friends, poor boys like me, who understood my problem and were willing to help me out. These boys earned their living any way they could: one sold newspapers; another, bagels; a few simply stole. As soon as the days became warmer, instead of going to the tailor shop, I began going to the city to meet them. I told no one at home what I was doing. I didn't even tell Chaim Zecherman, my kind boss, that I was quitting. I was too ashamed.

I followed my friends to the Jewish Market. It was their favorite hangout because of the wealth of merchandise displayed in the open, and the tumultuous confusion of people selling and buying. As we strolled casually among the stalls, one of the boys moved away from our little group. The others told me to keep my eyes on him. Suddenly the boy grabbed a pair of pants off a merchant's table and ran off with it. It was all done so quickly that if I hadn't been told to watch him, I would never have seen it.

With my limp, I knew I didn't have the speed or agility to carry off a job like that. Nevertheless, when I became hungry later that day, I picked up an apple and a pear from a fruit stand while the owner was busy with a customer. My friends cheered me when we had gotten away from the stall.

The next day I became a little more daring and lifted a hat and a scarf from an outside rack. One of the boys sold them for me. He and I split the few zlotys. At night, I gave Babbe all the money and told her that I had made many deliveries that day and been especially lucky with tips.

The following morning, I worked with another boy. We walked up to a stand with cheeses. The boy quickly squatted down under the stall, out of sight. As soon as the merchant had turned his back, I knocked a big piece of cheese off the table into my friend's hands.

When we had gathered in the early afternoon to eat the cheese, I noticed that two of the boys were missing. I asked where they were.

"Where do you think they are?" one of the older boys asked me.

"I don't know," I said.

"Guess," he said.

"Yes, guess," said another boy, smirking and winking.

"They went home sick?" I said, innocently.

All the boys laughed.

"Idiot!" the older boy said. "The coppers caught them with their hands full. They're in the slammer."

This news stunned me. It suddenly hit me that if I continued to work at the Jewish Market with them, I could also end up in jail. I told them to go on without me.

Some of the boys called me a coward, but the others just wished me luck.

I spent the next day alone, walking around the city, thinking. Without the help of those boys, I didn't know what to do to make money. A bagel peddler passed me and I wished I had a few groschen to buy a bagel. After hours of aimless wandering without eating, I was starved. I felt my pockets even though I knew they were empty. If I had some money, I thought, I could have become a bagel peddler myself. By law, a street peddler needed a permit from City Hall. The permit, however, was so expensive that few could afford it. Suddenly, the delicious smell of fresh hot bagels began to gnaw at my stomach. I looked up, saw that I was standing next to a small bagel shop, and without giving myself time to think it over, I walked in.

The shop was empty. I looked around the counter and, in the back, at the oven, I saw the baker. He was a short, round Jew with a red face and beard. He noticed me and came out, wiping his hands on his apron. How could he help me, he asked. He seemed to be a kind person. Driven by hunger and my hopeless situation, I poured out my heart to him. I didn't spare him any detail of my troubles. As he listened to me, the compassionate baker shook his head up and down and from side to side.

"I believe you, little boy," he said, "and I would even like to help you. But what if I trusted you with a basket of bagels without taking any money from you, and you never returned? I don't know you. It's happened before that as soon as I trusted somebody with a basket of bagels, they disappeared with the bagels and the basket. I'm not saying that you would do that, but you know what they say, 'Burn yourself once on a hot pan, and you'll blow even on a cold one.'"

"But I need to make money *every* day," I tried desperately to convince him. "I told you that I have to support my little sister and my crippled Babbe. I swear to you by the Holiest that I'm not lying. I beg you to trust me."

He was moved by my words. "If you promise to be an honest boy," he said, "maybe I will help you. It's too late to start today. Come in tomorrow morning and I'll see what I can do for you."

"I'll be here early," I said.

As I lay in bed that night, I decided that as soon as I had enough money I would travel to Warsaw to find my mother. When I fell asleep, I dreamt of hot bagels and money.

I woke up before anyone else in the house, dressed quickly, and ran out. At the bagel shop, the baker sized me up again, rolling his eyes over me from head to toes. He gave me another sermon on honesty, to which I nodded my head vigorously to let him know that I was in complete agreement. Again, I assured him that I wouldn't run off with the goods. He asked me for my name and address and wrote them down on a piece of old newspaper.

At last, the baker went to the back of the shop and came back with a large wicker basket.

"Hold it," he said, "and help me count." As we counted aloud, he placed each bagel in my basket.

"Thirty-six bagels. That's enough for now," he said. "You have to charge five groschen for each bagel. If you sell these, when you come back—and I pray that you will come back—you'll get more."

As I was stepping out the door, he called me back. "Good luck," he said, "and watch out for the police. Don't let them catch you."

I knew that if a policeman caught me, I would be fined for peddling without a permit. On top of that, I would be kept at the station the whole day, and the police would eat my bagels. Naturally, some policemen were bribed into blindness by the bagel bakers but one had to hide even from the bribed police so that it wouldn't seem that they were overlooking anything. Somehow, the police knew which bagel peddlers were 'kosher' and which weren't.

The moment I came to a busy corner, people going to work began to put five groschen coins into my hand for the bagels. In the sudden excitement of selling, I forgot myself and began to shout, "Bagels! Hot Bagels! Buy Hot Bagels!"

"What're you screaming so loud for?" one customer asked. "Nobody's deaf."

"Stop yelling," another warned me. "There are policemen lurking."

I shut up at once and looked all around me. No police yet. I was lucky. Quickly, quietly, I sold the rest of the bagels. Then I rushed back to the shop.

The baker was overjoyed that I had returned.

I took the coins out of my pockets by the fistfuls and tossed them into a paper bag which the baker held.

"Now, since it's still early morning," he said, "I will give you six dozen." He stopped, looked at me solemnly, and repeated, "Six dozen! May no evil thought befall you to lead you astray with those bagels. I don't have to tell you what I mean, do I? Don't even think of stealing those bagels. When you come back after you sell them, we'll figure out how much you made."

As I was leaving the shop, the wicker basket heavy with bagels, the baker shouted after me, "Remember, careful!"

I was more cautious now. To sell six dozen, I would have to go to the busier streets of the city where there were more customers but also more policemen. I walked at a fast pace, constantly on the lookout.

At the first major intersection, just as I had expected, I began to do a brisk business. Three hands at a time would reach into my basket and grab bagels as the coins were pressed into my open palms. Suddenly a policeman appeared on the opposite corner. I turned and dashed into the first doorway I found. Every few minutes, my heart in my mouth, I glanced out to see if he was still there. When he was gone, I came out and continued selling—one eye on the basket, the other on the street.

By eleven o'clock that morning, I had sold the six dozen bagels, except for a few broken ones on the bottom of the basket. The baker was standing outside his shop looking for me when I rounded the corner of his street. When he saw me, he waved happily and went back in.

"Did you have any trouble?" he asked as I stepped through the door.

"No, I sold everything. There are just a few broken ones left," I said, putting the basket down.

I took the coins out of my bulging pockets and spread them out on the counter.

The baker counted them one by one. Satisfied that I hadn't stolen any of the money, he smiled and patted my shoulder.

"Do you know what most bakers pay peddlers for each bagel they sell?" he asked.

"One groschen," I said. I knew because I had been told by my friends from the Jewish Market who sometimes did this work.

"That's right. But because you're an honest boy, I'm going to pay you two groschen for every bagel you sold. You had nine dozen altogether, one hundred and eight bagels. That makes it two zlotys for you for today's work."

I had never in my life earned so much money in such a short time. I thanked the baker. I was truly grateful to him for his generosity.

"I will come in even earlier tomorrow morning than I did today," I said. I put the money in my pocket, thanked him again, and started to leave.

"Wait a minute," he called after me. He took a brown paper bag from the shelf behind him and put all the broken bagels from the basket into it. "Here, this is for you also."

I walked out munching on a bagel, feeling like a businessman who had just made his first big deal.

By the end of that week, working from six to eleven o'clock every morning, I had earned *twelve* zlotys. It was enough to feed Babbe, Ruchele, and myself. We no longer had to take any money from Uncle Yankel. From now on, I thought, I would be able to take care of my family. I was a man at last.

During my first week as a bagel peddler, I still didn't tell anyone at home about my change of jobs. I wanted to be sure that it would work out. That Friday, however, after a meager Sabbath-eve supper, as I held the twelve zlotys in my pocket, I announced to Uncle Yankel that I had decided to stop working at the tailor shop.

"What are you talking about?" he interrupted me.

Everyone at the table stopped eating and looked at me.

"I'm going to make money, Uncle I want to help you out," I answered proudly.

He began to laugh. "Listen to this big shot. How are you going to make your fortune?"

"Selling bagels."

"Bagels? What a crazy idea!" Uncle Yankel scoffed. "Where do you get bagels to sell? You need money to buy them first."

"Maybe a baker will trust me."

"Ridiculous," Uncle Yankel waved me away with his hand.

"Stick to your tailoring. You make a few zlotys a week there, that's plenty of money for now."

Aunt Simke looked nervously back and forth between us and said, "Schloimele, dear heart of mine, enough talk already. I beg you. Let's enjoy this meal in peace and quiet."

I certainly didn't want to upset her. I thought that Uncle Yankel would be proud of me when he found out what I had accomplished on my own.

"Well, I already found a baker who trusts me. I sold bagels this whole week and I made twelve zlotys." I pulled the money out of my pocket and held it up for everyone at the table to see.

"What are you saying, Schloimele?" Babbe asked. "Did you stop learning to become a tailor?"

"Babbe, I can earn money and help out in the house with expenses."

Uncle Yankel grabbed the twelve zlotys from my hand and threw them down on the table.

"Are you out of your mind?" he shouted. "This is stupid! Can't you see what you're doing? Instead of learning a trade, you want to become a bagel peddler? You'll end up turning into a thief next!"

I was so surprised by this reaction, I didn't know what to say.

"Tell me, big genius, what's going to happen when you get older?" my uncle continued. "Someday you want to get married, no? Who's going to take you without a trade? With your strength, you won't even be able to become a porter. Schloime, you know I want what's best for you. Listen to what I'm saying. Throw away the bagels and go back to work for the tailor. If you're ashamed to ask for your job, I can speak to your boss for you. I'm sure he'll take you back.... I know that I said some bad things to you. I wish I had kept my mouth shut. Believe me, I am very sorry. But you see, we managed through the winter anyway, right? Don't worry. I can take care of all of you until you become a tailor. Promise that you're going back to the shop.... Well?... Promise!"

I couldn't promise because whether my uncle liked it or not, I had made up my mind to earn as much money as I could.

"Answer me!" Uncle Yankel yelled, banging his hand on the table.

Aunt Simke let out a moan.

"I'll throw you out of the house if you don't do what I tell you!" Uncle Yankel threatened. "Do you hear? Then you can do whatever you want. I have enough troubles of my own."

I braced myself and said, "I'm very sorry, Uncle, but I can't go back to work for Reb Chaim. I've decided to save up money and travel to Warsaw. I have to find my mother."

"You're talking like a stupid baby," said Uncle Yankel, trying to control his anger. "You think Warsaw is a little town like Lublin? Warsaw is a big city. You'll get lost there and nobody will ever find you again. Get this nonsense out of your head. I know what I'm saying. Learn a trade. When you get a little older, you can do whatever you want."

"I'm very sorry, Uncle, but..."

"You can't talk to this stubborn idiot," he said and stormed away from the table.

I did not return to the tailor shop, and my business venture turned out well. After a few weeks, I no longer took bagels from the baker on trust; instead, I bought them each morning with my own capital. I even began to save a little money.

Uncle Yankel remained angry and wouldn't talk to me. When he realized that he couldn't change my mind, he worked on Babbe and Aunt Simke to get them to convince me to do what he wanted. Again Aunt Simke's life was made miserable by her husband. She was always sobbing and groaning. It hurt me to see her like that, and I kept reassuring her that everything would change just as soon as I had enough money to leave for Warsaw. But this only seemed to make her cry harder, so I stopped saying anything. What mattered most was that with the money I earned, Babbe, Ruchele, and I didn't have to depend on Uncle Yankel anymore for food.

The summer and fall of 1926 slipped away. Winter approached. I kept peddling until snow, and the cutting wind forced me to stay indoors. We began to live off my meager savings. The money I had been putting aside to go in search of my mother, we now used to buy bread. My savings, however, did not last long. Again we had to depend on my aunt and uncle. As the winter grew worse, so did Uncle Yankel's temper. Whenever he couldn't work, we didn't have enough food, and it was bitter in the house. Somehow we managed to survive, but often, as we were eating, I wondered where the meal could possibly have come from.

Luckily, Ruchele and I did not have to spend our evenings in the kitchen listening to Uncle Yankel ranting at Aunt Simke that her family was killing him. At the beginning of that winter, I became friendly with a boy who lived a few houses away from us.

Beirel Feinman was my first close friend since my friendship with
Leibel. Through me, Ruchele befriended Beirel's sister, Toba.
And soon we were spending almost every evening with our new
friends at their home.

Beirel was my age, fourteen, as thin as I, but much taller. Under
a mop of black hair that bunched up on one side, he had a long
face, serious brown eyes, a fine, long nose, and a wide mouth with
thin lips. He was polite, kind, and like everybody else in his
family, he loved to play games. Besides his sister Toba, Beirel
had four brothers. His family lived above a bakery in a large,
comfortable apartment on the second floor of a big building. It was
a happy home. His parents also often had friends over in the
evening. The adults played cards; we, the children, played dominoes
and checkers; and everyone was always treated to delicious cookies
and tea. It was heavenly.

Beirel's father, Chemie Feinman, was a tailor and his two oldest
sons worked with him in his workshop, which was one of the rooms
of their apartment. Chemie was a good-natured man, tall, and so
skinny that one could count his bones. His wife, Feige, was also
tall, but very fat. I was amazed by the many folds of her flesh and
the size of her huge breasts. Unfortunately, there was one thing
drastically wrong with her. She couldn't stop farting. It was a
disease; she simply couldn't control herself. Her children were
embarrassed to go out in public with her and would turn bright
red with shame whenever they heard her sounding off around
strangers.

One winter evening, Chemie Feinman asked me why I wasn't
learning a trade. "You're a grown boy already," he said. "Aren't
you ashamed to sell bagels on the street? You see my Beirel? He
didn't want to be a tailor, so he's becoming a carpenter. A boy
must learn a trade."

I told Chemie about my decision to save up money and travel
to Warsaw.

"But you don't sell bagels the whole day, do you?" he asked.
"Why don't you come in every afternoon after you've finished
selling and learn a little tailoring?"

Chemie's offer, I realized, was the perfect solution to my problems
at home. I could continue to earn money in the mornings and in

122

the afternoons, learn a trade. This would ease Uncle Yankel's mind, and Aunt Simke would be able to breathe a little easier too. I told Chemie that I would be happy to learn from him.

"Then let's not waste any time," he said. "I have a lot of work to get out. You can start tomorrow afternoon."

I went home at once to tell Babbe and Aunt Simke about my new apprenticeship with Beirel's father. The good news lightened both their hearts.

"Tell your uncle," my aunt said, "the minute that he sets foot in the house. Please. Maybe we can have some peace at last."

When I did tell Uncle Yankel about it, he embraced me and we became friends again on the spot.

Later that night, as I sat at the table telling Uncle Yankel about the Feinmans, he said, "I'm glad to hear that you and Ruchele have such good friends. Do you want to know something?"

"What, Uncle?"

"I always thought that you were a good boy, Schloime. Even when I was angry with you, I knew it in my heart. Because if I ever thought that you were bad, I would have already chased you out of the house long ago."

He said this half in jest. We smiled at each other, both of us glad to be friends again. But as Uncle Yankel leaned back in his chair, I noticed that his expression changed. He began to look very troubled. He rubbed his face with his calloused hands and murmured, "But your mother, Schloime... I don't know... Your mother..."

My heart jumped. "What about my mother? Have you heard something?"

"Yes," he said almost in a whisper, "there are rumors about her in the city. But don't get excited. I'm not sure what is going on yet. As soon as I find out, I'll tell you first of all."

"What rumors?" I begged him. "*Please* tell me what you know!"

"But I told you already, I don't know anything yet!" he flared up. "How many times do you want me to repeat myself? If you don't stop pestering me, I won't find out anything else either."

I didn't utter another word even though I was a knot of questions inside. I was sure that my uncle wasn't telling me everything he had heard. But I didn't want to anger him. I controlled myself

123

with all my strength, hoping that eventually he would confide in me.

Every evening after that, I could hardly wait for my uncle to return from work. When he came in through the door, I was the first to meet him. Although I never asked him outright whether he had any news of my mother, just the way I greeted him gave away all the questions that were seething in me. But Uncle Yankel's only reply was his weary, cross-eyed smile. He shook his head sadly and walked through the kitchen into the living room.

I waited a week, and then I couldn't hold myself back anymore. One night when everyone in the house was asleep and Uncle Yankel was sitting alone at the table in the dim light of the living room, I walked in quietly and sat down next to him.

"So, what is it, Schloime?" he asked in a low voice.

Afraid to anger my uncle but desperate to know more about my mother, I whispered, "Please, Uncle Yankel, don't be mad at me for asking. I just want to know if my mother is all right."

He put his hand on my head and held it there for a moment. His face was so sad, I thought he was going to cry.

"I don't know," he said and closed his eyes. He kept his eyes shut for a while, as if he wished the world would change when he opened them again. "I heard that she's in a little town outside of Warsaw. I don't know where exactly..." He stopped, his jaw set, and finally he said, "They say that she got married..."

"Married?..."

"Yes... That's what they say.... They say she got married to some sort of a scoundrel." Suddenly shaking his fists in the air and gritting his teeth to keep from screaming, he uttered, "The Devil knows what's got into her! If I find her she'll be sorry for what she did."

I felt sick as I stood up from the table. I couldn't stay in the apartment. I walked out and wandered aimlessly through the dark, deserted streets of Lublin. Married?... To a scoundrel?... But why?... How was it possible?... What had happened?... All the horrible suspicions which had been dispelled by the two bright, hopeful letters from my mother, returned. Only now, the suspicions had turned into a real nightmare.

CHAPTER THIRTEEN

Shame

THE NEXT EVENING, as soon as I had a private moment with my uncle, I asked him what else he had heard about my mother. He looked at me sadly and said that he knew nothing more. Night after night I received the same answer from him. I began to suspect the news was so bad that he couldn't even tell it to me. I was convinced that Uncle Yankel knew where my mother was living, whom she had married, and what had happened to her.

I realized that my search for my mother would not be an easy one. It would probably take me some time to find her, and even if I found her, I could not depend on her for my survival. I needed a trade with which to earn a living. Bagel peddling, as I had found out that winter, was unreliable. Tailoring, on the other hand, was good anytime and anywhere.

In the few months I had been working for Chemie Feinman, I had picked up many new skills. He had already taught me how to sew in a lining, make a sleeve, and put pockets on pants. And Chemie was so pleased with my hard work, he began to hint that he would like me to work longer hours for him.

One afternoon, I told Chemie that I wouldn't mind giving up selling bagels if only I could earn a little money from tailoring.

"How about six zlotys a week to start?" asked Chemie at once. "And later, when you can do more, I'll pay you more. What do you say? Is it a deal?"

"It's a deal," I said, happy to have a good job at last.

We shook hands.

"I had wanted to ask you before," Chemie said, "but I didn't think you would give up the bagels."

Beirel, who had been ashamed to have a bagel peddler for a friend, was especially pleased that I had decided to work for his father.

Above all, I hoped to gain Uncle Yankel's respect and make him willing to confide in me. But even though my uncle praised me and said I had become a man in his eyes, he still insisted he knew nothing more about my mother.

One evening, tired of my uncle's evasions, I kept pressing him for answers. He quickly became exasperated and blew up at me. When he had stopped screaming, I told him I would never again ask him another question. As soon as I had the means, I said, I would go away and find my mother on my own. Uncle Yankel's only response was a weary sigh.

But as much as I missed my mother, I was afraid to take off in search of her. Almost two years had passed since she had left, and I still hesitated. Fear of winter, of getting lost, lack of money, not knowing where she was, all of these kept me back, but most of all, I was afraid of what I might discover when I found her. Towards the end of that winter, however, one incident left me with such an overwhelming feeling of shame that all my fears were wiped out at once.

One Saturday afternoon, as I stepped into the living room from the kitchen, I heard our apartment door close. I went back into the kitchen and noticed that Babbe had just left without saying a word. This struck me as odd. I asked Ruchele if she knew where Babbe had gone. My sister shrugged her shoulders.

"Let's go to Toba and Beirel's house," Ruchele suddenly said.

"But what about Babbe?" I asked, puzzled by Ruchele's lack of concern. "Where do you think she went?"

"Maybe she's getting some fresh air. Let's go," Ruchele urged me as she put on her coat.

"Why would Babbe go out in the cold?"

"I don't know, Schloime. Maybe she went to visit a friend."

"Who does she visit?"

"She has her old friends." Ruchele opened the door and said, "Get your coat because I'm going now."

"No. I'm worried about Babbe."

"Stop worrying and come have some fun," said Ruchele as she left.

Hoping to catch up with Babbe, I quickly put on my coat and ran out.

The day was cold and gray. I looked up and down our street but all I saw were a few children playing. I decided to take a walk around the neighborhood. As usual, my mind was filled with thoughts of my mother. The rumors which had spread about her made me feel uncomfortably self-conscious. I sensed that people were talking about us behind our backs. Lost in these thoughts, I suddenly looked up and found that I had also lost my way. I had wandered into the richer streets of the city. I would never find Babbe there, I realized. I started to turn back but after a few steps I noticed, about a block ahead of me, an elderly woman who looked like Babbe. I ran towards her; when I came closer, however, she stepped into a wealthy house. I knew at once that it couldn't have been Babbe. What rich people did she know? I continued to head home. I hoped that in the meantime Babbe had returned. As I walked, I again became engrossed in thoughts of my mother and lost track of where I was.

When I finally turned the corner of Tchwarteck Street, I saw Babbe walking towards our building from the opposite direction. She was carrying a small basket over her arm. Because of her weak eyes, she didn't recognized me until I was almost in front of her. When she saw me, she became upset.

"Where have you been so long?" I asked. "I've been looking for you for over an hour."

"What do you mean, Schloimele?... Where have I been?" she said nervously. "I...I went out...to visit a friend of mine."

She was about to walk past me, when I realized that something didn't make sense.

"How come you are carrying a basket today?" I asked her. "You're always telling me what a big sin it is to carry anything on the Sabbath."

Babbe's lips began to tremble. She lowered her eyes. Her bad arm, which was pressed against her chest, began to shake.

"What's the matter, Babbe?" I asked her again. "Why are you carrying the basket?"

She began to cry.

I reached out and took the basket from her arm. She didn't try to stop me. When I looked inside, I was so revolted by what I saw that I threw the basket into the gutter. Babbe had every reason to be crying. If I could have, I would have cried with her. But I was too angry. I shook with rage and my guts felt on fire. At that moment, I could have burned down the whole world. Babbe and I stood facing each other, drowning in shame. When I had regained some control and saw Babbe's grief, I felt deep pity for her. I wanted to stop her bitter crying, but when I opened my mouth to comfort her what came out were horrible, gasping shouts.

"I don't want you to beg! Do you understand? I don't want to eat begged bread! I would rather starve to death!"

Alarmed by my outburst, Babbe began to plead with me, "Don't scream, Schloimele. Please stop. No more. I promise you. No more."

I grabbed the basket off the street, ran into our courtyard, and threw the dried crusts of bread into the first garbage can I found.

After this humiliation, I decided to look for the quickest way out of Lublin. I was too ashamed to continue living there. I felt that the whole city knew I ate begged bread. At night, in my dreams, crowds of people chased after me, pointing and jeering. As I ran to escape, I cursed back at them. I thrashed around so much in my sleep that Babbe and Ruchele would be awakened almost every night. When these nightmares began to haunt me during the day, my life had become so insufferable that I turned again to Uncle Yankel for help. I confessed everything to him. I told him about Babbe's begging, how I had found out, and the terrible dreams and feelings that I was plagued by. Uncle Yankel listened sadly although none of what I said seemed to surprise

128

him. I suspected he had known about Babbe and her walks with the little basket. I implored my uncle to help me get out of Lublin and find my mother. If we could go live with her someplace where no one knew us, I said, maybe we could leave this shame behind us. He assured me that he would help in every possible way to locate her.

Days passed. Whenever I turned to Uncle Yankel, he shrugged his shoulders and said that he was asking around but still had no news. I soon realized that his assurance to help me meant nothing. He simply didn't want me to know what had become of my mother. If I would ever find her, I would have to do it on my own. Above all, I needed money to travel. Working for Chemie, it would have taken me a half year or more to save up enough. I had to find more profitable work.

Luckily, I didn't have far to look. The Feinmans lived above a bakery owned by a Jewish woman named Sheindel Knobel. Sheindel, who was in her late fifties, was short and skinny, with a shriveled face of leathery skin, half-covered by a large babushka. She was a widow with five children, and her two sons and three daughters, all adults, still lived with her. It was to this Sheindel that I turned for a job.

Purim had just ended and, like most Jewish bakers, Sheindel was getting ready to bake matzohs for Passover. It was an operation that required many workers—an assembly line of sorts: a person to knead the unleavened dough; a few people to roll it; a person with a spur-like roller to make holes in the flattened dough so the matzohs wouldn't swell up during baking; someone to shovel the dough into the oven and then take out the matzohs; a person to deliver the matzohs to the customers; and also people to measure out the flour, wash the pans, and pour water over the dough while it was being kneaded. The job of pouring water was usually given to children.

The moment I heard that Sheindel was preparing for the matzoh season, I went to her and offered to fill three functions: to measure out the flour, wash the pans, and pour the water. Sheindel thought it over and liked the idea. For her it was cheaper to hire one person than three. For me, it meant that I could earn more than if I were doing just one job.

129

I was sorry to have to stop working for Chemie, but at the bakery, at the end of four weeks, I had earned forty zlotys—a small fortune. I contributed ten zlotys to prepare for our Passover. I spent another fifteen zlotys for our food expenses. And I was left with fifteen zlotys.

The time had come for me to leave Lublin. I had begun to notice when I walked down our street that people were actually pointing their fingers at me and whispering to each other. Whenever I approached, they immediately became silent, but as soon as I moved away, I could hear them behind my back, whispering again. They had plenty to gossip about, I was sure. I imagined they knew more about my mother than I did. And how could they not have known about Babbe's begging? I couldn't wipe out from my mind that basket with the moldy, dried-out pieces of bread. Every time I remembered it, I was possessed by anger and shame.

I confronted Uncle Yankel again and told him that people on the street were gossiping about me. I asked him what was being said. He shook his head and said he didn't know.

On the first day after Passover, 1927, I bought a small, secondhand brown suitcase.

The instant that Babbe saw me at the door with the suitcase in my hand, she understood, and her eyes filled with tears.

"May the Almighty keep you from harm, Schloimele," she said. "What could you possibly be thinking of?"

"I'm going to find Mamme," I said as I laid the suitcase down on the bed.

Ruchele came running into the kitchen from the living room followed by Aunt Simke. "When are you going?" Ruchele asked, excited.

"Tonight," I said. "Now." I opened our old trunk, took one of Frau Liebe's letters, put it in my pocket, and began to pick out my clothes.

"Take me with you, Schloime!" Ruchele shouted. "Please take me too!"

"Dear God in Heaven, a disaster!" Babbe cried out. "I will die from worry, Schloimele! Have pity on me! You were always such a good child!"

I didn't want to hurt Babbe, but I also couldn't let anything stop me now. "Don't cry, Babbe. Please don't cry. I'll be careful. Nothing is going to happen to me." I turned to my sister. "I can't take you with me, Ruchele. I don't have enough money."

"Poor innocent child," said Babbe, "how can you do this without money?"

"I have enough for myself," I told her as I packed the clothes into my valise. "I saved fifteen zlotys from the money I made working in the bakery."

"But you don't even know where your mother is," Babbe insisted. "How will you find her? Where are you going to go?"

"I have a place to go—Frau Liebe, our old neighbor from the Tchurtic. I have her address from her letters. She is Mamme's best friend. I'm sure that Mamme will visit her if she comes to Warsaw. Please don't worry, Babbe. We have to do something, once and for all."

"Let him go, Babbe," Ruchele stood up for me. "Maybe Schloime will find Mamme."

"As soon as I find her, I'm going to come right back," I tried to reassure Babbe. "And I'll bring Mamme back with me."

Babbe stifled her sobs, and while I finished packing, she prepared a bag of food for me to take on my trip.

Through all of this, Aunt Simke stood at the kitchen door looking in sadly and said nothing. Uncle Yankel, however, hadn't even budged from the living room.

When I was all packed and ready to go, I embraced Babbe and kissed her. "Goodbye, Babbe. I'll be back soon."

"May God watch over you, Schloimele," she said tearfully. "And may He help you find your mother, and bring both of you safely home."

Then I kissed Ruchele.

"Find her and bring her back with you," Ruchele said. "Tell her that I miss her very much. Tell her that I dream of her every night."

"I'll tell her, Ruchele. I will," I said to my sister. "And I'll bring her back."

Finally I kissed Aunt Simke. She embraced me and wept, unable to utter a word.

Uncle Yankel still didn't show his face in the kitchen, not even to say goodbye. I was too angry to go to him. I picked up my small suitcase and the paper bag with food, and I left.

As I walked out of the building, I thought to myself that I would never forgive my uncle. Even though I was grateful to him for all he had done for us, I still hated him for not having been honest with me about my mother. I began the long walk to the train station. I didn't care anymore who pointed at me on our street or who whispered behind my back. After I had found my mother, I would decide what to do. But just the thought of her filled me with fear. What was everybody talking about? What would I find, if I found her?

Suddenly, I heard a shout behind me.

"Schloime!"

I turned around and far down the street, I saw Uncle Yankel running towards me, waving his hands over his head.

"Schloime!" he shouted again. "Wait!"

I stopped.

When he reached me, Uncle Yankel clasped me in his arms in a tight embrace. He was out of breath from running, but he kissed me and cried as he pressed me to his chest. At last he let go of me and gasping for air between sobs, he looked at me and tried to say something. His face was twisted from crying. He struggled to speak, but each time he opened his mouth, only another sob burst out. I had never seen a grown man cry like that. Finally, Uncle Yankel reached into his shirt pocket, pulled out a slip of paper, and handed it to me.

I took it. The writing on it was in Yiddish.

"That," Uncle Yankel finally managed to say, "is your mother's address."

I felt as if I were in a dream. That little piece of paper, which I was grasping tightly in my fist, was suddenly my dearest possession in the world. I threw my arms around my uncle's neck. I couldn't stop kissing him. Now we were both crying.

"You have to forgive me, Schloime," Uncle Yankel said. "I was only thinking of your own good. I wanted to spare you some pain."

I couldn't understand what my uncle was trying to say.

"Thank you, Uncle Yankel," I said. "For the rest of my life, I'll be grateful to you for this."

Uncle Yankel picked up my suitcase and took my hand.

"Come," he said. "Let's go." And he walked with me to the train station.

"Itzhak Copperstein. 33 Reimanta Street. Otwock."

I reread the slip of paper which shook in my hands as the train, with a shrill blast of the whistle, rushed out of Lublin. It was past midnight. Uncle Yankel had explained to me that Otwock was a small town, about fifty kilometers outside Warsaw. It was a healing center that only the rich could afford. The ride there would take the whole night. I turned to look out of the window, but outside all I could see was the reflection of my own frightened face flying over the darkness. I could still hear my uncle's parting words to me just a few minutes earlier at the station.

"When you get there, Schloime," Uncle Yankel had said, looking at the ground to avoid my eyes, "you'll understand why I didn't want to tell you about your mother.... I hope that all of what I heard turns out to be lies...believe me."

"Please tell me what you know, Uncle," I begged him.

"I can't, Schloime. Don't ask me.... It hurts me too much to talk about it," he said, still not looking at me.

My uncle's words troubled me deeply; but now that I had my mother's address, I would soon find her and know the truth for myself. That thought ran through me like a spike of ice. All I knew from Uncle Yankel was that my mother had remarried, and that her new husband was a scoundrel. Was Itzhak Copperstein, whose name was written on the slip of paper, her new husband? What kind of a scoundrel could he be? And why was my mother in Otwock? Was she sick?... Trying to answer these questions, however, was like trying to look out through the window of the train. All I could see were reflections: the coach, the people in it, and my own pale face staring back at me—like ghosts in the darkness.

The compartment in which I sat was only half full. Some passengers had stretched out on the empty seats and gone to sleep. Across from me sat a very elegant, middle-aged woman, wearing a beige, tailored suit. She must have been wealthy. Her shiny blonde hair was carefully combed. Her face was lightly powdered and painted pale blue over her eyes, pink on her cheeks, and red, like ripe apples, on her lips. She caught me staring at her and gave me a look as if it didn't suit her to be sitting in the same car with me. Then she reached into the red leather handbag lying beside her, took out a Polish book, and began to read.

I opened the paper bag with the food. I had eaten one sandwich at the station, but I still had a piece of bread and an apple left. I decided to eat them together. The rustling of the paper bag disturbed the rich Polish lady. She put her book down and glanced at the luggage rack over her seat. She had an expensive, red leather valise, no larger than my own suitcase.

"Rosumiesh po polsku?" she suddenly asked me. She wanted to know whether I spoke Polish.

"Nye," I answered. No.

"In that case," she said, "I will speak Yiddish to you."

I was very surprised. It hadn't even occurred to me that she might be Jewish.

She leaned forward and whispered, "I would like to ask you to keep an eye on my valise while I'm gone." She thanked me and left the compartment.

I took a bite of the fresh rye bread and a bite of the apple, sweet and juicy, and chewed them slowly to enjoy the taste longer. I was thankful to Babbe for making sure that I would have something to eat. As I ate, I wondered if the lady really was Jewish or whether she just happened to know some Yiddish. If she was Jewish, then it seemed to me that she was trying to hide it.

When she returned, she took a glimpse at her valise. "Thank you," she said. "The last time I traveled, I left my seat for a minute and my valise grew a pair of feet and walked off. Do you know what I mean?"

"Yes," I said.

She picked up her book and continued to read.

When I had finished eating, I sat back in my seat, closed my eyes, and tried to sleep. Almost everyone in the coach was already sleeping. I was so excited, however, that I didn't even feel tired.

I unfolded the piece of paper with my mother's address and read it again. I found that I already knew it by heart and put the paper back in my pocket.

The woman sitting across from me looked up from her book.

"Where are you traveling?" she asked me in a low voice.

"To Otwock." I spoke as quietly as she did, not to disturb those who were sleeping.

"Why are you going to Otwock? Are you sick?" she asked.

"No.... I'm going to visit my mother."

"Where is she?"

I pulled out the slip of paper from my pocket and handed it to the woman.

She read the address aloud. I realized that she had to be Jewish.

"I know where that is. We'll walk together," she said, returning the slip of paper to me. She closed her book and laid it down on her lap. "I'm going in the same direction.... I am on my way to visit my youngest son, who is in a sanatorium. He's very sick. He just wouldn't listen to me. Whole nights he ran around, gambling, drinking, dancing, until he developed an inflammation of the lungs. I took him from one doctor to the other. Everyone said the same thing: rest, nothing but rest." She sighed. "If only he had taken care of himself in the beginning. But he wouldn't even listen to the doctors. He kept on running until he ran his health into the ground. Now he lies in a sanatorium. He has already cost me a fortune. His own father doesn't even want to hear of him. Because of that wild boy, my husband has almost gone bankrupt twice. I remember days when my husband stood in the empty store, without any goods on the shelves. Once, out of sheer despair, my poor husband even tried to hang himself. Lucky thing that the maid noticed that something was wrong and called me—just in time. I'm at my wit's end. Sometimes I think I'm going to go crazy. But what can I do? A mother is still a mother."

We sat in silence for a few moments.

"And what about your mother? Is she sick?" the woman asked.

"I'm not sure...."

"Why did she go to Otwock then?"

"I don't know.... When she first left our home, she went to Warsaw."

135

"To Warsaw?... Why did she leave your home?"

"To find a place for us to live."

"Who was taking care of you then? Your father?"

"I don't have a father.... He also left us.... We were staying with my Uncle. He helped us as much as he could, but it was very hard for him. He has a wife and six children of his own. Sometimes we didn't even have enough food in the house..."

"Oh, my... Oh, my..."

I could see the rich lady becoming uncomfortable with the story of my poverty. She didn't ask any more questions and went back to reading her book.

The rest of the trip continued in silence.

I turned back to the window just as the day was beginning to dawn. The sky had a faint glow of gray light. I could finally look out. In the distance, I saw fields with little houses and barns rushing past.

One by one, the passengers in the railway car began to wake up.

Suddenly the woman stood up, stretched, and smoothed out her skirt. Then she looked out the window.

"We're almost there," she said, putting away the book into her red leather handbag.

"Otwock?" I asked.

"Yes, of course, Otwock," she said. "My Goodness, what's wrong? You look so pale."

CHAPTER FOURTEEN

A House of Strangers

WE STEPPED OFF THE TRAIN to a bright morning. The sky had turned deep blue and the breeze was sharp and refreshing. The station, a squat pink building with white trimmings, stood on a low hill. Above the entrance door, a sign in large letters announced, "OTWOCK." From the station, a gravel path stretched down the grassy hill towards the town.

With a smile, the elegant woman handed her red valise to me and said, "Come, I will show you where you have to go."

I was glad that her valise turned out to be even lighter than mine, and I carried both easily. We started down the path of the hill. It was a short walk into town. The houses we passed were pretty cottages painted in pale blues, yellows, and pinks, each surrounded by a large garden. I didn't see any tall buildings, as in Lublin, except for the few sanatoriums scattered in the distance, two- and three-story white buildings which sparkled against the enveloping dark green woods.

Soon we were walking on the main street past small shops. It was about seven o'clock and the street was still almost empty. The few people who were out, I was surprised to see, didn't seem at all sick. Dressed in light colored clothes, they looked more like rich people on vacation.

After a brisk, ten-minute walk, the elegant woman suddenly stopped. "Look down this block," she said. "Do you see that first street on the right?"

"Yes," I said as my heart began to pound like a drum.

"That is Reimanta Street. Number thirty-three should not be very far from here." She took her valise from my hand and wished me good luck in finding my mother.

As I watched her walk away, I couldn't move. I felt dizzy and faint. I was so frightened that I even considered turning back. Was it possible, I asked myself, that I had become so afraid of my own mother? I waited awhile. Then, I picked up my suitcase and began to walk. With every step I took, my pace quickened. By the middle of the block, I was running. Paralyzed as I had been just a few minutes earlier, now nothing could have stopped me. I ran wildly, my eyes fixed on the corner of Reimanta Street. At the end of the block, I turned right and found myself on a shady, tree-lined side street. Except for smaller gardens, it had the same pretty cottages as the rest of Otwock. I wondered whether my mother could really be living in such a rich neighborhood. I began to search for number 33. Suddenly, in the middle of the block, I spotted a small house of unpainted red bricks. It was strangely poor and run-down compared to its surroundings. That poverty looked so familiar to me. I ran across the street, approached the house, and above the unpainted wooden door, just as I had expected, I saw roughly brushed in black paint, "33."

I was so excited that I forgot to knock. I pushed open the door and walked in. The room seemed dark at first and I couldn't see anything. When my eyes adjusted, however, I stepped back. Two surprised women, seated at a table, having breakfast, were staring at me. The older one, a thin, dark haired woman who must have been in her late thirties, had her mouth pursed in anger, while the younger one, who was short, plumb, and probably in her early thirties, was smiling. Both were very beautiful, but neither one was my mother. Uncle Yankel had lied again, I immediately thought. He had given me the wrong address.

"What do you want?" the thin woman asked. She had a bony face with large, dark, angry eyes, one of which seemed covered by a gray film of tissue.

I reached in back of me for the door, ready to leave.

The other woman stood up. "Who are you looking for?" she asked with a friendly smile.

I stood confused, unsure of what to say.

The younger, smiling woman approached me. She wore a simple housedress which had a few buttons open at the top, showing part of her large breasts. She had long, curly hair, a round face with large brown eyes, a small, thick nose, and a painted mouth.

"Come in," she said, trying to put me at ease. "What is the matter with you? You are so upset and out of breath...." She closed the door behing me. "Now tell us, who are you looking for?"

I took out the slip of paper with the address and handed it to her.

She read it and went back to the table to show it to the other woman. While they whispered back and forth, I looked around me. There were only two small windows in the dark one-room house, one to Reimanta Street, the other to a backyard. The furniture was old and shabby. Up against three of the walls stood three small beds. Against the fourth wall there was a shoemaker's work-bench. Next to it was a small iron stove. In the middle of the room was the table with five chairs, where the two women were sitting. In one corner of the kitchen stood and old baby carriage: the wheels were rusty; the red paint had mostly peeled off.

"Where did you get this address?" the angry woman asked. "What do you want with Itzhak Copperstein?"

"I don't want anything with him," I said. "I'm looking for my mother."

"Who is your mother?" the kind woman asked. "Is her name Roise?"

"Yes, Roise!" I said immediately.

"Are you from Lublin?" she asked.

"Yes, yes, from Lublin!"

The two women looked at each other as if now they understood everything. The kind one walked over to me, took the valise from my hand, and placed it in a corner.

"Come and sit down with us," she said. "You must have been traveling a whole night."

I was in the right place after all. I sat down at the kitchen table between the two women.

"Are you hungry?" the kind woman asked. "Don't be shy. I'll make you something to eat."

"I'm not hungry. Where is my mother?" I asked her.

"Right now she's in Warsaw, to see a doctor," she answered. "She may be back later today."

"Is she sick?"

"No," the woman said and exchanged another look with her friend. "She went with someone else. You look so tired. Come and lie down a little."

Her suggestion that I lie down surprised me, but I was exhausted and I didn't know what else to do. The kind woman showed me to a bed. I took off my jacket and shoes, lay down, and she covered me with a blanket. I fell asleep at once.

When I woke up, the angry woman was standing at the table ironing clothes while the other sat and folded. They had been whispering but stopped as soon as I got up. My mother still wasn't back from Warsaw.

"Do you feel rested now?" the kind woman asked. "Come, you must be very hungry. I have food ready for you."

As I put on my shoes, the angry woman cleared off the table and the friendly one lit the small iron stove and began to set a place for me.

"Did you come alone?" the angry woman asked me after I had sat down next to her at the table. "Why didn't you bring your sister along?"

Her question surprised me. How did she know about Ruchele?

"It was too far for her to travel," I said.

The kind woman brought me a plate of hot soup with matzoh balls. I was starving now and began to eat at once.

"Look how hungry he is," she said. "Here, have a piece of matzoh, too." She put two pieces on a plate for me.

I thanked her.

"And how is your grandmother? Asked the angry woman while I ate. "Is she sick?"

140

"No. She's fine."

"Didn't she want to come along with you?" she asked.

"No."

"Is everything all right with your uncle?" the kind woman asked.

"Yes." How did they know so much about us? I wondered.

When I had finished the soup, the kind woman took away my empty plate, refilled it with a small piece of chicken and mashed potatoes, and served it to me. I thanked her again and continued to eat hungrily.

As I ate, they asked me what I did in Lublin, what Babbe and Ruchele did, in what kind of an apartment Uncle Yankel lived, and how big his family was. They even asked me if I had heard from my father. I felt suspicious and told them as little as possible.

"Would you like some tea?" the kind woman asked at the end of my meal. "Let me make some for all of us."

She took away my plate and put the kettle on. Rather than face the angry woman, I began to look out one of the windows.

"Do you need to go out?" the kind woman suddenly asked me.

"What?" I asked.

"Are you looking for the toilet?" she asked again. "It's out there." She pointed through the window to a small outhouse in the backyard.

I did have to go. I walked out the door and went around the house to the back. The sun was shining warmly. It must have been about two o'clock. The large backyard, overgrown with wild grass, was enclosed by a wire fence. I noticed the angry woman's face glaring at me from the window. I went into the outhouse, which stood in a corner of the yard farthest away from the house. It was a small dirty hut, no more than a sheet of tin for a roof and a few loose boards nailed together over a deep hole in the earth.

As I came back into the house, the kind woman was setting tea glasses down on the table.

"Sit down," she said. "We'll have some tea. It's getting late. Your mother may not return today. But don't worry. If she doesn't come today, she'll be here tomorrow morning for sure."

I sat back down at the table.

The angry woman frowned at me. "Why did you wait so long?" she said. "If you had come sooner, it would have been better for all of us."

I was puzzled by her strange remark, but before I could ask her what she had meant, the door opened. A tall, gaunt man stepped in, followed by a haggard-looking, gray-haired woman carrying a small child in her arms.

My mother.

She stood frozen at the open door. She was shocked, dazed. She stared at me, her green eyes enlarged as if she were trying to remember who I was. I took a step closer to her, but I also had to stop. I had to reassure myself that this old-looking, worn-out woman, holding a year-old baby in her arms, was my own young and beautiful mother. She was so thin and frail she seemed to have grown taller. Her face was so drawn that her eyes looked larger, her nose longer. Her hair, which had been so black and thick and curly, was now tightly pulled back, thin, and gray. What terrible things had happened to her to change her so much in less than two two years?

She must have read this question in my face because she began to shake her head from side to side as her eyes instantly filled with tears. Before I could say anything, she turned away, buried her face in the child she held, and started to cry. Her muffled sobs quickly turned to loud wails. As my mother pressed the frightened baby tightly to herself, it began to scream and flail its little arms to free itself. Blindly, my mother stumbled into the room, tripped, and began to fall. The tall man, who had quickly followed her steps, caught her just as she was about to hit the floor. The plump woman ran up and pulled the shrieking child out of my mother's arms. My mother collapsed against the man, and he dragged her over to a bed. She couldn't even stand on her own feet anymore.

The angry woman went to the door and slammed it closed. "Shut them up," she spat out, "before we have the whole neighborhood at our doorstep!"

But even with the door closed, my mother's and the baby's anguished cries must have filled the quiet street with horror.

142

The man sat down next to my mother on the bed. He held her and whispered in her ear.

The plump woman paced back and forth as she rocked the baby in her arms and shushed it soothingly. Soon, the child's screams had become whimpers.

My mother also calmed down somewhat. Without looking at me, she reached out to the plump woman and took the baby back. When she had it in her arms, my mother caressed and kissed the child.

I stood alone and forgotten in that house of strangers. I didn't move or make a sound. I felt more lost, more frightened, and sadder than I had in any of my nightmares.

The man stood up. "Get the table ready," he said to the two women. "It's late and we didn't eat anything yet."

At once the two women started to prepare the food.

"So you must be Schloime," he said, turning to me. He bent down and whispered, "Don't worry about your mother. You surprised her, and she became a little upset. Just leave her alone for a while."

Under a head of wavy, iron-gray hair, his face was long and hard. He had deep eye sockets, light brown, watery eyes with drooping bags under them, hollow cheeks, jaw muscles that were tense like taut rope, and a chin like the head of a hammer. He was probably under forty, but he looked at least ten years older.

He straightened up. "Let's eat," he commanded.

"I already ate," I said.

"Sit down anyway," he said as if my answer had annoyed him. "If someone gives you food, you should eat."

Even though I wasn't hungry, I sat down at the table again. I was afraid to disobey him.

The man took a quick glance around the room and walked out. I soon heard him in the backyard, banging the wooden door of the outhouse.

I looked at my mother. More than anything, I wanted to speak to her. The two women were busy warming up the food and setting the table. I stood up and slowly walked over to the bed where my mother sat holding the baby.

She lifted her head. Looking at me with swollen, red-rimmed eyes, my mother whispered hoarsely, "Forgive me, Schloimele. Forgive me," and immediately she turned away and started to cry again.

I looked at her bent head and inside of me I felt as if all my blood had turned into tears and still my heart couldn't stop crying.

The door opened abruptly. The man walked back in and scowled.

"What are you all waiting for?" he said sharply.

My mother stifled her sobs. I moved away from her.

The man sat down at the table, followed by the two women, and without saying a word, they started to eat.

"Come here and sit down," the man said to me.

He looked at my mother, who had her back turned as she prepared to change the baby's diapers.

"Come, Roise, you didn't eat all day," he said. "Leave the child for later."

Without turning around, my mother shook her head no.

It made him angry, but he gritted his teeth, then continued to eat. He sat hunched over his plate, both arms on the table, and ate quickly. His movements were abrupt. When he wanted a matzoh, his hand flew out and grabbed one from the plate as if he were stealing it. With a snap of his large fingers, the matzoh crumbled into the soup. I recognized that he had shoemaker's hands, scarred and blackened. Every now and then, as he put a spoonful of food in his mouth, his eyes shot up, first to one woman, then to the other. He glanced at me like that once and I was startled—it was the look of a madman.

I forced myself to eat. As often as I could, I stole glances at my mother although she didn't turn around even once to look at me. After she had changed the diapers, she gave the baby her breast. Why didn't she speak to me? I kept wondering. Was she so ashamed of herself?

The whole meal was eaten quickly, in complete silence. When it was finished, the two women started to clear off the table.

The man went to my mother, sat down on the bed, and whispered to her. I didn't dare move from my chair. I looked around me trying to understand where I was and what was going on. As quickly and quietly as they had prepared the meal, the two women cleared

144

off the table and washed the dishes. When they were done, they put on their coats and, without a word, left the house.

The man suddenly stood up from the bed and said to me, "Why don't you lie down and go to sleep. You must be tired."

Although I did still feel tired, I wanted desperately to speak to my mother. I told him that I had already slept while I was waiting for their return from Warsaw.

"I can see how red your eyes are," he said. He pointed to the bed in which I had slept. "Lie down over there."

"Mamme?" I called to her softly. "Mamme, I want to..." but I had to stop because she had started to cry.

The man gave me a sign with his finger to his lips not to say anything else. I took off my shoes again and lay down on the bed. I closed my eyes, pretended to fall asleep, and tried to overhear their conversation. But whenever they spoke, they whispered so quietly that no matter how hard I strained, I couldn't make anything out. And soon, even against my will, I was fast asleep.

A soft tapping noise woke me up. Slowly I remembered where I was. For a while, I lay without moving. All I heard, however, on and off, was that soft hammering. When I opened my eyes and lifted my head, I saw the man sitting at the shoemaker's bench, a boot on his lap, working. The room was lit by a large naphtha lamp. The windows were dark. It was night.

"Can't you sleep anymore?" the man asked me.

"No," I said.

The baby was asleep on the bed next to the man while my mother cooked at the small iron stove. She looked at me as if she wanted to say something, but unable to help herself, she let out a sob and started to cry again.

"Enough crying," the man ordered her, his jaw tight and his eyes wild. "Put on your shoes," he said to me, "and let's go out for a walk."

He laid his work aside as I slipped on my shoes. I didn't trust him, but I felt that I had no choice. After we had put on our jackets, he told my mother to stop worrying, and we left.

Outside, the man started to walk quickly. He was soon far ahead of me. When he looked back and saw that I was running to catch up, he slowed down.

The night was as beautiful as the morning had been. The air was cool and thick with the smell of the woods. The sky was clear, black, and full of stars. The big round moon covered the houses, gardens, and trees on Reimanta Street with a dark yellow light.

We walked in silence to the end of the block.

"Give your mother a little time to settle down," he said after we had turned the corner of Reimanta Street. "We didn't expect to see you. Did your uncle send you?"

"No," I said. "I came on my own."

"But didn't your uncle give you the money for the ticket?"

I wondered whether I should tell him how hard Uncle Yankel had tried to keep me from leaving Lublin altogether. I decided it was best not to say anything.

"I saved my own money from working," I said.

"So, you earn your own money already?" he said with obvious interest; this fact seemed to please him. "Your mother told me that you were apprenticed to a tailor."

"I had to quit the tailor a while ago because I couldn't earn enough for our needs," I told him.

"Then, how did you make the money?"

"I worked in a bakery, making matzohs for Passover."

He nodded his head with understanding and asked, "So, Schloime, how is your uncle doing these days?"

"He's very well."

"Are you and Ruchele and your Babbe Zlate still living with him?"

"Yes."

"And how are your sister and your grandmother doing?" he asked.

"They're also well."

"I'm glad to hear that."

I wondered if he really meant what he said.

The main street, when we came to it, was lit by lights from the shop windows. Many people were out now, strolling. As we passed a small tea house, the man put his hand on my shoulder and said, "Come, let's have a bite to eat."

Inside there was the happy sound of people talking and enjoying themselves. They sat at little round tables full of delicious desserts

146

and drinks. The man led me to a small table in a corner. We sat down and almost immediately a pretty, young waitress came and asked us what we wanted to have. The man ordered a glass of milk and a piece of cheesecake for me. For himself, he ordered only tea. When the waitress returned with a little silver tray, she set down a big slice of cake and a tall glass of milk in front of me. My first bite was a surprise, I had never tasted such a delicacy as that heavy, sweet cheese. And the milk was as thick as cream. I thanked the man.

"Good," he said, smiling for the first time. "Eat and enjoy it." He quickly looked around himself and in a low voice, he said, "I'm very glad that you finally came. I told your mother many times to send for you and your sister, but she wouldn't listen. She didn't even want to write a letter to you. We're not settled enough, she said.... Of course, with that baby on top of everything else..."

Again, he quickly swung his head from side to side, as if to check whether anyone had come too close to overhear him and then, quietly, he continued, "I know your mother for a long time. You weren't even born yet when I became friends with your parents in Lublin. Your father and I worked in the same shoemaker's shop, even before he married your mother. When she told me how he left her with you and your sister after the war, I thought he was a bastard."

He became silent and watched me.

I didn't look up from my plate. I spooned the cake into my mouth, but it had lost all its taste for me. As soon as I had finished eating and drinking, he picked up his tea and drank it down like a glass of water. He got up at once, paid, and we left the tea house.

On the street, after we had walked in silence for a while, he asked me, "How do you like Otwock?"

"It's beautiful," I said. I held myself back, however, from telling him how ugly their house was and how terrible and unhappy my mother looked.

He stopped, took hold of my arm, and looking right into my eyes, he asked, "How would you like to stay here with us?"

I felt the cold grip of his strong hand on my arm. I was frightened by his offer, but I couldn't leave my mother. I said yes.

147

"Good," he said, letting go of me. "Then it's settled. It's what your mother wanted all along. I hope that now she'll stop crying. You don't have to be afraid of me, Schloime. I'm going to help you out in every way I can. First I'm going to make a good shoemaker out of you. And when Ruchele comes, I'll decide what to do with her. It's a good thing that you're here finally. At least we can get rid of one problem."

I noticed that he hadn't mentioned anything about sending for Babbe. But I knew that it would have killed Babbe on the spot to have seen how my mother looked.

When we reached Reimanta Street, it was very dark. The lights were out in all the houses. I had many questions I wanted to ask him which only fear stopped me from asking, but there was one thing I felt I had to know before we went back in. I took courage and said, "Who are those two women living in your house?"

"My sisters," he said. "They work in a sanatorium around here. They're staying with me for a while. But now that you and Ruchele will be living here, maybe they'll leave."

How could the two women be his sisters? I wondered. The women looked as different from each other as night and day, and neither one of them resembled him in the least.

We walked back into the dark house quietly. My mother and the baby were already asleep. The two women, dressed in nightgowns, got up from the table where they had been sitting. They pulled out a folding cot from under one of the beds and quickly set it up.

"Tonight you sleep here with me," the man said, pointing to a bed.

The angry woman lay down on the cot, and the plump woman took the other bed. When they had turned their backs, I undressed quickly and lay down as close to the edge of the small bed as I could. The man also undressed, turned off the lamp, and took the other side.

I tried to convince myself that maybe the man wasn't really as bad as Uncle Yankel had said he was. This man was a shoemaker, after all, not some kind of a scoundrel. Could my uncle have been wrong? Did my uncle say that just to keep me from traveling to Otwock? But what was wrong with my mother? Was she ashamed that she had had a baby? But if she was married to this man, it was a normal thing for them to have a child. I wanted hard to believe that maybe things could still work out. But how could I deny that something was terribly wrong with my mother? She was like another person. And the two women, they were not the man's sisters. Why did he lie to me? How could I and Ruchele live with them? And Babbe, how could we leave her? What would happen to her?

In the house, everyone had fallen asleep and the darkness slowly filled with sounds of their snores, grunts, and sighs, but as I lay awake, thinking, soon all I heard was the beating of my own confused and frightened heart.

CHAPTER FIFTEEN

Fallen into Hell

IN THE MORNING, although my mother and I could finally look at each other without her starting to cry, she still seemed to avoid speaking to me. Her shame and sorrow were wrapped around her like a shroud and kept us apart.

The man, the two women, and I ate breakfast as we had eaten dinner: quickly, silently, and without my mother; she busied herself with the baby.

As soon as he had finished eating, the man sat down at his workbench. From the few scattered shoes that lay on the floor near him, he picked out a pair and started to fix them.

The two women cleared the table, washed the dishes, and left.

I continued to sit quietly at the table, waiting to speak to my mother.

When she finished changing the clothes on the baby, my mother laid it down on the bed next to where the man worked. The baby began to make gurgling noises to itself as it played with its little fingers.

My mother walked into the kitchen and took down a net bag hanging on a nail near the door.

"Do you want to come with me to the market?" she asked me.

"Yes," I answered at once.

"Then get ready," she said, "and we'll go now."

I put on my jacket, and she, her coat.

"We're going to the market," my mother told the man.

"Roise, don't leave the baby," he said without looking up from his work.

"But Itzhak, you heard the doctor's words," my mother said anxiously. "The child is sick. He can't go out."

"Wrap him in a blanket," the man said, becoming angry, "and put him in the carriage."

"Itzhak, I just changed him. He's as quiet as a little angel. He won't bother you. Just for—"

"I don't want to be tied down to the house," he cut my mother off.

"But you have so much work to finish," said my mother, a look of panic on her face. "Itzhak, you can't—"

"I told you to take him!" he shouted.

"Itzhak—" my mother began to plead, but Itzhak Copperstein jumped up suddenly from his chair and threw the hammer down with such anger that she stopped, her mouth open. The baby, frightened by the noise, let out a cry.

"All right, I will take him," my mother said quickly. "You just stay here and finish your work. Please, Itzhak. I beg you."

He sat back down at his bench, picked up the shoe and hammer, and went back to work.

My mother wheeled the old carriage out of the corner in the kitchen. She picked up the baby, put him inside, and covered him with a small blue blanket. I opened the door for her, and we left.

The day, once again, was beautiful. A few clouds floated in the blue sky like huge white birds. The sunshine made every blade of grass and every leaf sparkly like a green gem.

My mother pushed the carriage rapidly, walking away from the house as if escaping from it. The wheels squeaked mournfully on the quiet street. Self conscious of the noise, my mother glanced uneasily around herself. After a few steps, she asked me anxiously, "How is Ruchele? And Babbe? Are they all right?"

Before I could answer her, however, my own questions began to pour out. "Why did you leave us like that?" I asked her. "Why did you stop writing? Mamme, what's happened to you? Why do you look so awful?"

"*Stop.*"

She lowered her head, and then almost in a whisper, my mother said, "Don't ask me, Schloimele, because I can't tell you. When you get older, I'll explain it to you...but not now. You're still only an innocent child."

"I am not a child!" I said. "How can you say that to me? A child? Mamme, don't you know what I went through after you left? Did you forget how we struggled because Tatte abandoned us? How did you think we could survive without you? Did you know that a whole winter Uncle Yankel kept screaming to Aunt Simke to throw us out of the kitchen? Babbe went around with a basket on her arm begging for bread. I almost turned into a thief to make some money to feed ourselves. I finally became a bagel peddler. I'm ashamed to walk out on the street in Lublin. People point their fingers at me and whisper behind my back. How can you still call me a child after all that? I understand life, Mamme. I'm not a child! I understand life very well!"

"You're right, Schloimele, you're right," my mother said, as she fought back tears, some of which nevertheless began to run down her caved-in cheeks. "I know this isn't an answer for all the misery that I made you and Ruchele and Babbe suffer. But have pity on me, Schloimele. I'm too ashamed to say anymore. If you stay in that house any longer, you'll see for yourself why I stopped writing...why I turned into such an old hag. What can I tell you, Schloimele?" Overwhelmed by pain, she started to cry. "*I have fallen into hell and I will never escape from it again.*"

My mother stopped in the middle of the narrow sidewalk, covered her face with her hands and burst into terrible sobs.

A well dressed, elderly couple, who had turned the corner, crossed to the other side of the street. As they passed, they looked at us over their shoulders and shook their heads in disgust. Not even in Otwock could I escape our shame.

My mother took a handkerchief from her coat pocket, dried her eyes, and without looking at me, started to push the carriage again. Her face was white, drained of color and life.

152

We walked to the market in silence. I didn't ask her anything else because I saw how my questions tortured her. I realized that for now she had told me everything she could.

At the market, we spent a long time going slowly from one stand to the next while my mother bargained with the vendors for the lowest prices. She didn't buy much. She put a few of the groceries in the carriage at the baby's feet and when there was no more room there, she used the net bag, which I immediately took from her hand and carried for her.

She looked at me, tried to say something, but had to stop. I understood. She couldn't even thank me without crying.

On our way home, I decided that I would have to talk with Itzhak Copperstein. Since my mother couldn't tell me, I would ask him what kind of a hell my mother had fallen into. No matter how frightening he was, I had to know the truth.

On Reimanta Street, as we approached number 33, I noticed my mother becoming more and more uneasy. At the door of the house, she stopped and told me to wait by the carriage on the sidewalk. Warily she went up to the house, opened the door, and looked in.

"Come in," she finally said to me.

I pushed the carriage into the kitchen. The house, to my surprise, was empty. My mother quickly took out all the packages and put them on the table.

"Where is he?" I asked my mother.

"I don't know," she said nervously. "Schloimele, do you remember Frau Liebe, the woman who had the basement of the house on the Tchurtic?"

"A little," I said. "I was very young then."

"I met her in Warsaw again. She's such a kind woman, and such a good friend."

"I know, you wrote to us about her."

"She always asks about you and Ruchele. She would like to see you so much. Wouldn't you like to go and visit her?"

"Maybe we can go together, you and me."

"I can't. But you go to Warsaw and stay with Frau Liebe for a while. I beg you."

"Why? I don't want to leave without you."

"Please, Schloimele," my mother said, wringing her bony hands. "You say that you're not a child anymore. Can't you see what this place is like? How can I let you stay here?"

"If you don't want me to stay then why do you?"

"How can I leave? I can never escape again. Forget that you ever had a mother! I'm a damned woman, Schloimele! *Damned!*" she cried out bitterly.

The baby, frightened by my mother's shouts, began to cry. She took him in her arms, kissed his face to quiet him down, and tried to control herself.

"Do you need money?" she asked me. "I have a little. Let me give it to you. I'll walk with you to the station right now. Take the first train to Warsaw. Or go back to Lublin. Go back and don't—"

A sudden noise made her stop.

The door creaked open and Itzhak Copperstein, leaning heavily against the wall to keep from falling, staggered into the house. A foul smell came in with him. He had thrown up on himself and his pants were slimy with vomit. Unaware of us at first, he stood near the door in drunken confusion, dangling a half empty bottle from his hand. After a while, he turned around and stared at us with squinting eyes. Full of hatred, he spat out a filthy Polish curse at my mother. Then, laughing crazily to himself, he stumbled over to a bed and collapsed on it.

I understood from my mother's frantic looks that Itzhak Copperstein was dangerous in his drunken stupor. We stood dead-still, waiting for him to pass out on the bed. Fortunately, the baby had stopped crying. But moments after the drunkhard had lain down, he staggered back to his feet, cursed viciously again, and screamed that he was going to kill us.

My mother grabbed the blanket out of the carriage and threw it over the baby in her arms at the same moment that the drunkard lunged at us. We ran for the door. He tripped over a chair, fell, and we had just enough time to escape.

On the street, my mother stopped in front of the house.

"*Run!*" I screamed, pulling her by the arm. "Don't stand there!"

"No, you run away! Go home, Schloimele! Save yourself!" Her lips were ash-gray, and she was trembling like a twig in winter.

From inside the house came the noise of chairs being thrown and dishes crashing. A black iron pot came flying through the window, spraying broken glass on Reimanta Street. Then, quite suddenly, there was complete silence.

"Please don't stay here," I begged my mother. "He's going to kill you!"

"He won't kill me. I know him all too well. I only wish he *had* killed me long before this. But you must leave." She reached into her coat pocket and took out some bills. "Here's money. It's all I have, but it's enough for a ticket. Take it and go."

"I don't want your money," I said, pushing back her hand. "How can you stay with him?"

"I don't deserve any better!"

"I'm not going to leave you. If you're not going, then I won't go either."

From the surrounding houses, I heard doors being opened and slammed shut loudly in protest. All around me, I noticed faces in windows staring at us.

"I have to take a look," my mother said. "He must have passed out already."

I followed my mother as she walked carefully up to the house. Slowly she pushed the door ajar. I couldn't believe what I saw through the crack. The drunk, seated on a bed close to the wall, was rocking back and forth, banging his head against the wall while tearing at his flesh and clothes with his hands and teeth. Blood ran from his head and down the wall. As I watched spellbound, he ripped open his shirt, dug his fingernails into his bare chest, and tore at himself until red lines of blood crossed his flesh.

Silently, my mother closed the door and we walked back to the street.

"Why is he so crazy?" I asked my mother.

"He's drunk to death, that filthy bastard."

"Why does he drink like that?"

"He has enough reasons," she said bitterly.

Before I could ask her what those reasons were, my mother said, "The whole street is staring at us. Let me take another look. Maybe he has finally beaten his brains out."

We crept up to the door again, but now, out of nervousness, I pushed it a little too hard and it creaked open. He looked up from the bed where he sat drinking and saw us.

With a savage scream, he jumped to his feet and came rushing at us with the bottle.

"He's coming!" I shouted to my mother as I ran from the house.

An instant later he flung open the door and stood there, his head battered, his shirt torn and bloodied, waving the bottle over his head.

"Stop, Itzhak! Stop it!" my mother screamed. She hugged the baby closely to her breast as she backed away in horror.

With an inhuman cry, he threw himself at me. I shouted for help and ran across the street. I heard my mother yelling at him to stop. Then I heard her shouting, begging for help from the people who were watching from their windows. But no one came to my rescue. I ran as fast as I could, knowing that if he laid his hands on me, he would kill me. Only his drunkenness kept him from catching up to me in a few quick steps. Nevertheless, with my limp it was hard for me to keep outrunning him. I soon heard his heavy footsteps and animal grunts growing louder in back of me. The perfect day had turned into a dark haze before my eyes. As I was nearing the end of the street, all of a sudden, a sharp pain shot through my right knee, it buckled under, and I went rolling on the ground. Lying on my back on the pavement, I saw Itzhak Copperstein above me, flailing his arms like a demon, drops of blood flying from his head. He lifted his foot to trample me. I rolled away. He brought his leg down heavily, lost his balance, and fell. I scrambled to my feet, ran around the corner and barely able to stand up anymore, I opened the door of the first house I found and stumbled into it.

As I leaned against the wall of a dark corridor, catching my breath, I heard the soft rustle of footsteps. An elderly gentleman wearing a blue satin smoking jacket suddenly appeared and was startled to see me in his house.

"What are you doing there, little boy?" he asked.

Gasping for air, I whispered, "A drunk...is chasing...me."

"What? Are they carrying on again?" he said angrily as he walked past me to the door and locked it.

An elegant, white-haired lady also appeared in the corridor. "Yasha, what's going on?" she asked.

"Nothing to be alarmed about. Everything is all right," the gentleman said. "This little boy has to catch his breath and calm down a little. He was being chased by a certain drunk. Bring him a glass of water, Rivka."

"How terrible! Let him come inside," said the woman as she went to the kitchen.

The man led me into the living room.

"You are limping," he said. "Did he hurt you?"

Still gasping, I explained to him that I limped because my right leg was shorter than my left.

"Sit down on the sofa and rest a little," the gentleman told me.

I saw at once that these were rich people. On the living room floor, under my feet, there was a thick, yellow carpet with a colorful design of flowers and birds. The sofa on which I sat had a carved wooden frame and a red velvet cover. On the walls, there were paintings of peaceful landscapes. Rows and rows of delicate figurines stood in a fancy glass cabinet.

The lady brought me a glass of water. I thanked her and drank it at once.

"Why was the drunk chasing you?" the gentleman asked me.

I was too ashamed to tell them the truth. How could I have told anyone that this drunkard was my mother's husband?

"I don't know why," I said. "I was walking along the street and suddenly, without any reason, he ran out of a house and started to chase me."

"You know who that must have been, don't you?" the lady said to her husband.

"No doubt that human garbage on Reimanta Street—him and his women," he said to her.

"What do you mean?" I asked.

"They are terrible people," he said. "The lowest of the low. They are not even worth talking about."

"How I wish we could be rid of them, Yasha. They frighten me terribly."

"They won't go on like that much longer, Rivka," the gentleman said to his wife. "The police will put a stop to them soon, you can be certain of that."

He turned to me and said, "Are you feeling a little better now? Come, let's take a look. He is probably gone already."

We walked back to the corridor.

"You wait here," he said. "Let me make sure first." He unlocked the door, stepped out, and looked around. "It's all right," he said. "You can come out now. The drunk is gone."

I thanked the gentleman for his help.

"Don't you worry," he said. "You can go home safely now." He went back in and closed the door.

There was no one outside. I walked cautiously towards Reimanta Street. At the corner, I hid against the wall of a house and looked around the bend. A large crowd was gathered in the middle of the block. My heart suddenly began to beat violently again. I became afraid for my mother. How could she have defended herself with a baby in her arms if the drunkard had gone after her? I had to find out what was going on. Cautiously, I approached the crowd. I didn't have to get too close, however, before I heard the drunkard cursing in Polish.

Hiding behind the people, I crept up until I caught a glimpse of Itzhak Copperstein. He stood in the doorway of the hideous red brick house, suckling the mouth of his empty, broken bottle.

"That animal," I overheard one man in the crowd say to another, "is the head of that scurvy gang that's ruining this whole town."

"Roise!" the drunk suddenly called out. "My only love! Where are you? Come back, my darling Roisele! Please come back!"

She had escaped! I realized with a great wave of relief.

"He's calling for the thin one," I heard someone behind me say. "The one with the baby."

I turned around. "Do you know where she is?" I asked the man who had spoken.

"No," he answered. "Only the Devil knows where she is."

I decided that I wouldn't discover anything else by standing there. What mattered was that she had escaped from him. I walked away as fast as I could. Somehow I had to find my mother and get

158

her away from the drunkard. I understood now why she called her life a hell.

I had no clue where she might be hiding, nor did I know anyone in Otwock who could help me find her. The first thought that jumped at me, however, was the train station. It was the last place that she and I had talked about. If she had insisted on taking me there to help me get away, why couldn't she have gone there herself to make her own escape?

I ran up to the first passer-by I saw, a young nurse, and asked her for the quickest way to the train station. She began pointing and naming streets which I didn't know. When she saw how confused I was, she pulled out a pencil and a small notebook from her pocket. She opened the notebook to a clean page, marked an X for the spot where we stood, then quickly drew streets and arrows pointing the way. The station, she marked with a circle on her little map. She tore the sheet out and showed me how to hold it.

I thanked her and ran off.

The directions were well drawn, and after I had run through a few streets and turned some corners, I found myself on the main street. Now I knew, more or less, where I was. I had to walk straight to the end of the main street and from there I would see the hill on top of which stood the station.

As I walked, I prayed to God that my mother would be there. If she was too ashamed to go back to Lublin with me, I thought, then I would travel with her to Warsaw. We could stay at Frau Liebe's house until we got back on our own feet. My mother's cousin Yakob was sure to help us out. I would go to work immediately. I knew that I could make money to support us. My mother would rest and recuperate. As soon as we had our own home, we would send for Babbe and Ruchele. Above all, I would never let that disgusting drunk get near my mother again.

As I walked up the gentle slope of the hill, I looked up ahead to the train station's platform. There was no one out there. I began to pray harder.

If God knew everything that happened in the world, I thought to myself, then He must know how much I loved my mother, and how much Ruchele, Babbe, and I missed and needed her. What could Mamme possibly have done to deserve such a terrible fate?

And even if she *had* done something, hadn't she suffered enough? How much more pain could she bear? And what did we, Ruchele, Babbe, and I, do that was so sinful that we had to suffer the loss of my mother? Couldn't Mamme be given back to us now? It was with this prayer filling my heart that I opened the door of the train station. The room was empty. I walked up to the ticket window and asked the clerk if a woman with a child had been there recently.

"No one has been here since early in the morning," he said.

I turned around and decided to walk back into the town.

I wandered aimlessly from one street to the next, looking for my mother. I kept getting lost and finding my way. I passed the market where we had shopped earlier that morning. Somehow, I reached the end of town again and saw in the distance the low green hill of the train station. A little later, I found myself once more on the main street, close to Reimanta.

I searched every store, every alley, every corner. The day slowly turned into night. The sky was again brilliant with stars. The streets slowly emptied of people and soon were deserted. I was tired and hungry. I knew that I couldn't continue wandering around the whole night.

As I walked along the main street, reluctantly heading towards Reimanta, I saw a man on the corner who was dangling a bottle from his hand and arguing loudly in Polish with a street lamp. He spat on the wooden pole, kicked it, then he heaved back his arm and smashed his bottle against the lamppost. He stood wavering awhile under the pale light and began to cry. Suddenly he walked up to the lamppost, embraced it, and began to kiss it passionately.

I was too far away to be sure that it was Itzhak Copperstein, but I didn't go any closer to find out. I began to run in the opposite direction. I felt as if I had just seen the Devil.

My uneven footsteps echoed along the dark, empty streets as I ran away. After a few blocks, exhausted, I stopped running and continued to walk. I couldn't go back to my mother's house. The drunkard would kill me. If not that same night, then the next time he got drunk and was able to catch me.

Besides being tired, I hadn't eaten the whole day, and my jacket was not enough to keep me warm from the cold night air. Chilled through and through, I remembered my small brown suitcase with my clothes. I realized that I had to give it up for lost.

Now I had to decide where to go. My mother had wanted to send me to Frau Liebe in Warsaw, and I still had her address with me. But what could I expect from Frau Liebe in this situation? She had moved to Warsaw while I was still very young, and I only remembered her vaguely. All I knew was that she had been a good friend to my mother, and that her children, Leibel, Tsutel, and Elke, were the ones who had overturned the cradle that broke my leg while they were baby-sitting for me and Ruchele. After everything that I had just gone through, I wanted to return to a familiar place where I could feel safe again. As much as I didn't want to leave my mother behind, I decided to take the first train back to Lublin.

During my two days in Otwock, I had roamed over so much of it, that I knew my way around. I followed the main street to its end, walked through a few smaller streets, and I was soon at the foot of the low hill of the station. I walked up the gravel path towards the squat building with bright yellow light shining in its windows.

The train station, late at night, was deserted. I urgently needed to go to the bathroom and luckily I found one right near the entrance. When I came out, I went up to the ticket window. It was empty. On the counter, however, I saw a small bell. I rang it once. The clink echoed loudly through the empty room. After a few minutes, a sleepy clerk appeared, his hair disheveled, eyes half closed. He yawned. "Why are you bothering me at this hour of the night?" he asked.

"I would like a ticket to Lublin, please."

"A ticket costs six zlotys," he said, ready to go back to bed.

Immediately, I took out my money and put it on the counter.

"The next train doesn't leave until seven o'clock," he said as he handed me the ticket. "Don't lose your ticket because they won't let you on the train without it." Then he disappeared again behind the window.

I was completely drained of strength, my feet ached, and I was grateful to see a large, comfortable wooden bench with raised back and sides in the middle of the station. I leaned into a corner of the bench and fell asleep at once.

As if it were a dream, I heard my name being called and felt someone shaking me. It took me a while to tear myself awake. When I opened my eyes, I was startled to see the the drunkard's 'sisters' standing over me.

"Why are you sleeping here? Why don't you come home?" the plump woman asked me, smiling as if she really didn't know why I had run away. "Come with us."

"Yes, come back with us," the angry woman said, forcing a smile. "It's very late already and you should go to bed."

"I don't want to go back," I said. "I don't belong there."

"Did Itzhak upset you?" the plump woman asked. "You shouldn't judge him by what happened today. This happens very rarely. He really is a very good man."

"Once you get to know him better," the angry woman said, "you will like him."

"Come back now." the plump woman said and took my left hand.

"Yes. Come with us," the angry woman said and took my right hand.

"I can't stay in Otwock," I said, trying to pull myself free. "I only came to see how my mother was doing. Now I have to go back. I already have my ticket to Lublin. My grandmother and my uncle are expecting me to return tomorrow. Please let me go. I don't want to go back to that house."

"But why are you so afraid?" the plump woman asked, holding on to me. "There's nothing to be afraid of, believe me. It will be so nice to have you with us. Didn't you already tell Itzhak that you wanted to stay here. And didn't he also say that you could bring your sister along? Wasn't that nice of him?"

"Oh yes," said the angry woman, "he is so nice once you get to know him better. And it will make your mother so happy to have you and your sister with her. She misses the two of you so much that she can't live without you."

There was no one to help me. I thought of shouting for the ticket clerk, but I was afraid of what the two women might do to me before the clerk came.

"All right," I finally said. "I'll go back with you."

162

With one woman on each side of me, I stood up. Near the entrance, I said to the plump woman, "I have to go to the toilet."

"Wait until we get back home," said the angry woman.

"I *can't* wait that long," I tried to convince her.

The plump woman opened the door of the small room and looked inside. "Go ahead," she said. "We will wait for you here."

I walked in and locked the door. There was no place to hide, nor was there another door by which I could escape. Above the sink, however, I saw a small window. I climbed up on the rim of the basin and pushed at the glass. It didn't move. I thought of breaking it with my shoe, but I knew the women would hear the noise and come after me. As I tried to push harder, I noticed a small hook in one corner of the wooden frame. I unlatched it, pushed again, and now the window swung open. I pulled myself up and found that the opening was too small for my shoulders. By wriggling my arm, I was just able to fit my head and one arm through, and then with great pain and difficulty I pulled through my other shoulder. I was now leaning halfway out the window. The only way I could get to the ground was to dive head first. Propelled by fear, I pushed myself through, broke the fall with my hands, and landed on my back. I jumped up at once and ran down the hill into a nearby wooded area. In the woods, I hid behind the first wide tree. I waited till I caught my breath, then I looked to see if the women had followed me. In the moonlight the little station appeared very peaceful. There was no one on the hill. I sat down on the large roots of the tree and leaned back against the bark. I was shivering with cold and fear. Even though I wanted desperately to stay awake, my eyes slowly closed, and I fell fast asleep.

A loud whistle jolted me awake. The daylight hurt my eyes. I closed them but suddenly I remembered where I was. I looked around the tree. A long train was loading at the station. I jumped to my feet and ran. On the platform people were getting on and off the cars.

I ran up to a conductor and asked him if this was the train to Lublin.

"It is," he said, "but only for people with tickets."

I pulled out my ticket and showed it to him.

"Get right on," said the conductor. "We're leaving soon."

I ran up the small steps of the coach. With great relief, I sank into a seat next to a window.

"Schloime!"

I suddenly heard a man's voice shouting my name from the platform.

"Schloime!"

I looked out of the window and saw Itzhak Copperstein in clean clothes, sober, running up to the windows of the train. I became so frightened that I slid off my seat to the floor and began to shiver.

"Schloime!" he shouted just over my head.

People in the coach noticed that something was wrong and began to stare at me.

"What's the matter with you?" asked a young woman in the seat opposite to mine.

Another passenger, a well dressed man with eyeglasses, walked over to me and bent down. "Do you need help?" he asked as he pulled me up from the floor.

Still afraid to be seen, I immediately lay down on the seat.

"I don't think he should be traveling," the man said to the young woman and the other passengers. "He needs a doctor. They should take him off the train before we leave." But a shrill whistle suddenly drowned out the man's voice and with a lurch that made him lose his balance, the train started to move.

CHAPTER SIXTEEN

The Small Wicker Basket

IN THE COACH, a small group of passengers gathered around me.

"What's wrong with him?" someone asked.

"He's sick," said the man with the glasses. "Look, he can't even sit up straight. He needs a doctor. Somebody call the conductor."

I sat up at once. "You don't have to call the conductor," I said. "I'm all right now."

The train had picked up speed quickly. Through the window I saw Otwock disappearing.

The young woman sat down next to me and took my hand. "What is the matter with you?" she asked again. "Why are you trembling?"

"I'm very tired," I said. "I haven't slept the whole night."

"Why don't you lie down and rest," she said. "I'll make you a little pillow."

I stretched out on the seat. She took her jacket, folded it, and put it under my head.

"Are you feeling better?" the man with the glasses asked me.

I nodded to him.

"I'll keep an eye on him," said the young woman, sitting down across from me.

The passengers, including the man with the glasses, finally returned to their seats.

I began to calm down and slowly stopped shivering. Soon, rocked by the swaying of the speeding train, I fell asleep. I found myself immediately thrown back to Otwock. On the main street, I saw my mother running alone, without the baby. The look of fear on her face filled me with pity. I caught up to her and begged her to return to Lublin with me. She would go anywhere, she said, but she could never go back to Lublin. When I asked her why not, she wouldn't answer me. I didn't press her; I was just grateful that she had decided to leave Otwock with me. I told her that it didn't matter where we went as long as she left the drunkard. In an instant we were sitting in a train. As we tried to make up our minds where to travel, I woke up.

Still half asleep, I struggled up on my elbows to look for my mother.

The young woman noticed that I was up and asked, "What is it? What are you looking for?"

I realized at once that it had only been a dream. I sank down on the seat. "Nothing," I said. I turned my back to the young woman and without making a sound, I cried. A little later, I fell asleep again.

When I woke up it was already past noon. I returned the young woman's jacket.

"How would you like to share my lunch with me?" she asked. She opened a paper bag and gave me a sandwich of dark bread and cheese.

I hadn't eaten in almost two days and was starving. I thanked her and as I ate, I tried to make sense of what I had gone through.

I arrived back in Lublin in the evening. On the long walk from the station to Uncle Yankel's house, I decided that I would not tell anyone but my uncle what had happened in Otwock. I couldn't hide anything from him. It had been Uncle Yankel, after all, who had warned me not to leave Lublin in the first place. To Babbe and Ruchele, however, and to anyone else who might ask, I decided to say that I had not found my mother.

When I opened the door to our apartment, I saw Babbe sitting on the bed. She was alone in the kitchen and so deep in thought that she didn't even hear me open the door.

"Babbe," I called to her.

166

Startled, she looked up. "Schloimele," she said, her kind wrinkled face filling with joy. "Come to me and let me embrace you. I was just thinking of you and praying to God for your safe return. I'm so glad to see you." She held me close with her good arm and kissed my head.

I also was glad to be embracing her again.

"Schloime is back!" Ruchele screamed out from the living room and ran in. She threw her arms around me and kissed me.

Everyone else followed my sister into the kitchen.

Aunt Simke embraced me next. "Welcome back, Schloimele. We were so worried about you."

Uncle Yankel came over to me and looked sadly and knowingly into my eyes. He took my hand to shake it, but then threw his arms around me in a bear hug and lifted me off the ground. "Welcome back, you big adventurer. Welcome back," he said as he held me. "Are you in one piece still? Are you alive and well?"

"Yes, Uncle Yankel, I'm all right."

"Did you find Mamme? Did you see her?" Ruchele asked impatiently.

Uncle Yankel and I exchanged a quick glance.

"No, Ruchele," I said, feeling guilty for the lie.

The sudden look of sadness that swept over Ruchele's and Babbe's faces hurt me deeply.

"What happened, Schloimele?" Babbe asked. "Yankel told us that he gave you an address in Otwock."

"I went to the address, Babbe, but she wasn't living there anymore."

"Where is she then?" Ruchele asked.

"Her next door neighbors told me that she had moved away. They didn't know where to, only that she had moved."

"Didn't you try to find out?" Ruchele asked.

"I did, Ruchele. I tried to find out. That's why I didn't come back right away. These neighbors put me up in their house overnight so that I could go around Otwock and ask questions. But nobody knew where Mamme went."

"When did she move?" Babbe asked.

"They didn't know exactly…. Maybe a month ago…"

Ruchele put her arms around Babbe and began to cry. Aunt Simke and Uncle Yankel went back into the living room.

"Schloimele, what happened to the suitcase with your clothes?" Babbe asked.

"I went to the bathroom on the train," I said, "and while I was gone from my seat, someone stole it." It was the last lie I had made up on my way home.

"Let the suitcase and the clothes be lost forever," said Babble, "as long as you are back, safe and sound."

Later that night, when everyone else was asleep, Uncle Yankel said in a whisper to me, "Don't worry, Schloime, I'm not going to throw you out. I'll make believe that I have one more son. If there'll be enough for all the others, there'll be enough for you too. All I ask is, be a good boy. Find decent work, and I'll help you out as much as I can." To spare me pain and embarrassment, he never mentioned my mother.

I thanked him for his kindness.

I spent a good part of that night awake, sick with worry over my mother. The thought of her living with that insane drunkard in Otwock was unbearable. I had no doubt that she had fallen into a hell, as she herself had said. I almost fell into it myself. And what I had seen must have been only a small part of her horrible life. What baffled me, however, was how Mamme could have ever become involved with such a hateful man. It was so unlike her. Why had she done it? What kept her from leaving him and that hell? Why didn't she want to escape with me?... When I finally fell asleep, I had nightmares that I was being chased by Itzhak Copperstein.

I woke up in the morning feeling nervous, sad, and angry. I realized that if I kept on thinking about my mother and Otwock, I would drive myself crazy. I had to start thinking of earning a living for us again.

After breakfast, as I left the house to look for work, my sister followed me out the door.

On the street, Ruchele stopped me and asked, "Schloime, tell me truth. Where is Mamme?"

"I told you yesterday; I don't know. She wasn't in Otwock when I got there."

"Then tell me where she went."

"Didn't you hear what I said yesterday? Her neighbors didn't know. Nobody knew where she went."

My sister didn't seem to believe me. "Well, what *did* the neighbors tell you about Mamme?" Ruchele insisted. "Who was she living with?"

"The neighbors didn't know anything."

"How could the neighbors not know?"

"Because they're old, sick people and they don't go out of their houses much."

Ruchele looked down and said, "You don't have to lie to me, Schloime. I know everything."

"What do you know?" I asked her.

"That Mamme is married again," Ruchele said quietly. "And that her husband is a bad man."

"Who told you?"

"Uncle Yankel."

I was surprised and angry at my uncle for having told Ruchele. "If you already know, then why do you keep asking me?"

"Because I can't believe it. Is it true Schloime?"

"It's true," I finally had to admit. "Does Babbe know this?"

"No."

"Don't ever tell her, Ruchele. It would kill her. I wish you didn't know it either."

Although Ruchele was already thirteen and understood the basic realities of life, I could not tell her everything that I had seen in Otwock. I said nothing about our mother's baby, the two sisters, the man's drunkeness, or his violent temper. Nevertheless, even the little that my sister did know had a powerful effect on her. She looked pained and troubled.

"It's better to forget about it, Ruchele. It will make you sick if you keep on worrying."

"How can I forget?" she asked. "I can't put it out of my mind."

"I know. I can't either. But it won't do us any good to get so disturbed about it. We are on our own now. First we have to learn to stand on our own feet. Then we'll think of how to help Mamme."

After I left my sister, I went straight to the city to look for Uncle Yankel. I knew the area where he stayed between jobs. I wanted to know why he had told Ruchele about our mother.

When I found him, Uncle Yankel, who was talking with the other porters, was surprised to see me.

"Schloime, what are you doing here?" he asked.

"I want to ask you something in private."

He took me away from the porters.

"Why did you tell my sister about Mamme?" I asked him at once.

"How do you know what I did?" asked my uncle.

"Ruchele just told me."

Uncle Yankel looked at me with deep sadness and resignation. "I didn't want to tell her, Schloime. Believe me. I didn't want to tell her anymore than I wanted to tell you."

"The why did you?" I asked angrily.

"Because she heard about it from somebody else," said Uncle Yankel. He hesitated a moment and then said, "She heard it from some damned gossiper. After you left, she came crying to me and asked it it was true that your mother had remarried and that her husband was a thief. I couldn't believe my ears. I was so angry that someone would say that to such a young girl. What could I do? If I had told her that it wasn't true, she would have gone back and started fighting with the gossipmongers. And if I had told her that I didn't know, she would have kept on listening to them, driving herself crazy. I would have preferred not to have said anything·at all, but she kept crying and crying.... I had to tell her. Do you understand?"

I understood all too well. "Yes, Uncle," I said.

"I'm sorry, Schloime."

I had no doubt that my uncle was telling the truth. Hadn't he tried to protect me also as long as he could?

Uncle Yankel went back to his spot to wait for a delivery.

I knew that I could not waste any time before finding a job. In spite of my uncle's best intentions, he couldn't feed all of us. I went to see Chemie Feinman to ask if I could have my old job back. I had been able to early six zlotys a week working for him before I had quit to work in Sheindel's bakery. Although I was received warmly at the Feinmans, Chemie told me that he didn't even have enough tailoring to keep his own two sons busy.

When I left the Feinmans, I began to walk around Lublin, stopping in at tailor shops to ask for work. Most tailors told me at once they didn't need any help. A few, however, who were interested enough to talk to me, seemed to change their minds as they questioned me about my background. As soon as they heard that I lived with my uncle, they wanted to know what had happened to my parents. I told them that I had lost my father in the war, and that my mother had moved to Warsaw to work. Apparently, this background wasn't good enough for them. One tailor didn't even bother to ask me anything else after I had told him my name. It was as if he had already heard the gossip about me and didn't want to know anymore.

The days I spent looking for work were so frustrating that I began to think of peddling bagels again. I knew, however, that Uncle Yankel would be upset if I did that. We needed my uncle's help now more than ever and I didn't want to anger him. I kept looking and after a full week of endless searching, I was finally hired by an excellent tailor who had a busy shop.

I worked hard to please my new boss. Everything I was given to do I did quickly and carefully. Nevertheless, on the morning of my third day, my boss told me that he couldn't keep me on.

"Why?" I asked him.

He took me aside and said, "I can't lie to you and tell you that I don't have enough work. You can see for yourself that I'm very busy. And I can't tell you that you're a bad worker, either. I see that you work hard and try to do your best." He became embarrassed. "Let's just say," he finally went on, "that I heard something yesterday that didn't sound right to me. I don't like gossips, and I don't know if what I heard is true or not. Even if it were true, I wouldn't blame you for it. You seem to be an honest and hardworking boy...but this tailor shop is my business and I can't take chances with gossips.... I'm sorry."

I said nothing else.

The tailor paid me two zlotys for my work and I left feeling angry and humiliated.

On the street, I quickly went into the first grocery I came across and for two groshen bought myself a cigarette: a Wanda. Since I had started to work, at the age of eleven, I had been smoking occasionally, whenever someone gave me a cigarette. Now I felt the need for something to calm me down and help me forget the pain. As I roamed around Lublin, smoking the Wanda, I realized that I couldn't affort to let my bad feelings overwhelm me. I had responsibilities to Babbe and Ruchele, and my first concern had to be to earn a living for us. I began to feel hungry and tired from my aimless wandering. Since it was still early in the afternoon, I decided to return home to eat and rest, and afterwards, to go out again to took for work.

As I came to Tchwarteck Street, I saw Babbe ahead of me, leaving our building. Over her arm I noticed she was carrying a small wicker basket. With a feeling of dread and disbelief, I began to follow her. As soon as she came into the better neighborhood, Babbe stopped at a large house and rang the bell. I couldn't watch anymore. I knew what was happening. Babbe was begging again.

I looked quickly for a grocery store and bought myself a few more Wandas. As I smoked the cigarettes and calmed down, I decided that I had to go back to peddling bagels. It was agonizing for me to see Babbe going out on her *walks* again. As much as I didn't want to anger Uncle Yankel, I felt that I had no choice. I went straight to the bagel baker for whom I had once worked.

The red-faced baker not only remembered me, he was actually happy to see me again. I didn't even have to ask for my old job. He simply handed me a basket with a few dozen bagels, wished me good luck, and I was back in business.

After just a few days of peddling, I had enough capital to start selling newspapers in the early evening. And soon I was earning enough money again to pay for our food.

At the end of the week, I handed Babbe the money I had made. She took it with tears in her eyes. I told her that I knew what she was doing and I warned her never to go begging again or I would disappear forever and she wouldn't even know where I had gone.

Babbe swore that she would never do it again.

Uncle Yankel, however, was angry with me just as I had expected. Although he said nothing to me directly, I could see his displeasure from the way he looked at me. To appease him, I promised my uncle that the moment I was able to find tailoring work, I would quit peddling. I knew, however, that looking for tailoring was useless.

And so we got through the summer and autumn of 1927. I didn't make any great fortune, but at least we didn't starve, and Babbe didn't have to take any more *walks* with her little wicker basket.

CHAPTER SEVENTEEN

A Man with Empty Pockets is a Corpse

IN THE SPRING OF 1928, almost a year after my trip to Otwock,
memories of my mother still tortured me. Not a day passed that I
didn't think of her and her strange fate, a fate which I couldn't
fully understand but which I knew was horrible. I was completely
alone with these thoughts. I had no one with whom to share them,
and there was almost nothing in my life to take my mind off them.
I was too ashamed to continue my friendship with Beirel and the
few other nice boys I had known, just as they were ashamed to
be friends with a bagel peddler. My only friends were the boys
from the Jewish Market who, like myself, earned their living on
the street.

During the week, I kept busy selling bagels in the morning and
newspapers in the early evening. During the afternoon, between
my two jobs, I would meet my friends at the Jewish Market. On
the Sabbath, however, the Day of Rest, I felt very lonely. Since
the Market was closed and I didn't go to synagogue—I hadn't
gone since I was thirteen—I usually spent the day alone, walking,
smoking Wandas, and thinking. After my return from Otwock, I
began to smoke about five or six cigarettes a day. It gave me a
little pleasure and helped me bear the memories of that trip. To
light a cigarette on the Sabbath, however, was considered a great

174

sin and to avoid being seen by anyone who knew me, I had to be careful and take my walks far away from Tchwarteck Street.

One Sabbath evening in March, as I was coming home after a long and tiring walk, I saw Ruchele running towards me. She looked distraught.

"Don't go up, Schloime!" said my sister. "Uncle Yankel is screaming that he never wants to see you in his house again!"

"Why not? What did I do?"

"Someone told Uncle Yankel in synagogue that they saw you smoking cigarettes today. He is furious with you. He said he'll break all your bones if he catches you. Aunt Simke and Babbe are trying to talk to him." Ruchele began to pull me by the arm. "Let's not stand in front of the building. Uncle Yankel could come down and see you. Let's go in the back."

Our building had a large courtyard where the garbage cans were kept and where the landlord had built several small, wooden storage sheds for the tenants. Ruchele and I hid behind the sheds.

"Is it true, Schloime? Were you smoking cigarettes on the Sabbath?" my sister asked as we crouched down.

"Yes, but I didn't think anybody would see me. I went far away."

"What are you going to do? Where will you live if Uncle Yankel won't let you back in?"

"Don't worry. I'll talk to him when he calms down a little. I'll promise him that I won't do it again and he'll let me back into the house." In spite of the reassurance I gave my sister, I knew that my uncle was a stubborn man, and I didn't really think that he would forgive me so fast.

"You wait here," said Ruchele. "I'll go upstairs to see how Uncle Yankel is feeling. Maybe he has calmed down already."

My sister ran back into the building.

I waited behind the sheds in the courtyard. What made me feel even worse than my uncle's anger was Babbe finding out that I smoked on the Sabbath. She was very religious and I knew that it must have hurt her badly. Old and weak as she was, Babbe spent all her strength looking after me and Ruchele. I couldn't forgive myself for hurting her.

It was soon dark. The Sabbath was over. To relieve my misery, I took out my last Wanda and smoked it as I waited. More than an hour had passed before I heard my sister's voice again.

"This way, Babbe," Ruchele said.

"My God," said Babbe, "where is he hiding?"

I stepped out from behind the sheds.

"Schloimele, what have you done?" Babbe asked, putting her arm around me. "Tell me that it isn't true. Tell me and I will go to Yankel and swear by my old, wretched life that you didn't do it."

"Please forgive me, Babbe," I said. "I'll never do it again."

"May the Almighty forgive you for your sin, Schloimele, as I forgive you," she said. "But I'm afraid that we're finished now. Yankel doesn't want to listen to Simke, and he has no pity for my tears. My dear God, what are we going to do?"

The sight of Babbe in such agony tore at my heart.

"Don't worry, Babbe," I tried to comfort her. "I can go to a friend's house to sleep tonight. And tomorrow Uncle Yankel will let me come back home."

"I pray to God that he will," said Babbe, "but you know your uncle. He keeps on screaming that he doesn't want you to teach his children to smoke on the Sabbath."

"When he's calmer, I'll promise him that I will never do it again."

"In whose house are you going to sleep?" Ruchele asked.

"At a good friend of mine. You've never met him, Ruchele. He lives in a big house and I'm always welcome there."

"I brought you a little food," Babbe said, handing me a small bag, which she had been holding against her chest with her bad arm. "You didn't eat all day. You must be starving."

I kissed Babbe's hand. I was very hungry. I hadn't eaten since the morning.

"Don't worry, Babbe," I said. "Everything will be all right tomorrow. Now you and Ruchele go back and let me go to my friend's house before it gets too late."

"How will I be able to sleep tonight?" said Babbe. "May the Lord watch over you, Schloimele."

176

Reluctantly, Babbe and Ruchele left me and went back to the apartment. I took a walk around the block and returned to our courtyard. I had lied to spare Babbe more aggravation; I didn't have a single friend in whose house I was welcome. As I sat behind the sheds, eating the food that Babbe had given me, I tried to figure out where I would spend the night. I couldn't go to an old friend like Beirel Feinman because I was too ashamed. Nor could I sleep in the building because if the neighbors saw me, they would tell Uncle Yankel and Babbe. I finished eating and then by the pale light that streamed into the courtyard from the apartment windows, I checked the storage sheds to see if I could get inside of one.

All eight sheds had rusty metal hasps that were padlocked. I looked for a sharp stick of wood, and then I chose the shed with the loosest hasp. I wedged the stick between the hinge of the metal clasp and the wooden board to which it was nailed and pried the hinge loose. I easily pulled out the two rusty nails that kept the hinge in place and without even having to take off the padlock, I opened the small door.

Inside the musty shed, I lit a match. A sack of coal was propped up in one corner. On the ground, I saw some scattered firewood, two large empty sacks, and a bundle of rags. I put out the match. By the light from the courtyard, I began to clear the floor of the shed. I stacked the wood to one side and fixed the empty sacks and rags into a bed. At last, I closed the door of the shed and lay down. There was just enough room for me to stretch my legs. In a fit of anger, I cursed my bad luck and Uncle Yankel. I was very tired, however, and quickly fell asleep.

In the middle of the night, I woke up shivering with cold and so uncomfortable in my hard, lumpy bed that I found it impossible to go back to sleep. I finally rearranged the rags on which I was lying and used the least dirty of the sacks to cover myself. Soon I fell asleep again.

The next time I woke up, gray light filled the cracks between the wooden boards. I threw off the sack and rose at once. I had to be gone before our neighbors saw me. Outside the shed, I swung the metal clasp, which still had the padlock on, against the door and pushed the two nails that kept it in place back into their old holes. The door of the shed looked untouched.

I ran across the courtyard and stole away from our building.

I didn't work on Sundays, but at least the Jewish Market was open, and I spent most of the day there with my friends. Luckily, I still had fifty groschen in my pocket to buy some food and cigarettes. Towards evening I went back home.

At our building, I didn't go up, but waited instead for my sister to come down. When I finally saw Ruchele, her sad expression and the little bag in her hand told me the bad news at once. As she handed me the food, which Babbe had again packed, Ruchele said that no matter how much they all begged him, Uncle Yankel refused to change his mind to let me return home.

After my sister had gone back in, I stole quietly into the shed, closed the door, and ate my food in the dark. When I had finished eating, I took out my last Wanda, which I had saved just in case I had to sleep in the shed again. As I smoked, I seriously began to consider what to do next. If Uncle Yankel didn't change his mind soon, I thought to myself, I would have to find a new place to live. But where I would go, or how I could afford to live on my own, I didn't know. I simply wasn't earning enough money to pay rent and buy food. And in Lublin I couldn't hope to earn much more than what I was already making. Almost a year had passed since I had started to look for tailoring work, and I still hadn't found any. No matter where I went, everyone seemed to know about me and nobody wanted to give me a decent job. Perhaps in another city, I thought, where nobody knew who I was, I could struggle my way to a better job and a better life. Eventually I might even make enough money to bring Babbe and Ruchele to live with me. I could set up a house for us and maybe even rescue my poor mother from her hell.

These thoughts excited me. As soon as I began to think of starting a new life, I thought of Warsaw. It was a large city with many tailor shops. I probably wouldn't have trouble finding work there. I remembered Frau Liebe, Mamme's best friend, who lived in Warsaw. She had always been kind to us. Hadn't my mother wanted to send me to Liebe to get me away from the drunkard in Otwock? But what if Liebe had moved, I wondered, and I wasn't able to find her? Or suppose that when I found her, she couldn't help me? I was miserable in Lublin, but at least I survived. In Warsaw, alone and lost, without help or a job, I could easily starve to death. It was a frightening thought. I mulled over these possibilities a long time before I finally fell asleep.

The next day, Monday, I peddled bagels in the morning, spent the afternoon at the Jewish Market, and sold newspapers in the evening. When I returned to our building, Ruchele greeted me with a fresh bag of food and the same bitter news. Babbe kept crying and pleading with Uncle Yankel, my sister said, but he was still angry and stubborn as a brick wall.

To spare Babbe some pain, I asked Ruchele to tell her that the friend at whose house I was staying had told me that I was welcome to live with his family as long as I wanted. After Ruchele left, I returned to the shed, ate in the dark, thought over my plans, and went to sleep.

This continued for a whole week. I slept badly, ate badly, went around unwashed and dirty, until finally my life in Lublin tasted as bitter as gall to me. I decided that it was time to take action. I made up my mind that somehow I was going to Warsaw to start a new life. But first I needed money. I knew well enough that a man with empty pockets is a corpse.

Purim was approaching and the Jewish bakers were once again preparing to make matzohs for Passover. As the year before, when I had needed money to travel to Otwock, I went to see Sheindel the baker for work. She looked at me from under her large babushka and shook her head.

"A boy who breaks the Sabbath by smoking cigarettes," she said, to my surprise, "isn't allowed to help bake matzohs for Passover. The whole street knows about you. What will people say? As it is, I already earn a plague. If I let you work here, nobody is going to buy even one matzoh from me. I'll be finished for good." Sheindel turned around and went into the rear of the bakery.

My anger quickly overcame my feelings of hurt. I became even more determined to get out of Lublin. As if the gossipers hadn't

179

done me enough harm with the garbage that poured out of their mouths, they didn't seem to miss a single opportunity to make my life more difficult and miserable. Without wasting any time, I went to see other Jewish bakers about work. But every one of them, instead of giving me a job, gave me an interrogation. "Who are you?" they asked. "Where do you live?" "What does your father do?" "Who is your mother?" And so on endlessly.

I couldn't tell them the truth because they would never have hired me, nor could I tell lies; I would have been found out very quickly. Instead I told them that if I had been Graff Pototsky's son, I wouldn't be looking for work as an assistant matzoh baker. Some bakers smiled when they heard my answer, but no one hired me.

Finally, as one baker was putting me through a complete examination, I got so disgusted with all his questions that I asked him why he had to know all these facts. I hadn't come to borrow money, I said, nor was I asking to marry his daughter. And suppose my parents weren't of the highest class? I asked. How was I to be blamed for that? Don't forget, I told the baker, I didn't make them. And because of them, did he mean to say that I didn't have the right to work and live? Instead of helping a person in trouble, I said, everybody turns away from him.

The baker, a little astonished by my outburst, stared at me in silence.

"You're not altogether wrong," he finally said. "But what can I do? That's how the world is."

"The world isn't like that," I said angrily. "That's how people are!"

When it became obvious to me that I couldn't get work with the bakers, I began to feel lost. I knew that peddling would never give me enough money to travel to Warsaw. Worst of all, if I went on living in the storage shed, it would soon destroy me. I wasn't a sack of coal or a bundle of rags. The weather was still warm, but soon summer would rush by, and in winter I would freeze to death in there.

In the evening, when my sister came down to meet me, I asked her to tell Uncle Yankel that I had to talk to him.

She raced back upstairs and a few minutes later was down again.

"Uncle Yankel wants you to come up," she said.

I realized that if my uncle was still angry with me, he could give me a good beating. Nevertheless, I went up.

Babbe was standing by the open door, waiting for me. When she saw how I looked, tears filled her eyes.

In the living room, I was surprised to see Uncle Yankel sitting calmly at the table as if he had nothing against me.

"Come in, come in," said my uncle, "and let's talk. We haven't talked for some time."

When I approached him, he told me to sit down at the table. With a shake of his head, my uncle told his wife to take the children out of the room. Aunt Simke led the children into the kitchen and closed the door to the living room behind herself.

I opened my mouth to speak, but Uncle Yankel cut me off at once. "Wait," he said. "You can talk when I'm finished."

I listened quietly.

"What the devil is it with you, Schloime?" he began. "You don't want to find decent work. You run around with hooligans. You smoke on the Sabbath. And who knows what else you do that's even worse. When I step into the synagogue they want to gouge my eyes out because of you. They say that I'm raising a pagan in my house. I don't have enough troubles of my own? What did I ever do to you? Is this how you repay me for giving you a roof over your head?"

When I was sure that he had finished speaking, I said, "You think that I don't want a decent job? But tell me, Uncle, how can I find such a job if nobody wants to hire me? Everywhere I look they throw it up in my face that I'm not good enough. And I don't have to tell *you* why. You don't want me to be a peddler? I never wanted to be a peddler, either! But what else can I do? I can't just sit around here waiting for you to give to us, or for Babbe to go out begging with her basket to bring back crusts of bread. Do you think that I smoke on the Sabbath for pleasure? The Sabbath doesn't feel like a holiday to me. Maybe if my life was a little easier, I wouldn't need to smoke on—"

"Shut up!"

Uncle Yankel's shout startled and frightened me. I crouched, expecting him to hit me next, but he didn't.

"You went to *cheder*, didn't you?" he asked angrily. "You studied the Torah, yes?"

"So what?" I asked him.

"You should know better than to speak like an idiot."

"I speak that way because that's how life has taught me to speak. Maybe if God would explain to me why my life has to be so hard I might speak differently."

"You're not the first one who wants an explanation," said my uncle, holding back his anger. "And you won't be the last. You think that my life is so easy? You think that I don't ask sometimes why I have to suffer so much? But what comes out of the asking? What good does it do? I don't stop keeping the Sabbath just because I don't have an answer. Only God knows the truth, blessed be His name." Upon mentioning God, Uncle Yankel lifted his eyes to the ceiling and raised his voice, as if God had rented the apartment above ours.

I said nothing.

After a long silence, my uncle asked me, "Ruchele said that you wanted to speak to me. What is it?"

"I want you to help me leave Lublin."

"Where do you want to go?"

"Warsaw."

"Why Warsaw?"

"I could get work there. Warsaw is a big city and nobody will know who I am. If I have to struggle so much, at least maybe in Warsaw I could get somewhere. You don't want me in your house, and I can't keep rolling around the streets forever. I don't have much more strength left. Warsaw is my last chance. What have I got to lose?"

With a pained expression on his face, Uncle Yankel thought over what I had said.

"Maybe you're right, Schloime. But tell me, when you get to Warsaw, how will you manage? Where will you sleep the first night?"

"If I can live in a storage shed in Lublin, don't you think that I could find a storage shed in all of Warsaw to sleep in?"

My answer hurt my uncle. He dropped his head in shame. "Is that where you have been living all this time?" he said without looking at me.

I didn't want to make him feel bad. "It's all right, Uncle," I said. "Even the most intelligent people can sometimes make a mistake."

"Are you calling me a fool?" he asked with a sad smile.

"Of course not. Do you remember Frau Liebe, Mamme's best friend from the Tchurtic? She's living in Warsaw now. I have her address. She's a very good woman and I'm sure that she would help me out."

"Listen, Schloime," my uncle said, "I don't have any money to give you, but what I can do is ask the wagon drivers who travel to Pullav with merchandise if one of them would take you along. From Pullav you could take a boat to Warsaw cheaply. I hear that the boat owners are in a competition war, and a ticket is costing only a zloty instead of five. That's almost like free. Think it over carefully. If you really want to go, I'll help you. Before you leave, I'll even give you a letter for Frau Liebe and ask her to help you. You may be right, Schloime. This could be the best thing for you."

"Thank you, Uncle Yankel," I said. "Can I ask you for one more favor?"

"Ask," he said. "What is it?"

"Can I sleep in the house tonight, please?"

Uncle Yankel didn't say anything. For a moment, his crossed blue eyes seemed to become even more crossed as he held back from crying. Then he simply nodded.

When Babbe and Ruchele heard that I could sleep in the house, they beamed with happiness. But later that night, when I told them that I was soon going to leave Lublin for Warsaw, Babbe became alarmed again.

"What will you do there?" she asked. "It's such a terrible place. Heaven preserve us from such a fate. They kill people there in the middle of the street! You will get lost. I'm so old already. I will die soon and I won't even know where you've disappeared. First my Roisele and now you." She started to cry.

I tried my best to stop her tears. I explained to her why I felt that I had to move. I told her that she didn't have to worry because I would be staying with Frau Liebe, who would help me out.

"Schloimele, will you write to me often?" Babbe asked.

"I promise you, Babbe. Please don't worry. I just want to get a good job so I can earn money and find a house for you and Ruchele and me."

My sister, however, was glad to hear my plans. She too was sick of Lublin and couldn't wait to get out of there.

"When you're settled in," Ruchele said, "don't forget to send for me. I could also get a better job in Warsaw and help out."

I reassured Ruchele and Babbe that just as soon as I could, I would bring them both to live with me.

Drying her tears, Babbe looked at me and said, "When you get to Warsaw, Schloimele, ask around, maybe you can find out something about your mother."

Babbe was the only one who still didn't know anything of what had happened to Mamme, and it was a good thing that she didn't. She wasn't very strong anymore, and the truth about our mother could have been a blow that she might not have survived.

"I'll find her, Babbe," I said, holding back my own tears. "I'll find her and when we have a new home, we'll bring her back to live with us again."

CHAPTER EIGHTEEN

1st of May, 1928

TWO DAYS AFTER OUR TALK, Uncle Yankel asked me if I was still set on going to Warsaw. I told him that I hadn't changed my mind. "In that case," he said, "I've found a wagon driver who can take you to Pullav."

Babbe and Ruchele made me a small travel sack for my bit of clothes.

A few days later, in the evening, my uncle walked with me to to see me off on my trip to Warsaw. When we came to the wagon, Red Chaim Leibish, the driver, had already begun to load the barrels, crates, and rope-tied packs that were heaped on the sidewalk. This time my parting from Uncle Yankel was quick. As we said goodbye, he handed me a letter for Frau Liebe.

"Don't forget to write," he said. His crossed eyes moistened as we looked at each other. "Take good care of yourself, Schloime. Don't get into any trouble."

Uncle Yankel thanked the driver and left.

"Hey, you! Come over here," the driver, out of breath and sweaty called to me. "If you give me a hand, we'll get out of here sooner."

Reb Chaim Leibish, who must have been in his sixties, was short and muscular. He had small blue eyes, a long thick nose, a pointed gray goatee, and a fixed scowl on his face. On his head he wore a black cap which was turning gray with age. For a belt, he had tied a wide red ribbon around his stomach. His clothes were no more than a colorful assortment of patches.

I put my own little sack down on the wagon and went to work. I carried whatever I could and dragged whatever I couldn't lift. The open wagon, although it wasn't large, had high sides, and by the time we had finished, it was heavily loaded to the top. I couldn't imagine how the horse, a small brown nag, more bones than flesh, would ever pull that load from Lublin to Pullav.

Reb Leibish tied the goods down securely, and we climbed up. The scowling driver took the reins, gave them a hard pull, and slapped them down on the horse's bare haunches. "Move, you Old Corpse!" he shouted.

Slowly, with painful creaks and moans, the wagon rolled out of Lublin. It kept on rolling as long as the road was level, but as soon an we approached the first hill, the wagon stopped.

"Do you see what this lazy bastard does?" Reb Chaim shouted as he jumped to the ground. "When he has to go down a hill slowly, he runs! But when he has to go up a hill, and give a little pull, he plays dead! You should drop dead right now, you Bag of Bones, and put me out of my misery once and for all!"

As it turned out the trip was not an easy one. The little nag was so weak and the load so heavy that on every uphill we had to get off and push the wagon, and on every downhill we had to get off and pull the wagon back to keep it from overturning. The driver, meanwhile, blamed everything on the horse, and since the road to Pullav was all hills and valleys, throughout our entire ride— during which we walked as much as we rode—the wagon driver didn't stop heaping deadly curses on the little nag. "Walking Skeleton!" "Old Cadaver!" "Blind Nag!" he shouted at it. "You don't even look where you're going anymore! Let a blight lead you to your grave!"

When he got a little angrier, Reb Chaim Leibish soothed his nerves by running the whip across the poor horse's bones. This went on the whole night. I became angry with the driver's abuse of the innocent animal. Towards dawn, I began to wonder how the cruel man expected that half-dead creature to keep on pulling the heavy load if ever since we had left Lublin, he hadn't fed it even

186

a handful of hay. I finally couldn't hold back anymore, and I asked Reb Leibish if he was waiting for the horse to tell him that it was hungry. If he waited much longer, I said, there wouldn't be any horse left to feed.

As I was speaking, I saw the driver's expression change from a scowl to a glare to a sneer. "Look at this," he said, turning towards me. "The world is filled with wise men. Listen, do you know the old saying, 'For borscht you don't need teeth'? Or how about this one, 'Nobody has to teach a father how to make children'? You follow the meaning? If I didn't feed that creeping skeleton maybe there's a good reason for that."

I realized at once that he himself hadn't eaten anything either the whole night, and why should the horse be better off than the driver? Both worked just as hard. I was ashamed and apologized for my remark. I told the driver that I understood the sad reason for their hunger.

But poverty, it seems, concerns only the poor. Our arrival in Pullav in the morning, the three of us soaked in sweat, was greeted by a small mob of angry businessmen who followed the wagon to its stop shouting that their merchandise was late and threatening never to hire Reb Chaim Leibish again. The wagon driver, for his part, put the whole blame on his panting and gasping horse, which looked ready to drop dead. He apologized to the businessmen, cursed the torturous road to Pullav, and shaking his clenched fists at the horse, he cried, "What can I do if this corpse moves like a fly in sour cream?"

The businessmen grumbled as they quickly pulled their merchandise off the wagon.

I stood aside watching, thinking to myself that while the wagon driver and his little horse had been killing themselves on the road, traveling the whole night long, these businessmen had been fast asleep in their warm, soft beds like lords. And now, how did they thank Reb Leibish and his nag? With curses and threats. I was disgusted by this scene. I picked up my travel sack and left.

Pullav was a small rural town. As I roamed around the streets, I asked people where I could catch the boat for Warsaw. Soon I was on the shores of a huge body of blue-gray water, Lake Visla. Surrounding the small port, I saw a crowd of people sitting among suitcases, wooden trunks, wicker baskets, and bundles tied with string. It made me think of the Jews of the Bible on their exodus from Egypt thousands of years ago.

I approached a man who stood cradling a baby in his arms and asked him if this was the place where the boats left for Warsaw.

It was, he said, whenever they came. It was clear from his comment that I might have a long wait ahead of me. I looked for a comfortable spot and found some stacked crates against which I could sit and lean. As soon as I settled down, I closed my eyes and fell asleep.

I slept for four or five hours. When I woke up, although there was still no boat in sight, the crowd had grown much larger. As I waited, more and more people kept arriving. It wasn't until the early evening that two small boats finally appeared on the water. By then there were so many people waiting at the port, it seemed that even ten boats wouldn't have been enough.

No sooner had the boats docked than people started to run, push, and shove. Everyone wanted to get on first. I raced along with the crowd towards the entrance of one of the boats, but it was impossible to get on. Men were fighting; women, screaming; and children, crying.

Suddenly two military guards came out, one from each boat, to make order.

"First old people and women with children will get on!" one of the guards shouted. "Everyone else stand aside until they have boarded!"

I was short and could still pass for a child. I approached an elderly woman and asked if I could help carry her bundles. She was grateful to have my help. Alongside the old woman, I got past the guards and on board.

But it was still hours before the boat was fully loaded. When it finally left port, it was already late at night. After most people had settled down, a man dressed like a French general appeared. He carried a revolver over one hip, a large leather bag for money over the other, and in his hands he held a booklet of tickets.

"*Za billet!*" he called out in Polish, "Get tickets!" as he went from passenger to passenger, collecting fares.

When he came to me, I handed him my zloty.

He looked at the bill and made a sour face. *"Pieintz zlote koshtuie!"* he shouted at me. "It costs five zlotys!"

I had no more money than that one zloty, and I was frightened. I didn't know what to say.

The ticket collector became angry and shouted something which I couldn't understand. Luckily, a Jewish man who was sitting next to me saw my problem and translated. "He's asking, don't you know that the price competition is over?"

Through my interpreter, I told the ticket collector that if I had known, I wouldn't have even bothered to come to Pullav. The ticket collector shook his head impatiently and said that he believed me, but this wasn't his boat, he was only a worker, and he had to collect the money.

Since my explanations weren't getting me anywhere, I reached into my pockets and turned them out to show him that the zloty was all I owned.

My Jewish interpreter didn't bother to translate the curses that came flying out of the ticket collector's mouth. I understood only his last few words. "You're lucky, you little bastard, that we're in the middle of the water!" Then, angrily, he threw the zloty back at me and moved on to the next passenger.

I put the zloty into my pocket. I was relieved the threat had passed and a strong feeling of exhaustion overtook me. I nestled into the corner where I sat and hugging the travel sack on my lap, I closed my eyes. The long journey was almost over; soon I would be in Warsaw. The gentle motion of the boat, as it rolled over the quiet waters of the lake, lulled me to sleep and I found myself sitting on a black horse, holding on to a rope tied around its neck. The day was sunny and as the horse galloped across a green field, a summer breeze blew in my face. I was riding towards home where my mother and father were waiting for me and I felt free and happy. I had never known such a sweet feeling in my heart before. In my excitement, however, I didn't notice that the horse kept galloping faster and faster. When I realized what was going on, I began to pull back on the rope as hard as I could, but it didn't help. I was soon being bounced so violently that the rope slipped out of my hands and I was almost thrown off the horse. Somehow I managed to grab the animal's neck and I clung to it for life until the pain in my arms became agonizing and my grip began to weaken. Suddenly, neighing madly, the horse reared and tossed me into the air. I screamed as a sharp blast of the boat's whistle tore me out of my nightmare.

It was morning. I sat panting, my heart racing like the wild black horse of my dream. We were approaching Warsaw.

After I had calmed down, I stood up and walked to the front end of the boat. Through the window, I saw a long iron bridge and running across it something like a single, red train wagon. An electric streetcar! I had heard about them in Lublin, but this was the first one I saw with my own eyes. It looked very odd. A long pole extended from the roof of the vehicle to a cable above it, and where the pole and cable touched, sparks of fire flew like small flaming birds.

Around me, people preparing to disembark gathered their belongings. I took my travel sack and climbed up the stairs to the upper deck. On one side of the lake, in a section of Warsaw called Praga, I saw streets with sidewalks shaded by big leafy trees, and houses which looked like little palaces with gardens covered by flowers. The boat, however, turned towards the opposite shore to dock. On this side, Warsaw proper, the ground was much higher, and all I could see were sections of streets climbing and falling steeply.

I had memorized Frau Liebe's address and as I was getting off the boat, I asked an elderly man where Muranovska Street was. He pointed to an uphill street and told me to walk to the top. There, he said, I should ask again for directions. I had far to go and he couldn't explain it from where we were. I thanked him and started the uphill climb.

I had expected Warsaw to be one of the most beautiful cities in the world, but the neighborhood through which I was passing was very poor. The little houses which I saw weren't any better than the houses in the poor sections of Lublin. Most windows instead of having glass panes were nailed over with wooden boards. Squalor is the same everywhere, I thought. On the concrete sidewalk and on the cobblestoned street, there wasn't even a trace of grass, flowers, or trees.

At the top of the hill, however, there was a sudden and impressive change of scenery. To the right, overlooking Lake Visla, I saw a mansion which looked like it could have been the home of the President of Poland. The entrance to that small palace was made of broad gravel pathways, winding through flower beds and sculptured shrubs. To my left, I saw a long, wide street crowded with tall buildings, some as high as eight stories. At street level, the fronts of these buildings had stores with large windows displaying all sorts of merchandise. On the roofs, I saw huge billboard advertisements in Polish with pictures of smiling men, women, and children holding up a variety of products.

I began to understand what it meant to be in a big city. I stood on the street corner looking around me in awe, searching for a Jewish face among the passers-by. I soon spotted a young man with a hat and a thick black beard. I approached him for directions. Muranovska Street, he said, was in the Jewish section, but I was still very far from it. Pointing to my right, the young man told me to follow the street to its end, where it would branch out. There, he said, I should ask someone else for more directions.

As I walked deeper into Warsaw, I noticed that the stores were closed. Everywhere, I saw men gathering in small groups. They would talk quietly but excitedly, then band into larger groups and rush off together. Further still into Warsaw, the groups of men grew larger and noisier. I began to see policemen on foot and mounted on horses. Finally, as I came to a wide square at the entrance to a park, I saw a crowd of hundreds of men, many carrying signs, standing closely packed together, listening to a speech. The speaker, seated on the shoulder of two other men, was shouting in Polish and gesturing wildly. I couldn't understand him, or the Polish signs, but a few of the signs were in Yiddish and I read, "STOP UNEMPLOYMENT!" "DOWN WITH POLICE!" "BETTER PAY AND WORKING CONDITIONS!" "DOWN WITH THE REACTIONARIES!"

A circle of policemen, waving rubber truncheons, stood surrounding the crowd of demonstrating workers. Instead of keeping order, however, the police would attack the workers from behind, hitting them on their heads and backs with the billy clubs. The demonstrators, who tried desperately to defend themselves with

191

bare hands, were no match for the police. Shots suddenly exploded over the crowd and a riot broke out. The police made a full attack and everyone began to run.

Terrified, without any sense of where I was going, I also ran. The shooting continued. From the rooftops, police armed with rifles picked off workers in the street. Mounted policemen trampled men with their horses. I saw bloody fights everywhere. A gang of men who must have been plainclothes police roamed about like a pack of wolves looking for demonstrators. I saw how they caught a young man, surrounded him, threw him to the ground, and clubbed him until blood gushed out of his face and head. I kept on running until I finally reached streets without police or demonstrators.

I still had to search for two hours before I finally found Muranovska. It was a wide street, one of the main streets in the Jewish section, with two silver rails stretching down its middle. The buildings, three to four stories high, were old and large. As I was about to cross the street, I heard a trolley car approaching. Afraid of being showered by the flying sparks of fire, I stepped back against a building. The red streetcar came charging wildly along the rails, making such a loud clatter as it passed that I felt the pavement tremble under my feet.

As soon as I crossed the street, I saw number 34, Liebe's address. It was an old building, like all the others on the block. I walked in through the large front doors and asked the children who were playing in the courtyard where Frau Liebe lived.

"In the basement," a little boy told me and pointed the way.

The stairs had no lights. Running my hand along the wall, I carefully groped my way down. Soon I heard the faint sound of voices and through the darkness I saw a line of light coming from the crack of a door. To avoid bumping into the door, I approached it with my arms outstretched, accidentally pushed it open, and found myself facing a room full of people.

The conversation stopped as everyone turned to look at me. There were four young men, two young women, and an older woman in the room.

"I'm looking for Frau Liebe," I said.

"I am Liebe," said the older woman, seated in the middle of the room.

192

Her plain, almost flat, face was deeply marked by the lines of a hard life, and although her expression was grave, her tone of voice was so kind and friendly that I felt immediately at ease. She was about fifty years old. I could tell that she was a pious woman from the dark-haired *sheitel* on her head. There was such a calm feeling about her that it was obvious she was at peace with herself.

"I'm Schloime," I said. "Roise's son."

"Schloimele!" a few voices shouted at once.

A tall, handsome young man put a strong arm around me and gave me such a hearty squeeze that I thought my ribs would crack. One of the two young women, the plain one, came up and took my travel sack from me. The other young woman, who was rounder and prettier, brought me a chair.

"When did you arrive in Warsaw?" asked Frau Liebe.

"I just got off the boat a few hours ago."

"You must have seen what is happening in the streets then?" she asked.

"Yes," I said. "I had to run away from the fighting. What is going on?"

"The government is giving the workers a May Day celebration that they will not soon forget," said the handsome young man angrily. "They sent in the police to smother any demonstrations for justice. Who knows how many people they killed today, those murderers. And what are the workers asking for that they deserve to be shot at? A little more money so they can afford to feed their families?"

"Such a madness," Frau Liebe said. "It's a lucky thing you didn't get hurt or arrested. But just look at you! When we left Lublin you were just a baby, and now you're a young man. I'm so happy that you came."

I had never imagined that Liebe and her children would welcome me so warmly. They made me feel at once like one of their family. I realized why my mother loved her so much and just what a wonderful friend this woman was to us.

The door from the other room opened and I saw a stooped old man, thin and sickly, standing in his nightshirt. "What's going on?" he asked in a strained, hoarse whisper.

"Hertzke, guess who this is?" Frau Liebe said. "Roise's Schloimele!"

A weak smile bent the old man's lips. "Welcome, welcome," he whispered, waved his hand, then turned around and shuffled back into his room.

"That's my husband," said Frau Liebe. "He's not feeling well and has to stay in bed. Do you remember when I got married? It was just before we left Lublin. And that house on the Tchurtic where we lived, do you remember that? It was such a long time ago. Do you recognize my children?"

My strongest memory from those days was how my right leg was broken, but I didn't mention it; nor did they, although they must have noticed my limp and known what it meant. But that didn't really matter anymore.

Slowly I found out who everyone was. The tall, strong young man who had embraced me like a brother was Leibel, the same Leibel who had engineered the system of baby-sitting that had ended in my broken leg. And the two young women were his sisters, Tsutel and Elke, the assistant baby-sitters. The other three young men, who also lived there, were Frau Liebe's husband's grandsons. They had come from a small town, not far from Lublin, to live with their grandfather because in their own town they couldn't find any work. In Warsaw, I was glad to hear, they had found jobs quickly. Frau Liebe's children also worked: Leibel in a leather handbag factory, Tsutel for a seamstress, and Elke as a salesgirl in a large dress shop. Frau Liebe herself no longer sold potato latkes, as she had done in Lublin. Now, she dealt in small fish, which she bought, cleaned, fried, and then sold in the market. Only Frau Liebe's husband, Hertzke Schneidleider, who was an invalid, didn't work.

After they had told me about themselves, Frau Liebe and her children wanted to know about me, Babbe, and Ruchele, and what had made me come to Warsaw. I felt so much at home with them, so much a part of their family, that I held back nothing of the miserable truth. When I told them what had happened to my mother, and of my painful visit to her in Otwock, Frau Liebe and her children sat in stunned silence, exchanging sad glances.

194

I saw how deeply disturbed they were by the story of my mother's life, and I tried not to dwell on it too long. When I finally told them that I had come to Warsaw to look for some decent work and a better life for our family, they immediately reassured me that I had nothing to worry about. There was plenty of work in Warsaw, they said. I would soon be earning a little money and be feeling much better. Without any hesitation, they invited me to stay with them.

Their kindness was so overwhelming that I couldn't find words to thank them properly. Liebe and her family, however, didn't even want to hear my thanks. Instead, Frau Liebe said that I must be starved from my long journey and told me to sit down at the kitchen table to eat. As Tsutel and Elke gave me dinner, Leibel suddenly ran out of the house.

In Warsaw, Frau Liebe and her family didn't have much better living quarters than they had had in Lublin. They lived in a dark cellar with two small rooms. Each room had two windows at street level that let in a little daylight, but most of the time the electricity had to be turned on. Since eight people were living there, the two rooms seemed filled with beds: three in the kitchen, two in the other room, and under the beds there were folding cots, which were opened only at night.

While I ate, Leibel returned, carrying a small straw mattress with one arm and a broad wooden plank with the other.

Later that night, when it was time to sleep, Leibel pushed two chairs towards the kitchen wall, put the wooden plank down across the chairs, and the mattress on top of it. Tsutel and Elke covered the mattress with a sheet, gave me a pillow and a blanket, and I had a comfortable place to sleep.

It was only after I had lain down that I remembered Uncle Yankel's letter. A few minutes later, when Frau Liebe came in from the other room to see how I was doing in my improvised bed, I told her that my uncle had written to her and gave her the letter.

She opened it and read it. When she finished, she folded the letter and put it back into the envelope.

"Don't worry, Schloimele," Frau Liebe said quietly to me. "You can trust us. We won't let any harm come to you. I know how much you have suffered from what has happened to your mother.... I loved her very much, too.... She was my best friend...."

CHAPTER NINETEEN

"Run As If from a Wildfire"

AFTER A FEW DAYS IN WARSAW, I wrote home to let everyone know that I had been warmly welcomed by Frau Liebe and her family. I also started to look for work. I read carefully through the job announcements of the "Express," a Jewish daily which carried notices for all trades. Within two days, I found an advertisement that called for a boy who wanted to become a tailor. The applicant, who had to be from a province, would receive full bed and board. The name and address given were: Mr. Kalmen Nagil, 8A Dluga Street.

When I got there, ten boys were already standing in line waiting outside the closed door of the house. I took my place with them. After a few minutes, the door opened a little and a man's voice asked the first boy where he was from. No sooner had the boy answered than the man behind the door said no, he wasn't what was wanted and sent him away. The next boy, who was the oldest standing in line, wasn't even asked where he was from; through the crack in the door, the man took a good look at the boy and told him to move on. A few boys were asked, "Who are you?" and "How long have you been in Warsaw?" but they weren't right either. By the time I stood in front of the door, another ten boys had already lined up behind me.

196

"Where are you from?" the voice asked me.

"Lublin."

"How long in Warsaw?"

"Five days."

The door opened a little more and two large eyes scrutinized me. Suddenly a hand reached out and pulled me in. When I regained my balance, I found myself standing in a dark corridor before a very short and strangely shaped man.

"You have been in Warsaw only five days?" he asked me again. "Did you come alone?"

"Yes."

"Do you have parents?"

I hesitated a moment and said, "No." I surprised myself with my answer, but I had to lie. He wouldn't have hired me if he had known about my parents.

"Who are you staying with?"

"My aunt," I said, lying again. My answers, however, seemed to please him.

"You're the boy I'm looking for," he said.

He opened the door slightly and said to the boys still waiting outside, "You can go home. The job is filled."

He closed the door and turned back to me. "Go home and tell your aunt that I want to speak to her."

"She isn't home now. She sells at the market."

"All right, later when your aunt comes back from the market," he said, "I want you to go and call her. Now come with me."

I followed the short figure through the corridor into a room which was both a kitchen and a tailor shop. Here there was plenty of light coming from a large open window, which looked out on the backyard. Under the window stood a sewing machine and next to it, a small table with tailoring supplies: spools of thread, buttons, chalk, tape measures, pins, scissors. There was a long work table against one wall, and against the opposite wall, a large brick stove, a wooden bin, an icebox, and a sink.

For the first time, I took a good look at the strange little man, Mr. Kalmen Nagil, my new boss. He was about thirty-five years old, although he looked much younger. He was very short and broad boned. He had a large bulging head with thin, light colored

197

hair, and big gray eyes. His short, thick legs were as crooked as a pretzel and he looked like a dwarf.

His wife who was in the kitchen preparing tea, had a friendly face. She was in her mid-twenties and taller than her husband. Her fiery red hair was curly, her face, lightly freckled, and her eyes were bright green. A little boy, about four years old, stood hanging on to her skirt and hiding his face in it. They had another son, the tailor told me, who was seven years old and went to school.

The other person in the room was an elegant young man, dressed in gray-striped pants, white shirt, tie, and vest, who was working at the sewing machine.

"And this is *Monsieur* Chaim Friedman," the short tailor said in a mocking tone, pointing to the young man. "He works here too."

The young man slowly looked up from his work and said, "I thank you for the *Monsieur*, Mister Nagil, but I won't need it until I get to Paris—which I hope will be as soon as possible. And as for my working here, for the wages you pay me, I would rather call it slavery." Then, smiling pleasantly to me, Chaim Friedman said hello and went back to work.

Mr. Nagil disregarded his assistant's comments.

"You'll work here with us," my boss said to me."Your first job in the morning, *every* morning, will be to light the stove."

He led me to the three flat press irons lying on a metal sheet on top of the brick stove. "The press irons must always be hot and ready for use. That's your most important responsibility for now. In here," he said, opening the lid of the wooden bin, "we keep coal and some kindling wood. When you see the bin getting empty, tell me and I will give you the key to the cellar so you can get more coal to fill it up again. Understood?"

"Yes, Mister Nagil," I said promptly.

"Besides that, you'll help us out in general. Don't worry, we'll keep you busy in one way or another. Alright, now sit down and watch carefully how tailors in Warsaw work."

My new boss picked up an unfinished jacket and moved a chair close to the long work table. But instead of sitting down, he stepped on the chair, hopped onto the table and sat himself down, crossing his twisted legs so strangely that he ended up sitting on his feet.

In the evening, the elegant assistant got up from the sewing machine and carefully brushed off the thread and lint that clung to his suit. He fixed his tie, and with a friendly smile to me, said good night.

"Tell me, Monsieur Friedman," Kalmen Nagil asked, "will you come to work tomorrow, or are you off to Paris already?"

"I will be in tomorrow, Mister Nagil. But, when I do leave for Paris, you can be sure that I will tell everybody *but* you."

"If you keep on talking to me like that," said Mr. Nagil, "I may send you packing to Paris much sooner than you're ready."

"I am so frightened by your threat, Mister Nagil, that I will go home now to recuperate so that I may be able to come back tomorrow morning," said the smiling assistant. And he walked out without even saying goodbye to the tailor.

Mr. Nagil's only response to his assistant was a disdainful snort.

A few minutes later, my boss told me to go home and bring back my aunt.

When I returned to the basement, Frau Liebe was already back from the market. I told her about my new job and asked her if she would speak with the tailor. With embarrassment, I also told her that I had lied and said that I had no parents and that she, Frau Liebe, was my aunt.

"Do you want to work there?" Frau Liebe asked me.

"Yes," I assured her.

"Then let's go see him," she said, "and don't worry. I think I know what he wants. I will take care of everything."

As soon as we arrived, Mr. Nagil took my 'aunt' into the other room of his house and spoke with her a long time.

When they finally came out, Mr. Nagil was smiling. He was obviously satisfied with the talk.

"Tonight," Frau Liebe said to me, "you will still sleep at home, and tomorrow morning you will start working and living here."

Frau Liebe and I left the tailor's house. On our way back, I asked her why the tailor had wanted to speak to her.

"He wanted to know," she said, "if you were an honest boy. Then he asked me what had happened to your parents, and who you had been living with in Lublin. I told him that you were very honest and hardworking, and that until you came to me, you had lived with your other aunt. Your father, I said, didn't come back from the war. I said nothing about your mother, so Mister Nagil asked me again what had happened to her. I told him that it was a very sad story and it would disturb me too much to talk about it. That was enough for him. Then I reassured him that he would be very happy with your work."

We walked in silence awhile and then Frau Liebe said, "It's not good to lie, Schloimele, but it's better that you told him you didn't have parents because if he had known about your mother, he wouldn't have hired you."

"What do you mean?" I asked her. "What do you know about my mother?"

"Don't ask, Schloimele," she said. "It's a terrible story. You have suffered so much already."

"Please tell me everything, Frau Liebe. I beg you. You can tell me the truth. Since my mother disappeared, I haven't had a moment's peace of mind. You were Mamme's closest friend. She must have confided in you. Maybe if I can understand what happened, I'll be able to find some way to help her. Please, Frau Liebe, don't hide the truth from me."

We walked in silence a long time while Frau Liebe carefully considered my words.

"I will tell you what I know," she said at last. "Heaven forbid that you should run into the people that have ruined your mother's life. At least if you know about them, you'll be careful not to let yourself get dragged into the same mire. But I can't tell you how your mother fell into their hands, or why. That I'll never understand. I wouldn't have believed it possible if I hadn't seen it with my own eyes.

"You know that when your mother came to Warsaw she went to work in her cousin's dry goods store. The first time she came to visit me here, your mother and I cried for joy. We were so happy to be together again. Every Sabbath, Roise would come to spend with us. We sat and talked. After nine years of not seeing each other, we had plenty to talk about. She told us how difficult it had been for her to earn a living in Lublin after she had lost

Pearl as her peddling partner and how you were all forced to move in with your uncle's family, into a cramped apartment.

"I don't have to tell you that she couldn't make a living in Lublin, no matter how hard she tried. Finally, her cousin Yakob offered her a job in his store here in Warsaw, and she took it. She came here to make a better life for her family.

"Your mother was happy with her work, she liked Warsaw, but she missed all of you very much. She never stopped talking about the day when she could bring you and Ruchele and her mother to live here.

"Her plan was to save up a little money and then to start peddling again. I thought it was a very good idea. I offered to lend her some money and I told her that if she wanted, she could bring all of you to Warsaw to stay with us for a while. No matter how crowded it is, there's always room for good friends. But Hertzke, my dear husband—may he live to be a hundred and twenty—has been very sick, and your mother didn't want to impose on us. She said that she was already sending money to you in Lublin and she had even started to look for an apartment. You don't know how happy we were that things were going so well for her. A few more weeks, we thought, and she would send for you. We didn't tell her this, but we had planned to welcome you with a party.

"And then, we didn't see her one Sabbath. We thought that she must be busy, had something else to do, or maybe she just didn't feel like visiting once—there's nothing wrong with that. But the next Sabbath, she didn't come again. When we didn't see her for the third Sabbath in a row, we became worried. I went to her cousin's store to see if she was sick. But Roise wasn't there anymore. Her cousin told me that she had left three weeks earlier, on a Sabbath, and she had never returned.

"Our first thought was that maybe she was so homesick that she had returned to Lublin, even though we still couldn't understand why she wouldn't have told us. A few weeks later, when we received your letter from Lublin asking if *we* had any news of your mother, it became clear that she hadn't gone back home. We didn't know what to think then.

"One day, a few months later, as I was standing in the market selling fish, I looked up and couldn't believe what I saw. I thought my eyes were deceiving me. I left my stand to move a little closer, and I realized that it was Roise, your mother, standing next to a tall, thin man. I walked towards her, but just as I came close, she and the man quickly walked away. I called after her, but they started to run and I couldn't catch up to them. I didn't know who the man was, but somehow he seemed familiar. Then I remembered that I had often seen him at the market, each time with a different woman.

"I started to ask my friends about him. Everyone seemed to know something different. One person told me that he was a thief. A second said that he was a terrible drunkard. A third said that he lived with four women. One good friend of mine, a woman who sells next to me in the market, told me that his parents are her neighbors. They live at forty-six Stafke Street, in a cellar. The tall man visits his parents often, and whenever he comes, he always brings his four wives with him. His parents are no better than he. His mother is an old thief. The whole neighborhood knows her, and there isn't a store owner on her block who lets her set foot in his store. The father is an old beggar and a thief. When he goes into a house, he grabs whatever he can get away with. All of this, my friend told me. She said that the household at forty-six Stafke Street doesn't know the fear of God.

"The tall man, my friend has heard, sends the women out to steal for him, to wash clothes, even to beg, while he himself is always lying around drunk. And on top of it all, he beats the four wives without any pity."

Frau Liebe stopped and looked at me. I was bewildered. She must have seen from the expression on my face how deeply hurt I was by these revelations.

"I'm telling you all these things," she said, "because I want you to be careful, Schloimele. Otherwise, I would never have told you. I know how much this hurts you. But they are dangerous people and God forbid that you should also be led astray by them. I want you to become the kind of man that your mother wanted you to be. Who knows what witchcraft they used to make Roise fall into their dirty hands? I have known your mother almost ten years, and I know that she wouldn't have joined them of her own free will. I can only think that somehow they drove her crazy.

202

That's how dangerous these people are. And now that you know, remember always, Schloimele, if you should see one of them in the street, run away—run as if from a wildfire!"

I didn't know what to say. Frau Liebe's description of my mother's life and of the people she was involved with left me too ashamed even to look up. I kept my eyes fixed on the pavement and walked the rest of the way to the basement in silence.

At Frau Liebe's home, everyone noticed how disturbed I was and left me alone. Later that night, after the beds had been made and the lights turned off, Frau Liebe came into the kitchen. As I lay on my makeshift bed, staring at the dark wall, she whispered to me, "I know how painful this is for you, Schloimele. But you are not alone. You can think of us as your family. We care about you and we will always be here to help you. Now try to sleep. Tomorrow morning you have to get up early to go to work."

I lay wide awake in the dark room where everybody else was already asleep, and went over everything I had heard about my mother. Even though I knew that Frau Liebe would never lie to me, I still found it impossible to believe what she had told me. It sounded so incredible. How could a man have four wives? And how could my mother live with a man who sent her out to steal and beg for him? Mamme—a beggar and a thief? Never! Even after all the horrible things I had seen in Otwock, I still couldn't believe that. But I knew that Frau Liebe was not a liar. I could easily believe that Itzhak Copperstein was a thief and that he beat women mercilessly. I already knew that he was a drunkard. Hadn't he attacked me in a drunken rage? And hadn't I known at once that the two women living with him weren't his sisters? But who would have guessed that they were his wives? How could my mother live with them? How did she ever get mixed up with such a bunch of criminals? My mother was so kind, decent, and honest. It could only have happened the way Frau Liebe had said. They must have deceived her somehow, maybe even bewitched her so that she didn't know what she was doing. They had turned my mother into a different person.

I went over my memories of Otwock, looking for new clues, trying to fit Frau Liebe's information with what I had gone through at 33 Reimanta Street. I saw my mother's face again—so pale, drawn, aged; that look of shame in her eyes when she first saw me—now I understood why. I remembered how she had cried and stumbled into the room, nearly falling and dropping her baby. *Forgive me, Schloimele. Forgive me,* she had cried out to me. *I've fallen into hell, and I can't get out anymore!* Now I knew what she had meant; why she had stopped writing to us; why she had wanted to send me away from Otwock as soon as possible. Now I knew what her hell was. But why didn't she run away? What kept her with them? Was she afraid that they would kill her if she tried to escape?

No matter how these thoughts frightened and upset me, I couldn't stop dwelling on them. As much as I wanted to get some rest to be ready for work the next day, I couldn't fall asleep. Hours later, when I was finally able to doze off, one thought kept recurring and pulling me out of my sleep with a shock that left my heart beating violently—46 Stafke Street! I couldn't forget that address.

At most, I slept three hours that night. When Leibel woke me up early in the morning, I was still very tired. Nevertheless, I dressed and went to work, taking with me the small travel sack with all my belongings.

When I walked into Mr. Nagil's kitchen-tailorshop, he and his assistant were already working.

"You're here finally," said Mr. Nagil as soon as he saw me. "Put your bag down and make the fire in the stove because we need to use the press irons. This is work, not a spa, and you're not here for a vacation."

"Good morning, Schloime," said Chaim Friedman. "Welcome to Egypt and to the rule of Pharaoh the Tiny. How are you feeling today?"

"Good morning, Mr. Friedman and Mr. Nagil," I said. "I'm fine, thank you." Hurriedly, I threw my bag under the table and went to the wooden coal bin. I opened the lid, took out some pieces of kindling wood, and put them into the stove. Next to the bin, I found a small can of naphtha with which I sprayed the wood. After I had put the can of naphtha safely back in its place, I lit a match and threw it on the wood in the stove. As soon as the fire was burning, I began to put in the coal: small pieces at first, and when

204

these were glowing, larger pieces. In a short while the press irons, lying on the metal sheet on top of the stove, began to heat up.

"Now wash your hands," ordered Mr. Nagil.

As I stood at the kitchen sink rubbing my blackened hands with a piece of perfumed soap, he asked, "How old are you?"

"I will soon be sixteen," I said.

He walked out of the kitchen to another room and quickly returned with a prayer book and a blue velvet pouch with gold embroidery, containing phylacteries.

"Every morning, after you make the fire," said Mr. Nagil, a solemn and pious expression invading his face, "you will go into the other room to put on *tfillin* and say your morning prayers. Now go and come back as soon as you're finished."

I entered the other room, which was the fitting room, living room, dining room, and bedroom, all in one. Mrs. Nagil and her children, who had been there, walked out. The oldest boy was late for school and his mother was rushing to prepare him a hot breakfast now that the stove was lit. I was left alone in the room. Although it had been years since I had put on *tfillin* and said morning prayers, I still remembered how to do it, and now, because my boss insisted on it, I went through the holy morning ritual again.

When I was done, as I was replacing the *tfillin*, Mr. Nagil suddenly appeared at the door. "What's taking you so long?" he asked. "What are you, a rabbi? Does this look like a synagogue? There's work waiting."

"I'm done," I said, quickly closing the blue velvet pouch.

"Now come into the kitchen," said Mr. Nagil. "You have to go out and buy some things for breakfast. Everybody is going to starve waiting for you."

The boss's wife told me what she wanted and exactly where I should go to buy it. The tailor gave me money and I left. It was the first time in my life that I bought so much good food at one time: milk, rolls, butter, cheese, sour cream, eggs, herring. I carried the large bag to the tailor's house with both my arms around it, hugging it as if it were gold.

Within minutes of my return, the tailor's wife had breakfast ready. Mr. Nagil pointed to the the small table with the tailoring supplies and told me to make room for myself there. I was then served such a breakfast as I had never eaten before in my life— a roll with butter and cheese, a large piece of marinated herring, and hot cocoa. It tasted delicious. Although I was aware of my boss staring impatiently at me from the table where he sat working, I tried to enjoy my meal as long as possible.

As I was taking my last bite of the roll, the short tailor hopped from the table to a chair, jumped to the floor, and said that I had to go out at once to buy tailoring supplies. He needed buttons, thread, and lining. He gave me money, samples, and instructions on how much and where to buy, and I was on my way.

The moment I returned with the supplies, the tailor's wife handed me a small bag with the oldest boy's second breakfast and told me to take it to him at school. Even though this time I only had to go around the corner, I felt so tired from my sleepless night that I walked slowly and the errand took me a long time. I returned feeling exhausted.

"I'm glad that you're back so fast," the sarcastic little tailor said as soon as I came through the door. "Now that all the nonsense is out of the way, let's take care of some real business. But first, don't forget the stove. The press irons are getting cold."

I quickly took care of the stove. What Mr. Nagil meant by *real business*, I soon found out, was to send me on endless errands with heavy and light packages to all parts of the city. First I had to deliver cut material to the pants-maker for sewing and finishing since my boss and his assistant only made the jackets of the suits. Next I had to deliver cut material to the vest-maker. Then, a finished suit had to be delivered to a customer. Afterwards, there were overdue bills to be collected from customers who either had forgotten to pay or outright didn't want to pay, and who weren't happy that I was bothering them about it. There was no end to the running around. I became so tired that every time I sat down to rest on the steps of a doorway, I would catch myself falling asleep.

What kept me going, however, was my desire to find 46 Stafke Street, the home of Itzhak Copperstein's parents. From what Frau Liebe had told me, I thought that it was very likely that my mother visited them whenever she came to Warsaw with the drunkard.

Everywhere I went, I asked passers-by for Stafke Street. I didn't come near it until late in the day, when I went to collect money from people who lived near Frau Liebe. Stafke Street, I discovered, was only two blocks away from Muranovska.

My first day of work didn't end until late at night. As I staggered in from my last errand, Mrs. Nagil told me to sit down and eat my supper. The lunch which she had given me earlier in the day had been better than breakfast, and supper turned out to be one of the best meals of my life. Mrs. Nagil served me chicken soup with noodles, a salad of tomatoes and onions, as much meat as I wanted, mashed potatoes with gravy, cooked carrots, bread, tea, and to top it off, a chocolate pudding dessert. For the first time in my life, my plate had more food than I could eat.

After my meal, when I could barely keep my eyes open, Mr. Nagil came in from the other room and said that now he was going to teach me a little tailoring. He started to show me how to sew two different types of stitches, but when he saw how tired I was, he told me to go to sleep.

"Rest up," said Mr. Nagil. "Tomorrow we have a busy day and I don't want you dragging yourself around like today."

I slept in the kitchen on a cot with a thin mattress so old and worn that the wooden frame of the cot poked through everywhere. When I woke up in the morning, from a night that seemed much too short, all my bones ached.

The days that followed were no different from the first. If I wasn't sent out on deliveries, I went to collect overdue bills; and when I wasn't running errands, I had plenty of work to do in the house. Unfortunately none of my work had anything to do with the craft of tailoring. It was clear that Mr. Nagil had insisted on a boy from the provinces because he needed someone easy to exploit.

One morning my boss noticed that the coal bin in the kitchen was getting empty. He gave me the key to the cellar and a large empty sack, and told me to go down and bring up more coal. The bin, although it looked small, was deep and held so much coal that I had to make four trips. On each trip, I dragged a heavy load up the long, dark stairway. As I finally brought up the last sack of coal, I was exhausted and completely covered with soot.

"Do you have to make so many trips?" asked Mr. Nagil from the table where he sat perched like a vulture.

Nevertheless, I tried not to get discouraged. Whatever else he may have been, Mr. Nagil was also an excellent craftsman who was paid some of the highest prices in Warsaw for hand-tailored suits. And even though my tailoring lessons took place late at night and were always short, I tried to learn as much as I could from him. I had a place to sleep, the best food to eat, and even a little pocket money from the tips I received from deliveries to customers.

A week flew by. Early in the morning of my first Friday with the Nagils, I realized that this was going to be a special day. After I lit the stove and finished praying, instead of being sent out on errands, I was told to help Mrs. Nagil prepare for the Sabbath. I went shopping with her and carried the grocery bags. I swept the house. While she cooked, I kept her little son out of the way. And when the food was on the stove, I watched that the pots didn't boil over or burn.

As I worked, memories came back to me of how I used to help my mother and Babbe on Friday afternoons. These memories made me feel sad and lonesome for the days when my family was together.

Mr. Nagil even stopped working early on Friday so that we would have time to wash up, change clothes, and get ready to greet the holy Day of Rest.

As evening fell, Mrs. Nagil lit the Sabbath candles and said the blessing over them. At last, it was time for the meal for which we had been preparing the whole day. I helped Mrs. Nagil bring in the dishes. She set four places on the table in the living room: for herself, her husband, and their two boys. And then she set one place at the work table in the kitchen for me.

After the food had been served on both tables, the door to the living room was closed and I was left sitting in the kitchen alone like a dog. Through the closed door, I heard Mr. and Mrs. Nagil singing little Sabbath songs for their children. I sat and looked at the food laid out before me, probably the best meal I had ever seen in my life, but I couldn't touch it. I had no appetite. Why did they shut me out? I kept asking myself. Did they think I wasn't good enough to sit at the same table with them? And where was

my own family? Why couldn't we have a table to sit at together—
my mother, Babbe, Ruchele, and I? Was that too much to ask
for? What kind of a life was this where those who had the best of
food also had beautiful homes and their families to enjoy it with
them, while others, who couldn't even beg enough to ease their
hunger, had to eat their bitter meals alone, forgotten in some
corner? I was suddenly overcome by such feelings of anger and
disgust that I picked up my plate and threw the food out the window
into the backyard. At least I could share my good fortune with all
the other stray dogs of the world.

CHAPTER TWENTY

46 Stafke Street

ON THE SABBATH, however, I was happy. Even though I was not supposed to work on that day, nevertheless, after I awoke and said the morning prayers, I had to make a small fire in the stove, boil water, and serve my boss and his wife tea in bed. For this they gave me a few delicious butter cookies to have with my own tea. After that I was free for the rest of the day to do as I pleased. And in Warsaw I had important things to do.

The whole business of being told to pray and then to make tea on the Sabbath struck me as funny. How could such pious people, who insisted that I put on *tfillin* every day, order me to commit such a sin as lighting a fire on the Day of Rest? But I resisted the temptation to ask Mr. Nagil about it. He probably would have thought I was getting too smart and thrown me out. Besides, I wasn't really bothered by a little hypocrisy anymore. And soon enough, only two weeks after the start of my Hassidism, everything was cleared up anyway. One morning while I was praying, Mr. Nagil charged into the room and accused me of praying slowly on purpose to avoid work. The day after this unjust accusation, I skipped the morning ritual altogether. My boss didn't seem to notice the difference. A week later, although he still didn't mention anything about my stopped prayers, Mr. Nagil did say that he thought my work was improving.

Every Sabbath I visited Frau Liebe and her family. Whenever she asked me how my work was going and whether my boss was treating me well, I always reassured her that I was very content with my job. I told her that I ate the best of food at Mr. Nagil's, that every night the tailor taught me a little of the craft, I had a good place to sleep, and I was even earning a few zlotys a week from tips. What more could I want? It made Frau Liebe happy to hear this because she was very concerned about me, and I saw no reason to burden her with my troubles. What good would it have done either of us?

Everyone at Frau Liebe's spent Sabbath morning sitting in the kitchen, sipping tea, discussing the current events of Warsaw and the world. Frau Liebe's children, especially Leibel, were very interested in the workers' struggle for unions, better wages and working conditions, and the improvement of the standard of living of all poor people. Not only did I enjoy these discussions and learn from them, they actually gave me courage to go on with my own life. I realized that I was not alone in my outrage at the painful existence that I and my family, and millions of families like mine, were forced to suffer. The more seekers for a better world there were, I thought, the quicker we might find a way out of our misery.

In the early afternoon, I would go back to Mr. Nagil's house to eat lunch. When I returned to Frau Liebe's, I took take a walk with her husband's grandsons. The three boys were about my age, and we became friends. On our walks we continued to talk about our lives. Their situation, I quickly found out, was a lot like mine. They complained of how little money they were paid for their hard work. If not for their grandfather's help, they said, they wouldn't have been able to manage at all.

But the time to which I looked forward most, although I also dreaded it, was the end of the day. After I had said goodbye to everyone at Frau Liebe's, instead of going straight back to Mr. Nagil's house, I walked to Stafke Street, where the drunkard's parents lived. I went there with the hope of running into my mother. I couldn't abandon her no matter how dangerous the gang of thieves was. I was sure that she was being held against her will. She could never have been one of them. I had made up my mind that the next time I saw her and could to speak to her alone, I would tell her that Frau Liebe had explained to me what was going on, and that I was ready to help her escape from those criminals.

Stafke Street was a little narrower than Muranovska, had no trolley car, but was just as crowded with large buildings. Number 46 was a four-story building with black iron front doors. With a chill of fear in my bones, I walked past the building, went to the end of the block, crossed over, and walked back again on the other side of the street. I repeated this walk until darkness fell, and I had to run back to my boss's house.

Sabbath after Sabbath I kept my watch on Stafke Street without any luck, without even a glimpse of my mother.

As I had promised Babbe, I kept in touch by mail. Soon after my first letter, I wrote again to say that I had found work as an apprentice to an excellent tailor at whose house I had bed and board. I also wrote that I visited Frau Liebe every week and that I was treated like a member of her family.

More than a month passed before I received an answer. In the letter, Uncle Yankel said that he was happy to hear I had finally found a good job. He urged me to keep up my courage. Ruchele said that she was still working for the dressmaker and was earning five zlotys a week, which was a great help in the house. Her life in Lublin, however, was miserable. Everywhere she went, fingers were pointed at her. People whispered such horrible things about our mother that Ruchele was ashamed to look anyone in the face. She couldn't wait to get away from there. She begged me to ask Frau Liebe if she could help her move to Warsaw. Worst of all, my sister said, Babbe had started having trouble breathing, fell ill, and had to be hospitalized. Babbe missed me very much and said that she hoped to live long enough to see me again.

I wrote back immediately asking my sister, Uncle Yankel, and Aunt Simke to take the best possible care of Babbe. I asked them to tell Babbe that I missed her even more than she missed me, and that at the first opportunity, I would come back to visit her. For now, however, I begged Babbe to take care of herself and get well quickly. I explained to Ruchele how crowded it was at Frau Liebe's apartment and that Liebe's husband was sick. I asked my sister to be patient just a little longer, until I had a chance to establish myself somewhat, and then I would help her move to Warsaw.

In the letters that followed, Ruchele wrote that Babbe had slowly recovered and although she was not fully cured, she had become well enough to return home. I felt grateful for this news.

Months passed. The summer of 1928 was almost over. On a Sabbath evening in September, as I was rushing back to the tailor's house after another useless watch on Stafke Street, I ran past a woman who seemed familiar. I stopped and turned around. To my surprise she had also stopped and was looking at me. She took a few steps towards me.

"Schloime!" she suddenly exclaimed, as a delighted smile spread across her plump face. "Is it really you?"

I recognized her voice, her round face, her false friendly smile. I had met her in Otwock. She was one of the drunkard's wives.

Frightened, I stepped back, but she grabbed my hand.

"Where are you running off to now, you foolish boy?" she said, holding on to me. "What are you doing in Warsaw? Have you seen your mother yet? Does she even know that you're here?"

At the mention of my mother, I tried to control my fear. "No, I haven't seen her yet," I barely managed to stammer.

"Then you must come with me," she said, pulling me by the hand. "You can see her right now."

I tore my hand free from her grasp and stood without moving. "Call my mother out," I said. "Tell her to come here. Tell her that I want to speak to her."

"What's the matter with you?" she said, laughing. "You're so jumpy. What is it? Are you afraid of Itzhak? He won't do anything to you. On the contrary, he'll be glad to see you. When you ran off in Otwock, Itzhak kept looking for you. He almost followed you to Lublin. You left your poor mother so distressed, she didn't know what to think. She's still crying and wondering what happened to you. Now don't be a fool and come with me to see her."

"No," I said. "Please ask her to come out."

"This is ridiculous," she said impatiently. "Your mother can't come out. If you want to see her, come with me; if not, then goodbye." She turned around and started to walk away.

"Wait," I called after her. "I'll go with you."

I followed her into the building at 46 Stafke Street. At the dark stairway to the basement, she took my hand to guide me through the pitch-black passageway. Finally, she pushed open a door and entered a dingy cellar.

The appalling sight and the stale air of the small, crowded room stopped me at the door. I couldn't breathe. I felt faint and leaned against the door frame.

Although the room was dimly lit by a naphtha lamp, I soon recognized the drunkard's gaunt face, the angry woman with the clouded black eye, and *my mother*. Her gray head was bent. On her lap she hald a small bundle of rags which, I soon realized, was a baby. She had two children now. The baby in her lap and the little boy, over two years old already, standing restlessly next to her, pulling at her dress.

There were many other people in the room: an old man and woman, who must have been the drunkard's parents, and six other men, dirty and unshaven, dressed in torn beggar's clothes. One of them was not even a whole man, just a head and torso propped up on a little wagon with wheels.

My mother didn't look at me although her tears, falling on the bundle on her lap, told me that she knew I was there.

"Mamme," I said, "come out with me. Please. I want to speak to you."

She shook her head. "I can't go out now," she said with a broken, cold voice, still not looking at me.

We were both silent for a long while.

"Tell me where you live," my mother finally said, "and I will come to see you."

I looked at the wretched criminal faces that were staring back at me, and I became afraid to give out my address. These people, I thought, could rob my boss's house and then kill me.

"I'll come back next Sabbath," I said to my mother, "maybe you'll be able to talk to me then."

I started to leave.

"When did you get to Warsaw?" Itzhak Copperstein asked before I could back out of the door.

"A few months ago."

214

"What are you doing here?" he asked, stopping me again.

"Working."

"Sit down awhile," the plump, smiling woman said. "You must be hungry or thirsty. Have some tea with us."

I still had not seen my mother's face, and it was clear to me that I wouldn't that day. She was too ashamed that I had found her in such a condition.

"I have to go," I said as I ran out the door.

"Wait a minute!" Itzhak Copperstein called after me. "I'm going too! Wait for me!"

CHAPTER TWENTY-ONE

"The Happiest Time of Our Lives"

As I GROPED BLINDLY through the dark staircase, I heard Itzhak Copperstein's footsteps behind me.

"Wait!" he shouted. "Don't run away again!"

I stumbled against a step and fell. A strong hand gripped me under the arm and lifted me to my feet.

"Where are you going?" Itzhak Copperstein said, holding on to me firmly. "Let me help you."

I couldn't escape him this time. He was sober now. Even if I did manage to yank myself free from his big hand, I could never outrun him. I saw light at the top of the stairs and decided to wait until we got outside. On the street, I would scream for help. Even if a policeman was not around, people would stop to find out what was happening, and Itzhak Copperstein would have to let me go. But as soon as we stepped out of the building, he released my arm.

"Schloime, why are you afraid of me?" he asked. "Is it because I chased you when I was drunk? Forgive me. I didn't even know I did that until your mother told me about it. But you didn't have to run away, I wouldn't have hurt you."

"I'm not afraid of you," I lied, slowly walking away.

"Then why don't you come back and stay?" he said, following me closely. "Don't you want to see your mother?"

"I very much want to see my mother," I said while I kept on walking, "but she couldn't speak to me now. So, I'll see her next Sabbath."

"Schloime, I have to speak to you," he said. "I want to explain some things."

"It's late," I said, still walking. "I have to be back already."

"You think that it's my fault that she is so unhappy, don't you?" Itzhak Copperstein said.

I stopped and turned around. I wanted to say, Yes! I wanted to damn him for destroying my mother's life and for breaking up our whole family. But all I could say was, "She has changed a lot since she left Lublin."

"I know," he said. "The years she has spent with me have been cursed, like my whole life has been cursed. If I could have prevented what happened, I would have. I don't want to see even a hair on her beautiful head harmed."

I felt revolted to hear him speak that way about my mother. My face must have shown him my feelings, because suddenly, looking into my eyes, he cried out, "I love her, Schloime! Do you understand? Just as much as you love her. I also love her.... You look at me as if I am not human... as if I have not suffered for all of the misery that I made your mother suffer.... You don't understand! Let me at least walk with you and explain what happened."

It was a trick, I thought, to find out where I lived or else to lure me into joining his gang and becoming a thief for him. I remembered Frau Liebe's words of warning about how dangerous he was. At all cost, I didn't want him to know where I lived. But I was also torn by the desire to know what had happened to my mother. I decided to hear what he had to say, but in my heart, I swore that I wouldn't believe a single word. He had already trapped my mother, I would never let him catch me, too.

"I have a long way to go," I said. "It's better to talk here."

"Schloime, I have to speak openly to you," he said, the wild look of his eyes piercing into mine.

I nodded to let him know that he could say anything.

"I never wanted to become what I became," he began. "And if my parents had been decent people, I wouldn't be what I am today. I grew up in a house that every night was full of thieves, whores, and murderers. My father, when he was younger, was a shoemaker, but he also had a little side business. He was a fence. Do you know what that is?"

"No."

"He bought stolen merchandise from thieves and sold it. That's the kind of house I grew up in. Now and then, even the police would drop by. When I got older, my father taught me shoemaking. As soon as I found a job and earned enough money, I moved out of my parents' house. I wanted to escape their crazy life.

"All of this happened in Lublin, and it was in the shoemaker's shop where I was working that I met your father. What a craftsman he was, the best, and so well liked. For a while we were friends, before all my troubles started.

"After I had been living on my own for a while, I fell in love with a girl. We decided to get married. Unfortunately, when her parents found out my past, they tried to stop her from seeing me. But my girl loved me too much to care what her parents thought.

"Just a few weeks before our marriage, my boss's house was robbed. I was the first one my boss suspected and questioned. I told him that I had nothing to do with the robbery. He ordered me to find out who had done it. If I didn't come up with the name of the thief, he said, I was fired. I had little choice and said that I would try. I asked around without any luck. I even asked my father, but he also knew nothing about the robbery. At least, that's what he told me.

"My boss was convinced that I had broken into his house, and he fired me. He even spread that lie to all the other shoemakers in Lublin, and it became hopeless for me. The minute I stepped into a shoemaker's shop to ask for work, I was treated like a thief. Maybe if I had other parents, the whole story would have been forgotten in time. But everybody knew my father and mother, and I couldn't clear my name again.

"As long as I was able, I looked for work and tried to survive on my own. Eventually I was forced to move back to my parents' house. Slowly I got dragged into their company of crooks, and I

218

went out on a few jobs. At first, I was just a lookout. I kept watch while the others did the robberies. But I quickly got used to the work, and I also started to steal. I became a thief.

"When my girl found out what I was doing, she threatened to leave me. I told her that I had no other way to earn a living. I wasn't any happier than she was about my work, and I promised her that I would quit as soon as we had enough money to move to another city. I hoped that someplace where nobody knew me, I would be allowed to live a normal life. My girl was understanding and she agreed to this plan. But before I could save up any money, I got caught during a break-in and was thrown in jail.

"My girl wanted desperately to help me. Most of all we needed money. Since she didn't have a job, she began to steal from her parents. She took out of their house what she could and sold it. She did everything possible for me while I was in jail, and for my trial, she hired one of the best lawyers in Lublin. He was so good that he managed to convince the judge that I was innocent. They let me out a free man.

"When I left prison, where could I go? The only place was back to my parents' house. I was still determined to make enough money to move out of Lublin and get married. I looked and looked for work, but nobody wanted to hire me. So I started to steal again, except that now my girl decided to help me out. We thought that the sooner we could get enough money to move away, the sooner we could start a normal life. She continued to take things out of her parents' house until her father caught her and threw her out for good.

"After that, we had to get married right away. We arranged a quiet wedding and rented a small apartment in Lublin. The only way I could support us was to continue to steal. It upset my wife very much. She became afraid to let me out of her sight.

"'The minute you leave the house,' she said to me, 'I start to worry that you'll be arrested again. If you're going to do this, then take me with you. I don't want to stay at home going crazy wondering what's happened to you.'

"When I refused to take her along, she started to follow me everywhere I went. I had to give in. But from then on, I did as few jobs as possible. The moment we had enough to live on for a few days, we would stop stealing. When the money ran out, we were forced to go out on a job again.

"We couldn't avoid making friends with other thieves. They started to visit us just as they visited my parents' house. My wife became friendly with a woman who soon became our partner. For a while the three of us worked together. Then, one day, my wife decided that I should stop going with them. She said that a man looked more suspicious than a woman.

"'You go back to shoemaking,' my wife said. 'We know many people now and you should have enough work to keep you busy. I'll keep doing jobs with my friend, but as soon as we can live off your work, I'll stop.'

"I thought my wife's idea could be our answer. I set up a little workshop in our apartment and started to work at my trade. I didn't earn much at first but slowly business picked up. In a few months I was doing so well that when we found out that my wife was pregnant, we decided that she should stop going on jobs. We started to live like normal, honest people.

"My wife gave birth to a beautiful little girl—Matelle. She is a young woman now, fourteen years old, and beautiful. She works for a friend of mine in a restaurant. But soon after Matelle was born, life became harder. There were times when I didn't have enough work and we went hungry. It got so bad that my wife wanted to go back to stealing. Her old partner kept asking my wife to join her on jobs. I didn't even want to hear about it. 'We'll manage somehow,' I said. And we did. Sometimes better, sometimes worse, but we lived happily. We even fixed up the apartment somewhat. Matelle, above all, was our joy.

"One night, my wife's old partner came to see us, all excited about a big job. She had a plan for a 'sure thing.'

"'A golden opportunity,' she told us. 'A once in a lifetime deal. It's going to make us rich without a single risk.'

"I told her that we weren't interested no matter how good the deal was. But my wife wasn't so sure. She began to get excited by the idea. I should have thrown the partner out right then and never allowed her into our home again. But I didn't, and that was my big mistake. The two of them sat up till late at night going over the whole plan, and then my wife tried to convince me to let her go.

"'Just one more job,' she said, 'and we could have everything we always wanted.'

"I told her that all I wanted was to get away from a life of crime, and that, we already had done. But the two women worked on me for so long that in the end, like an idiot, I let them talk me into it. My wife and her partner got ready, and they left at once to do the job.

"Less than an hour later, the partner came running back alone. She was frightened and crying. 'Run, quick!' she screamed. 'They got your wife! Go and save her!'

"Immediately I went to see a good lawyer. He assured me that he would take care of everything. Unfortunately, he wasn't able to get my wife out of jail before the trial.

"I was left to take care of Matelle by myself. I had to be father and mother to her, which meant that I didn't have much time for my shoemaking work. Between worrying about money for food and about my wife in jail, I almost went crazy. Just then, my wife's partner came to me and said that she felt guilty about the mess she had dragged me into. To make up for it, she offered to look after Matelle so I could work. I had always suspected that she had her eyes on me. You know what I mean? The whole business stank of a setup. But until my wife went to trial and they let her out, I didn't know what else to do. The woman started to come to my home every day.

"My wife finally went to trial. The lawyer I had hired to get her off wasn't as good as he was supposed to be. My wife was found guilty and the judge sentenced her to three years in prison.

"As long as she was doing time in Lublin, I visited my wife every week. But after a few months, they moved her to Pawiak Prison, here in Warsaw, and then I could only afford to see her two or three times a year. But I wrote to her often, and I sent her whatever I could.

"My wife's old partner came every day to help me in the house, and slowly that woman and I drew closer. The whole business got so out of hand that she moved in with me. We started to live like husband and wife. Soon she was pregnant, but she didn't tell me and I didn't notice it at first. When I finally saw what had happened, it was too late to do anything about it. I asked her why she hadn't told me as soon as she knew. She denied knowing anything until it was too late, and then, she said, she became afraid to tell me. I found out later that she was lying. She had planned the whole thing from the start, just as I had suspected.

"I had to find a way out of this mess. I told the woman that if she left my house, I would help her in anyway I could. She wasn't interested in moving out, she said. When I saw that I couldn't get rid of her nicely, I told her that I didn't want her in the apartment anymore. If she didn't leave on her own, I threatened to throw her out. She started to scream that she would write to my wife that I had raped her and forced her to live with me. And then she would tell the police a few things about me.

"I had fallen into her trap. The best thing to do, I figured, was to prepare my wife for the surprise she would find when she came home from prison. I wrote to my wife that her old partner had married, and because she and her husband didn't have any money, I let them live with me in our apartment. Then, after the woman had the baby, I wrote to my wife that her friend had given birth to a little boy.

"When I went to visit my wife in Pawiak, she started to ask me questions about her partner's husband. I told her that the man wasn't from Lublin, and I made up some other lies.

"A few months after my visit, I wrote to my wife that her partner wasn't able to get along with her husband, and they had divorced. I said that I was letting her friend and the baby stay in our apartment because they had nowhere else to go.

"When my wife was about to be released from prison, I asked the woman again to leave us alone, and I offered to support her and the baby if she moved out. But she wasn't interested in leaving. All I could do then was ask her to go along with the story I had made up for my wife. To that, she agreed.

"For the first few months after my wife returned, everything was quiet. My wife and I still loved each other and were very happy to be together again. It never crossed my wife's mind that I was the father of her friend's child. But soon enough my wife heard gossip from the neighbors, and when she found out the truth, life became sheer hell.

"My wife's partner blamed me for everything. She said that I had forced her to sleep with me, and that after she had the baby, I forced her to go along with my lies. I tried to tell my wife the truth, but she wouldn't believe me. If it were not for our daughter, my wife said, she wouldn't have stayed with me for another moment. I didn't know what to do. My wife began to yell and curse at me constantly. Then the two women started to fight with each other. I became so disgusted that I began to drink and was almost never home. Because I had stopped working, suddenly there wasn't any money in the house. The two women realized that they still had two small children to take care of, so they made up and decided to go back to their old trade.

"When I found out what they were up to, I became afraid they would both get arrested and I would be left with the babies. I tried to stop them. They told me that if I didn't like it, I could leave and go to hell.

"I became desperate. At once, I stopped drinking and went back to shoemaking. I hoped that if they saw me earning money again, they would stop stealing. But it was useless. They *liked* their work.

"On their fourth or fifth job, they were caught breaking into a house, and what I was most afraid of, happened. They were both arrested and sentenced to four years in prison.... Now I had two babies to care for. My friends helped me find a woman to look after the children and the house, and I went back to shoemaking to earn a living.

"Four years is a long time for a man to be alone. Within a few months, this third woman moved into my apartment. It was easier that way for both of us, and I was lucky that she couldn't have children. I worked; the woman took care of the house; the children grew; and that's how four years went by.

"When my wife and her friend came back from prison, the third woman didn't want to leave. The battles broke out all over again. I couldn't stand it anymore. I decided to put an end to that crazy life. I told them that I didn't need three women, and I gave them

223

one week to decide with which one of them I could stay. Otherwise, I told them, I was going to disappear and leave them all.

"A week later they told me that they had no other place to go, and they had decided to live together in the apartment. The next day, without saying a word to the women, I took the train to Warsaw and left them. Here in Warsaw, I found a job in a shoe factory and settled down. After a while, I went back to working for myself as a shoemaker. From time to time, I would travel to Lublin to visit my children, and when I could, I sent them money. I kept hoping that someday the three women would come to their senses and let me go back to my first wife.

"I waited four years, but nothing of the sort happened. When I had first left the three women, I couldn't believe they would let me get away. But after all those years, when they didn't try to get me back, I was sure they had forgotten about me.

"A few years ago, I met your mother here in Warsaw. She was working in her cousin's store. I had known Roise since the time your father and I had worked for the same shoemaker in Lublin. When she told me that your father had divorced her, I asked her to go out with me. She was lonely and said yes, and we enjoyed being together. We went to the theater, had dinner, we told each other our sad stories, and we got close.

"We liked each other very much, so much that I asked her to marry me. Roise turned me down because of the other women in Lublin. I told her that I was finished with that life. In the four years that I had been living in Warsaw, I told her, I often went back to visit my children, but I had nothing to do with the three women. And the women never mentioned that they wanted me back. On my last trip to Lublin, I told Roise, I had even tried to bring back my daughter, Matelle, with me, but her mother wouldn't let her go....

"Neither your mother nor I wanted to stop seeing each other. I kept trying to convince her that I was a free man and that she should marry me. She kept saying no.... Until one day she found out that she was pregnant, and then she agreed to come live with me.

"For the first time in my life, I was making a good living. I told your mother that if she didn't want to have the baby, I would pay for the best doctor in Warsaw. But when Roise saw how happily we were living together, she decided to marry me and have the baby. Immediately we began preparations to bring you and your sister to Warsaw. I even agreed to have your grandmother live with us. And your mother agreed that my children could come live with us too.... Your mother and I decided that just as soon as I got a divorce from my first wife, we would get married...."

Itzhak Copperstein stopped. As he had been speaking of my mother, his voice had been getting hoarser and lower, and now it sounded as if a great sadness had a grip on his throat and he couldn't get another word out. He turned away.

I waited without moving.

When he turned back to me, the puffy bags under his watery eyes were swollen. But he could speak again.

"Your mother and I were very happy. Schloime, you must believe me. The love that we felt for each other and the happiness that we shared was something that neither she nor I had ever known before in our lives. She told me so herself many times...many, *many* times...and I said the same thing to her.... This was the happiest time of our lives. After all of the suffering that your mother and I went through, we deserved it...and we enjoyed it....

"But our happiness didn't last long. My troubles started again the moment that the three women in Lublin found out that I was living with another woman. They wrote that they wouldn't let their children lose their father. If I didn't come right back to Lublin, they said, to fulfill my responsibilities towards them, the three of them would take revenge on me.

"I wrote back at once that I was never returning to Lublin. I told them to send the children to me and I would give them a good home.

"They wrote back that they didn't want their children brought up by a stepmother.

"Your mother and I became frightened of what those women could do to us. We decided that I shouldn't write to them anymore. I told your mother that they probably just wanted to scare me and that soon they would forget about me again. But we were both worried enough to put off all our plans.

"We let some time pass. Just when we thought that we could safely send for you and your sister and grandmother, the three women, all of a sudden, appeared at the door of our apartment. With them, they had brought all their belongings and the children. Your mother and I saw our happiness being destroyed in front of our eyes. I tried to talk to the three women. I told them that they couldn't expect to have me back after all that time.

"Why not? they said. If I was good enough for Roise, then I was good enough for them.

"I started to scream and tried to throw them out. They told me that if I didn't shut up they would go straight to the police and say that I had forced them to steal. They would also say that they had spent years in jail for me, and that now I wanted to throw them and the children they had borne me into the street, just so that I could live with another woman....

"I asked them why they hadn't said anything before. A long time had passed since I had left. Not even when I came to visit the children did they say anything. Why suddenly now did they have to have me?

"They told me that they had made a pact years earlier never to let me live with another woman.

"There was nothing that Roise and I could do. Unfortunately, by then, it was too late for your mother to do anything about the baby that she was carrying, and she was too ashamed to go back to her old life. The women took pity on her and let her stay. A few months later Roise had a baby boy....

"The neighbors in the building where we lived wouldn't stop gossiping about us. Soon the landlord came and threatened that if we didn't move out, he would call the police.

"We moved to a small nearby town, but there we were also hounded.... We still haven't been able to find a place where people would leave us alone.... Ever since those women came back into my life, I can't stop drinking....

"I live with four women...but the only one that I love and want is Toise, your mother...."

Itzhak Copperstein became silent. He had finished his story.

I suddenly noticed that a blackness had swallowed the street. It took me a while to realize that it was just the night, that the sun had gone down while he had been speaking.

"You have to believe me, Schloime," said Itzhak Copperstein, "that your mother loves you and your sister more than her own life. Nothing would make her happier than to have you two with her. You're always welcome to stay with us, if you want."

If I hadn't been afraid of him, I would have cursed him to his face for ruining my mother's life, as well as Ruchele's, Babbe's and mine. And I would have told him that I never wanted to be near him or see him again. Instead, I said that I would visit them when I had more time, but now it was already late and I had to go. We said goodbye, and I hurried away.

Every few steps, I looked back over my shoulder. When I was sure that Itzhak Copperstein wasn't following me, I slowed down and stopped. My head was spinning. For a few minutes, I stood helpless in the middle of the sidewalk thinking that I would collapse. I felt that I was tumbling through the very darkness of the universe.

Where was my family? What had become of us? Babbe and Ruchele were far away in Lublin. Babbe was old, had almost died, and who knew if I would ever see her alive again? My father had disappeared when I was so young that I never even got to know him. And now I had lost my mother too. My poor mother, who had struggled so hard for us, who had suffered so much, and whom I loved more than anyone....

I felt abandoned and adrift in the world, as lost as if my home had vanished from the face of the earth. I promised myself that soon, as soon as I possibly could, I would help Ruchele move to Warsaw. And then, my sister and I, working together, would bring Babbe to live with us. And the three of us, Babbe, Ruchele and I would make a home of our own again.... These thoughts soothed me. They gave me strength and the will to go on. I waited a little longer until my head stopped spinning and when I began to walk again, I saw the world dancing crookedly before my eyes to the rhythm of my limp.